W9-DAO-718

3 4028 07964 8375
HARRIS COUNTY PUBLIC LIBRARY

J Turner
Turner, Amber McRee
Sway : a novel

$16.99
ocn752909540
1st ed.   06/13/2012

SWAY

SWAY

A NOVEL BY
Amber McRee Turner

Ｄｉｓｎｅｙ • HYPERION BOOKS / NEW YORK

Copyright © 2012 by Amber McRee Turner

All rights reserved. Published by Disney·Hyperion Books,
an imprint of Disney Book Group. No part of this book
may be reproduced or transmitted in any form or by any means,
electronic or mechanical, including photocopying, recording,
or by any information storage and retrieval system, without
written permission from the publisher. For information
address Disney·Hyperion Books, 114 Fifth Avenue,
New York, New York 10011-5690.

First Edition

1 3 5 7 9 10 8 6 4 2

G475-5664-5-12060

Printed in the United States of America

Designed by Joann Hill

Library of Congress Cataloging-in-Publication Data
Turner, Amber McRee.
Sway / Amber McRee Turner.—1st ed.
p. cm.
Summary: Ten-year-old Cass's attitude changes after her mother,
whom she idolizes, leaves her behind, and her father who previously
seemed boring and practical, takes her on a summer road trip in
which he shows her the creative, magical side of himself.
ISBN-13: 978-1-4231-3477-0
ISBN-10: 1-4231-3477-X
[1. Fathers and daughters—Fiction. 2. Mothers—Fiction.
3. Loss (Psychology)—Fiction. 4. Automobile travel—Fiction.
5. Imagination—Fiction.] I. Title.
PZ7.T8534Sw 2012
[Fic]—dc23   2011032728

Reinforced binding

Visit www.disneyhyperionbooks.com

SUSTAINABLE FORESTRY INITIATIVE
Certified Fiber Sourcing
www.sfiprogram.org

THIS LABEL APPLIES TO TEXT STOCK

For Lainey

one

Momness

Being awake all night long is not such a good thing when it comes from eating spoiled mayonnaise or hearing raccoons fight over garbage outside your window. But being awake all night long is a perfectly fine thing when it comes from gladness beyond the stars that your mom is coming home for the first time in four months. Because when your mom is coming home for the first time in four months, you're not so concerned that your tired eyeballs feel like they've been rolled in corn-bread crumbs. And not so peeved when your weather alert alarm clock goes off for no reason every so often with its fake thunder sound. And not so upset when you lie in bed and, twenty-eight times in a row, fail miserably to make the Eiffel Tower out of finger string. Because your mom will soon be wiping the crust from your eyes. Your mom will soon be telling you her own stories of powerful wind and lightning. And your mom will soon be making your Awful Tower be Eiffel again.

It was the first Saturday of summer that I started my day just so, with almost no sleep, some gritty eyes, and a sparkling pile of excitement about my mom coming home that very day.

For as long as I could remember, Toodi Bleu Nordenhauer had been a Diamond Level Volunteer for the Southern Mobile Aid Response Team. If a twister struck or a hurricane swept or something the size of golf balls fell from the sky, there she went in her little white car, all loaded up with bottled water and first-aid supplies.

To me, though, her being gone was a lot like my favorite deep-dish pizza. When you take a piece away, it leaves behind a valley of no-cheeseness, but for just a moment, and then the other ooey-gooey stuff comes flowing in fast to fill up the space. The good work I knew my mom was doing always seemed to fill in the empty of her being away for so long.

That morning, with every smack of my snooze button, I'd already pictured what she might have been doing on this, her longest rescue mission ever. Mom and all her SMART associates rowing from house to house, pulling huddled families from the roofs they'd scrambled onto to escape the rising floodwaters. I'd wondered what it would be like to be right there alongside her on the next rescue, and how exactly I planned to convince her that a certain groggy, disheveled ten-and-a-half-year-old was more than ready to be her partner-in-rescuing.

As usual, despite my lack of skill, finger-stringing seemed a good way to fill up the wait, and to avoid other less productive habits. Like pulling at my eyebrows. Or clenching my teeth together to see if they still lined up. Or fiddling with my kiddy cell phone, the one with chunky MOM, DAD, and POLICE buttons that I'm only allowed to use if 1) my mom calls in from the road, or 2) my head falls clean off my shoulders. So that morning, to avoid tugging my brows mangy, gritting my teeth jagged, and rubbing that MOM button totally blank, I resorted to finger-stringing my own custom design. That is, until from outside my bedroom window came a holler so loud it sent a cold squirt of scared up my back.

"BAM!" someone yelled.

Following just a split second behind the *BAM!*, the entire upper half of my cousin Syd lunged right through my open window, stretching the screen with his face and hands till it gave way right onto my bed.

"BOO!" he shouted, landing with an *oof* on my lap, all tangled in my string like a bug in a red spiderweb. If my fingers hadn't been tied to his ear I would have thumped him hard on the forehead.

"Syd! You scared the daylights out of me! I thought you were a prowler or something."

"What?" He smushed at my cell phone with his nose. "You mean you don't have holler ID on this thing?"

"Very funny," I said. "Are you aware how wrong it is to crash into a delicate project like this?"

"Oh." He wriggled free of the string. "Are you saying I had me some *wrength*?"

"Some what?"

"You know. Like strongness is *strength*? And longness is *length*?"

"Okay."

"So wouldn't wrongness be *wrength*?"

"I guess it would be if it weren't so not," I said, trying hard not to let Syd muddy my excitement with his wandering thoughts. My cousin was twelve, but that fall he would be repeating the sixth grade—mostly because of these random notions of his.

"Come on, Cass. You've got to see what my dad's making for Aunt Toodi's welcome home party! It's so *awes*." To Syd, words like *awesome* are way more *awes* when they're split in half.

"Tell me what it is."

"Nope. You already got two hints."

"Well, let's see," I said. "You gave me a *bam* and a *boo*. Could it be something to do with . . . oh, I don't know . . . *bamboo*?"

"No duhyees, Einstein!" Syd slid himself back out my window hole and was gone in a dust-puff.

"I'll meet you in a sec," I yelled after him.

Hopping into the cleanest jeans I could find on the floor, I stuffed the phone into my back pocket and made my way to the kitchen. There I found Dad, for the third morning in a row, trying to lure a family of doves out of the vent above our stove. For bait, he had shoved stale hot dog buns into a paper sack.

"Breakfast?" he said, pointing toward a Pop-Tart with the charred edges pinched off. "I whipped you something up before the dove hunt."

The pastry looked like a big frosted postage stamp on a plate.

"No thanks, I'll just grab something at Syd's."

The mound of anticipation in my stomach had taken the place of food anyway.

"Yeah, I can't say I blame you for refusing that gourmet meal," Dad said with a grimace toward the table.

My dad's name is Douglas Nordenhauer, but the kids in my class usually call him "Sluglas" or "Buglas." As Olyn Elementary School's groundskeeper, Dad is in charge of keeping creepy-crawlies off the pansies that make up the big *OES* in front of the school, squirting bird poo off signs, and scrubbing graffiti from the bricks. In the summertime he works a second job as a door-to-door meat salesman in our neighborhood. And pretty much, that's my dad. Pansies, poo, paint, and pork chops.

"Are you coming to help decorate for Mom's party?" I asked, helping him hold the paper sack steady.

"Not this time, Casserole."

The scrunch of Dad's forehead showed off his constellation of chicken pox scars. When he concentrated like that, he bit his mouth in a way that made both lips totally disappear under his salt-and-pepper beard.

"But Syd says Uncle Clay is making something special." I even sang it all slow like *speshaaaaalll*, but Dad was unmoved.

"No doubt about that, Cass," he said. "But I really need to evict these little poopers before your mom gets here."

Dad had always been nervous about Mom's home-comings, but this time he seemed extra that way. All week he'd been doing stuff like pouring salt in his coffee, putting junk mail in the fridge, or spreading butter on a sponge. This morning, his unsure smile made it hard to tell whether he was feeling the Christmas kind of nervous, or the dentist kind of nervous.

"And besides," he said, "your Uncle Clay's not the only one who can brew up a surprise, you know."

"What? You mean you've got a surprise for today, too?"

"Perhaps."

A bonus blub of excitement squeezed its way into my gut. "For Mom or for me?" I said.

"Maybe both. You just wait till the party," said Dad. "Now go on out there before Syd breaks a window. We sure can't afford that."

As I walked out the door, I felt the little cell phone squeezing its way up out of my back pocket with every step. Unlike the MOM button on my phone, the DAD button is totally unsmudged. There's never really been any reason to press it because my dad is always right there. Right there melting my shirts with the iron. Right there asking me to play Scrabble every night. Right there trying to be mom enough and cool enough to make me not care that all the real momness and coolness is hundreds of miles away from little Olyn, Alabama.

"And speaking of not affording things," Dad added. "We may have to get rid of that phone of yours now that your mom's going to be back for a while."

Which was more than fine with me. I couldn't tell my dad this, for fear of nerving him right over the edge and making him pour his salted coffee into a frozen junk mail envelope and then having to clean it up with a buttered sponge. But the way I saw it, that day was going to be the last time I'd welcome Mom home from a rescue trip anyway. Next time, Dad would be welcoming *us* home.

two

Anywhere
to Alabama

Syd shuffled rainbow shapes with his feet into the dirt
outside our back door.

"Is your dad *ever* going to crank that grungy thing
up?" he said, nodding toward the old motor home that
filled my backyard. Hidden under a blue plastic pool
cover, that RV had been sitting there lifeless since March,
when Dad puttered it down our driveway for the first and
last time ever. It used to be The Roadstar, but some of the
letters fell off when he squirted it with the hose, so now
Dad just calls it The Roast.

"I don't know when he's going to drive it," I said.
"He's been working on it a lot."

Syd shot me a look of disbelief.

"I mean he's been working on getting it running," I
said. "Not so much on the grunginess part."

"You can say that again," he said, but I didn't see fit
to discuss The Roast any more than that.

"Hey! Watch out for the nevergreen!" warned Syd as we made the short one-Mississippi, two-Mississippi journey from my yard to his. He then leapt clean over the hapless little Castanea dentata tree that shares my name—a tree that could easily be mistaken for a branch jammed into the ground if it weren't for the tiny wire fence around it. I'm pretty sure the only way to even prove it's a Castanea dentata is the torn-off tag that stays at the bottom of my underwear drawer.

"So how long will it take Aunt Toodi to drive home from Misery?" asked Syd.

"Not Misery," I said. "*Missouri*. There was a big flood in a town called Gwynette. And I don't know how long it takes to get from there to Alabama."

In fact, I didn't know how long it took to get from anywhere to Alabama. I'd hardly even seen the next county.

"Well then, couldn't they call it the Flood of Misery anyway?" asked Syd.

"I guess they could." I shrugged.

"You going to show her your Book of Scribbles?" Syd asked, both of us swatting hard at a mess of curious gnats.

"It's called the Book of In-Betweens, Syd. And it's not scribbles. It's my *noodling*. My swirlies and jaggeds. You wouldn't understand."

"I don't think I want to understand," he said. "Besides, isn't noodling catching catfish with your bare hands?"

"To you, maybe."

Syd had some nerve insulting my Book of In-Betweens, the journal I'd filled with doodles of everything Mom might want to know from the days in between her being

9

at home. Only I don't call them doodles, but *noodles* instead, because I draw the dreams and memories straight out of my noodle, the way that Cass and only Cass thinks about things. The binder itself isn't much to look at; the front cover just an empty plastic sleeve I'd reserved for one of those photos where your mom is standing behind you with both her arms clasped around you tight like she's telling the world, *This one belongs to me, and don't you even think about messing with her.*

Syd kicked a dandelion bald. "If you ask me, your brain is swirly."

"Well, nobody asked you. And just wait. I'm going to cover my whole room in noodling someday. When Mom and I travel together, I'll ditch the book completely and noodle our big adventures right onto my own bedroom wall when we're home between rescue missions."

"Whatevs," said Syd. "Your dad isn't going to let you draw squat on those walls. I bet you haven't even busted open that pack of Sharpies we gave you."

"Sure I have."

Syd was right. I turned ten like eight months ago, and I hadn't even so much as uncapped one of those permanent markers, but not because of Dad. Truth is, I was scared of making anything permanent. Most all of the permanents in my life had so far been bad ones. Dad's permanent grass stains, Syd's permanent roof-surfing scar, Uncle Clay's permanent paralysis, the countless bad perms Aunt Jo had gotten at the salon. I'd always wanted to noodle a big something across the wall and have it be my first-ever *good* permanent, but I hadn't even put the first molecule of ink on there. I'd yet to come across anything permanent-noodle-worthy in all of Olyn.

"So where's your mom going next?" said Syd.

"She doesn't make the storms, Syd. She cleans them up. I'll let you know where she goes next when *we* get there."

"What do you mean?" he asked. "She's going to let you go with her?"

"No duhyees," I said. That is, if *no duhyees* means *man, I sure hope so.*

"But you don't even know how to rescue," said Syd.

"I know some," I said. "I bandaged your head that time. And I left cold water for the mailman. I figure I can learn the rest."

"Yeah, but that duct tape near snatched me bald," said Syd. "And if I remember right, that water spilled all over the mailbox and ruined your dad's bills."

There was no wrength at all in Syd's argument, but it still annoyed the stew out of me.

"You know, if you really want to learn about rescuing, you ought to watch *The Fearless Fenwick Show*," he said.

My left ear got itchy from the surge of aggravation in my head. "Syd, Fearless Fenwick does not rescue. Fearless Fenwick covers his head with bees and lets people shoot him in the backside with paint balls."

"Well, I bet he *could* rescue," he huffed. "Maybe even better than you and your mom put together."

Two itchy ears.

"I highly doubt that, Syd," I said. "Since my mom pulls kids from floating cars and grandparents from under

11

houses and dogs from the tops of trees, and since she is going to have months to teach me to do all that before her next trip, and since I'll learn it so fast we'll even have one whole month left over for nothing but finger-stringing."

"Well, whoopdeedoo dot com!" he shouted. Syd tacked a *dot com* onto a lot of things to try and sound cool, never mind that his computer was old enough to have a driver's license.

"Hey there! You two are just in time!" Uncle Clay waved from the screen porch. A few years back, when Uncle Clay had his stroke, everything on his right side quit moving. It made him half able to talk and even less able to walk. Syd tells people that his dad's left is all right, but that his right up and left him.

That morning, like usual, Uncle Clay sat squished into a beat-up gold corduroy recliner. In front of him on his workbench was a stick of green bamboo plucked right from their yard and squeezed tight into a vise. The vise pinched the bamboo steady while Uncle Clay's good hand carved into it with a pocketknife. "Where's that dad of yours?" he asked, in that gurgly way of talking that our family has come to understand. "Tidying up the Nordenhauer nest for Toodi's return?"

"Evicting poopers," I said.

"He's a little on edge this week, huh?" Uncle Clay said.

"More like the last few weeks," I told him.

"Well, you just be extra patient with your dad, Cass. He's trying to figure some things out." He tapped on his forehead.

I wondered what in the world could be so hard to

figure out that it would make a man accidentally brush his teeth with sunscreen.

"All I know is, poopers or not, the forecast for today calls for fun." Uncle Clay pointed over to Aunt Jo's clothesline. From a wire, there dangled the biggest cloud-shaped piñata ever. Fashioned from scraps of newspaper weather reports, the cloud, like all of Uncle Clay's home-made piñatas, had been customized for the celebration at hand. Across the picnic table below it, Aunt Jo and the wind played tug-o-war with a red tablecloth. Uncle Clay loosened the vise and handed the stick over for my inspection. There were tiny lightning bolts scraped into the tough green skin.

"I've named it Ye Olde Piñata Whacker," he said. "You think your mom can handle this thing, Cass?"

"Yes, sir. This is really neat," I said, tracing my pinkie over the lightning grooves. "My dad told me he has a surprise too."

"So I've heard," said Uncle Clay.

"You know what it is?" I asked.

Uncle Clay said "Nope," but he wasn't very convincing.

"Oooh! Can we try that out?" interrupted Syd. He swiped the bamboo stick and whacked at the air, way too close to me for comfort.

"In a little while," said Aunt Jo, stuffing soft drinks into a cooler of ice. "You two have your own jobs to do before the party. Syd, you're in charge of spreading this tablecloth. And Cass, will you close the storm cellar doors? We can't have someone falling through that thing like a tiger trap."

"Aw, how come I get the girlie job?" Syd whined.

Uncle Clay chuckled as he resecured Ye Olde Piñata Whacker to his worktable and began to carve its official name into it.

"Can it, Syd," said Aunt Jo as she handed me the railroad spike they used to fasten the cellar doors.

I loved any excuse to peek into Aunt Jo's storm cellar, that tiny underground room on the side of their house nearest ours. It's not a regular shelter, stocked with things their family can't live without. Instead it's full of things their family can't live *with*. Stacked on old shelves are dozens of jars with little notes crammed inside. Complaints. Bad ideas. Thoughts they don't want to think anymore. Instead of canned goods, they call them canned *bads*. When Aunt Jo and Uncle Clay and Syd tell each other to *Can it!*, it means to put it in a jar and get over it.

The sun through the open cellar doors put a shine on some of the topmost jars, and I leaned till my neck hurt to try and read one of the notes.

"You know you can add something to that collection if you ever need to," Aunt Jo said.

"Yeah, I know," I said. "But all I've got is good thoughts today."

"Well, we sure don't want to put away the good stuff," she said. "But if some bads ever show up, you know where to send them."

"Yes, ma'am."

Syd told me once that the first thing he ever canned was a napkin that said, *Okruh is grose.* Now I imagine Syd would write things like *I hate repeating the sixth grade.* Or *I sure wish my dad could play football with me.* The only complaint I could even muster at that moment was *I wish moms had faster cars.* It took my whole self pushing against those thick wooden doors, one at a time, to close up the cellar. Each thud made the jars tinkalink.

Syd waited for Aunt Jo to disappear into the house before he wadded up the tablecloth and stuffed it under the grill lid instead of spreading it on the table.

"If your dad is going to sell meat again this summer," he said, "you think he could score me some mud bugs?"

Syd had told everybody at school he could pull apart a crawfish and eat it in three seconds. I figured he wanted to prove it.

"Doubt it," I said. "Why don't you get Fearless Fenwick to find you some? Maybe he'd let you fling them at his behind."

Syd popped open a Fresca, gulped a mouthful, and skutzed it between his front teeth right at my face. "Flood of Misery!" he sputtered.

Scrambling to the cooler for something worse I could spit back, I caught sight of my dad standing puffed-up proud across the way on our doorstep.

"Got 'em!" he called out, waving a bulging bag of birds in the air like a winning bingo card. But no sooner did he stoop at the edge of the driveway to grant the dizzy birds their freedom, there came a little white Volkswagen Rabbit zooming up like a blur and stopping just shy of his feet. Panicky peeps came from every which way as Dad and doves scattered for their lives, the birds taking to the sky and my dad checking to see that all his parts were still there. When the exhaust smoke cleared, there was my mom, her knuckles wrapped tight around the steering wheel. Her car sat crooked on three good tires and one bad.

"You don't mean it," said Aunt Jo, holding a bowl of Funyuns and a fistful of bendy straws. Aunt Jo always said that when she could hardly believe something.

"Now, that's what I call disturbing the peace!" Uncle Clay garbled out.

My dad stood stunned, holding that empty paper sack like he might well need to breathe into it. The car door swung open and my mom stepped one foot out onto the gravel, her hot pink sandal more high-heeled than I ever knew a sandal could be. A cluster of shrunken fruits sat just above the toe hole, and her toenails were painted to match the cherries. She gave a *hold on a sec* finger-wave out the door and reached to the floorboard for her things.

"Mercy me," Mom said, unfolding herself from the driver's seat. She came out with stuffed-full grocery bags hanging from all her fingers and a pink plastic box under her arm. I'd never seen my mom so tall or so tan. There were more little fruit clusters printed all over her dress, and the light breeze made the hem of it flap against her knees. Her hair looked more on-purpose than it ever had before, with layers and layers of flowy flippiness and flippy flowiness. To draw it, you'd have to take out all six of the browns from the crayon box and hold them in your fist together.

"Aunt Toodi, you look like a model!" said Syd. Aunt Jo *mmm-hmmm*'d in agreement as she helped Clay out of his wheelchair and held him steady by the back of his belt.

"Syd, you're way too kind," Mom said, wobbling in my direction first, just like I'd hoped she would. When she got within hugging distance of me, her eyes got little shines in them. And not those window-shaped fake shines you put on drawings of apples and balloons, but *real* shines.

"My girl," she said, bending over me with her eyes closed and pressing her chin to the top of my head. I felt a tear land on my scalp and run right down the part in my hair. Mom smelled tons better than I ever imagined flood-water smelling. I held that first mom-air in my chest until it hurt.

"I'll have to take a rain check on the giant hugs," she whispered, nodding toward the grocery bags. "I'm losing the feeling in my pinkies."

I'd never heard of a rain check before, but hoped it was something storm rescuers bought bags of souvenirs for their kids with. Over my mom's shoulder I saw my dad across the driveway struggling to flick the last dove feather off of his sweaty arm. But when Mom turned in his direction, he suddenly got all frozen as she made her way toward him with the plastic bags bouncing off her hips.

"Sorry I almost flattened you," she said.

"Water under the bridge," said Dad. "Flood rescue has sure been good to you." Then Mom and Dad hugged like two wrong ends of magnets, an invisible wavy-wiggly force keeping them from getting too close.

"Can I help you with the bags?" Dad asked.

"Oh, it's a short walk, hon. I got it," Mom said.

"Then I guess I'll change that bad tire," Dad said, struck with a shyness that wouldn't let his eyes any farther off the ground than the tires anyway.

"Thank you," she said, spinning around and flinging a smile in Aunt Jo and Uncle Clay's direction.

"I see Funyuns. It must be a party," Mom said.

"All for you," said Aunt Jo.

"Can't wait," Mom said. "Would you all be so kind as to excuse me while I go put on my face real quick? The long drive's given me a terrible case of the greasies."

Aunt Jo lowered Uncle Clay back into his chair. Syd stuck a straw in each ear. Mom teetered back to the car and pushed the door shut with her behind.

"Come on, Cass. Let's be girly," she said over her shoulder, on the way up the back door steps. I moved so quick to catch up with her, the screen door didn't even graze me as it closed. I'd never heard my mom use the word *girly* before, and it was sure worth leaving some Funyuns behind to find out what she meant.

three

The Cheese

From the corner of the kitchen, I watched as Mom dumped her bags out all over the floor, sending halter tops and capri pants and flowered dresses piling up near as tall as our washer. Once or twice when I was younger and more tender about things, I'd ask why she had to go on these trips, and she'd always say, "Cass, they just need a smilin' face to help clean up the place." The first time she ever told me that, she went straight out and had it air-brushed on a tank top: *Here's a smilin' face to help clean up the place!* I looked for that shirt to land on the pile, but didn't see it.

"It smells kind of pet-store-ish in here," Mom said. She sniffed at the air as if something was burning, but I didn't mention the doves. Then she scanned the room from wall to wall, corner to corner, like when I check the shower for crickets.

"It looks like the church ladies haven't let you go hun-gry," Mom said, straightening the leaning tower of empty foil pans on the counter. "So what kind of potpies did you all get this time?"

"Mostly chicken and turkey," I said. "There was a bologna potpie too, but we threw that one out, pan and all."

"Well, speaking of wise moves," Mom said, spotting our game board still set up on a TV tray next to the fridge. "I see you and your dad have been at the Scrabble again."

"A little," I said. We had actually been at the Scrabble a lot, but in Dad's special way of playing, where he spells out a word like *hero* and then says something like, "You know, that mom of yours sure is one." In fact, Dad does lots of goofy things to try and make things okay when Mom goes away. Like twisting little storm rescue scenes out of pipe cleaners. Or putting paper drink umbrellas on *every*thing. Or making fog in a jar. My dad tries to fill in the empty part of the pizza when the Mom slice is taken away. Dad tries really hard to be the cheese.

"Sweetheart, would you mind carrying this last one for me, please?" said Mom, handing me the pink plastic box she had under her arm. It was like a mini pink version of the one Uncle Clay kept his tools in, and it had a squeaky handle.

"Whew . . . With all that weight off, my arms feel like they're floating," Mom said, play-flying her way down the hall.

"Come on, Cass. Fly with me!" she sang out, bumping framed SMART certificates and assorted "Thank you, Toodi Bleu, from the Mayor!" letters. I followed close behind, straightening each frame. In the bathroom, I

20

plopped myself onto the counter, where a new Response Team recruit is probably too big to be sitting, but it seemed okay just that one time. Then Mom gave me a sudden squeeze that was longer and tighter than any time she'd come home before, a journal-cover-worthy squeeze that made me wish someone behind the shower curtain had a camera.

"Now, let me have a look at you," she said, cupping my chin in one hand and smoothing my hair with the other. Even with a case of the greasies, my mom was so beautiful they could have designed a Storm Rescue Barbie after her.

"Cass, what's this sticky all over your face?" she said.

"Fresca."

Mom grabbed the washcloth and turned on the warm water. As she gently scrubbed my face, I closed my eyes and imagined that I was a poor storm victim she was helping. Like, if only I had some stuff for her to bandage, I could sit there all day with her tending to me. But without the actual blood and hurting, of course. When she stopped to wring out the dirty water, I let the questions flow like my own little flood.

"Did your cell phone not work in the storm area this time?"

"No phone reception in those parts, baby," she said. "No power, no nothing. They were hit really hard."

"So then, what's Misery, I mean *Missouri* like?" I said.

"You know, Cass," she said with a grin. "I'd really like to find out someday . . . when it's not covered in water, that is."

Mom dabbed at my mouth with the washcloth.

"There'll be plenty of time for my stories at the party," she said. "Now, you hold still just a sec."

I could smell fresh nail polish as Mom lightly scraped at my face with her pinkie. She held her finger so close to my eyes it made them cross trying to focus on the two eyebrow hairs she'd lifted from my cheek.

"A wish for each of us!" she said, blowing the tiny hairs to nowhere.

That's just like Mom. She's always wishing on things. But not just on regular stuff like fallen eyebrows or shooting stars or coins in fountains. On weird things, too. Like on typos in the newspaper. Or on broken pieces of glass. One time, I even saw her make a wish on a cereal flake that looked like her old gym teacher.

But unlike Mom, I don't make a habit of saying wishes out loud. I really only ever had one wish—to see the world with Mom—and Syd says that if you say the same words out loud over and over again, they're in danger of losing all their meaning.

"Know what I wish?" she said. "I wish you'd tell me about *Cass*. I do hope you've kept that journal of yours filled in for me to see."

"Sure did," I said. "I've noodled every day." And while Mom inspected every inch of her own face, with her nose almost touching the mirror, I was more than happy to tell her about Cass. In fact, I'd planned on my next words being, *Mainly, Cass would very much like to become a storm rescuer.* But instead, they came out more like, "I made a cyclone out of two Coke bottles for my final project last week, and the whole fifth grade thought it was cool except for Mean Maritucker Mentz, who called me a fartsy-artsy, thumb-sucking, goo-goo baby for talking about my weather-loving mom so much."

"Well, I'll be a monkey's patoot," Mom said, fussing a fog circle onto the mirror. I'd planned on her next words being, *Well, you just get me that girl's phone number and I'll make sure she doesn't mess with my baby again.* But somehow, instead, they came out, "I've got myself a zit."

She said it like *zeeyut.*

"I'm sorry to interrupt, hon," she said, with a pat to my knee. "But this here is one powerful blemish."

I had to agree with her. It was an enormo pink shiny one at the top middle of her forehead.

"Is that your first-aid kit?" I asked as Mom slid the pink plastic toolbox over toward us.

"Sort of," she said.

"Would you maybe teach me how to use that stuff?" I asked.

"I'll be happy to," she said. "Although, it may not be the kind of first aid you're expecting."

Mom undid the box's main latch and lifted the lid to reveal an array of lotions, powders, sprays, and every possible shade of makeup. The box got bigger as she unfolded level after level of beauty supplies.

"You were thinking gauze pads and peroxide, weren't you?" she said.

"Yeah," I said, like I knew what those were. "Where'd you get all this stuff?"

"Oh, from this precious lady whose salon was a mess of sludge," said Mom. "I helped her salvage some of her

23

chairs, and she gave me all her samples as a thank-you. I've been enjoying being kind of fixey-fixey ever since.

"So," she continued, "since we got folks and finger food waiting for us next door, how about I give you a few quick rescuing and beauty tips mixed together?"

I thought that was an awes idea.

"Let's see here," she said, rummaging through the bottom level of the box. "The lesson that's first . . . Be prepared for the worst."

I figured there might be a rhyme coming. My mom was born to rhyme. Dad says she burps, sneezes, and snores in rhymes.

"As a rescuer, you never know where you're going next, or what's going to be waiting for you there. But if you're well prepared, you can handle anything."

Mom unloaded a whole lineup of creams and said, "Take this bump of mine, for instance. A dot of this and a smear of that should cover it right up."

She held her bangs back with one hand and applied a zeeyut potion with the other. After re-lidding all the jars, she pulled a pointy-handled comb from another level of the box.

"Lesson number two . . . Comb all the way through."

Mom ran the comb through my hair so hard it made static crackle in my ears.

"After a devastating storm, never leave a house unsearched, no matter what a tangle it's in," she said, hitting a knotty speed bump at the back of my head. "Cass, I swear, you're just like your momma with this one piddly wave in your hair."

I figured if I couldn't have my mom's flippy flowiness, I could at least be proud of having one piddly wave in common with her.

After that, Mom grabbed a little roll-on deodorant from the box and said, "Lesson number three-o . . . Some deo for your b.o." We looked at each other and busted out laughing.

"In other words, don't let the people you're helping know that you're so scared your teeth are sweating," she chuckled.

Right about then, I saw the corner of something familiar sticking out from under a collection of lipsticks in the middle level of the pink box. I pulled at the corner to reveal my wrinkled old fourth grade school picture. When Mom saw it, a tear as tiny as a dewdrop formed in the corner of her eye.

"Just a little friend I always take along with me," she said, tilting her head toward the light to let the tear slurp back in. "And that, my friend, brings us to lesson number four, for when the tears start to pour."

From that same middle level, she picked out an eye shadow duo the colors of peas and corn, along with a long tube of mascara.

"Flood-proof eye makeup," she said. "Want to try a little?"

"Sure," I said, wondering if this would be our daily routine out on the road together.

As she applied the shadow to my lids in slow, smooth strokes, Mom said, "Just look at how this chartreuse and goldenrod shimmer on you." She kept having to smush her wrist to her cheeks to smear off some runaway tears.

Usually, you'd rather touch a slug than to see your own mom get all weepy-eyed, but it feels kind of nice when it's because she's been missing you so bad.

"Land sakes," she said. "That Alabama pollen has *already* got my allergies going, don't it?"

I couldn't remember my mom ever having allergies before, but as she dabbed and dabbed again, something else caught my attention real quick. Something that shimmered tons more than eye shadow. It was my mom's charm bracelet all crammed full of new charms, way more crowded than I remembered it being. A palm tree, a beach ball, a dolphin. It looked like her little Cass-head silhouette charm was squished between a seahorse and a sailboat.

Just about the time I finished studying the charms, Mom did the last swipe of shadow on my lid and reached over to open up a special side compartment of the pink box.

"I've got something here that you might want to have, Cass. It may still be a little big on you, but it seems fitting to go ahead and pass it on to someone who's well on her way to being another smilin' face to help clean up the place." From the little chamber, she pulled out something that needed to be unfolded in five directions before I could tell what it was. When she laid the airbrushed tank top across my lap, it felt like she'd covered me in a quilt made of fifty satiny first-place ribbons that I myself had won.

Without hesitation, I slipped the top over my shirt as quickly as I could and tugged the creases out as Mom looked on in a speechless, achy-proud sort of way.

"Thank you, Mom. I love it," I said.

"You ladies just about ready?" Dad called from the kitchen.

Mom took one last moment to puff her whole face with some powdery pinkness before collapsing the beauty box and latching it shut.

"You're welcome," she said to me as I stared in the mirror at my new shirt, the bright loops and swooshes of its lettering almost glowing.

"Hello?" Dad called again.

Mom and I found Dad standing at the kitchen sink with the faucet going, like he did a hundred times a day, waiting for the water to heat up.

"The flat tire is good as new," he said, flashing us ten little crescent moons of grime crammed up under his fingernails. "But now *I* need to degrease before the party."

If a thing about my mom is she's always wishing, then a thing about my dad is he's always washing. Always scrubbing off some mulchy, meaty evidence of the day's work. Every new bar of soap we ever opened was worn down to a sliver in record time.

"Cass and I were just discussing the finer points of rescuing in style," said Mom, scooting back a chair for me and one for herself at the same time. She propped an ankle across her knee to shake loose the gravel trapped between her sandal fruits.

"I noticed the nice new duds," Dad said. "But what's with the foo-foo stuff on your face, Cass?"

My dad wears an *It's a dirty job but somebody's got to do it* ball cap that has white waves of dried-up sweat salt on it. Mine and Mom's airbrushed tank top would want nothing to do with that hat.

"Oh, just a little something I shared from my beauty box . . . I mean, *our* beauty box," Mom said, giving me a wink. "We'd have offered you some too, Douglas, but you just don't seem the goldenrod and chartreuse type."

Dad looked perplexed, so I closed my eyes to show him better.

"My new favorite colors," I said.

"I see." Dad stooped and splashed some water on his face. "Don't you think you're maybe a little young for that stuff?"

"Mom was just telling me some things about being a rescuer," I said, feeling a sudden need to change the subject.

"Like what?" he sputtered.

"Exciting stuff," I said. "Like about not ever knowing where you're going next, and having to be ready for anything."

"It's all about putting yourself in someone else's shoes for a while," Mom said, slipping her sandals back on. "Trying to understand each and every person's needs.

"And *shoowee*," Mom added, pointing toward Dad's feet and pinching her nose. "From the smell of things, Douglas, you might want to put yourself in some other shoes too."

Honestly, I hadn't noticed any stink coming off of Dad, but I smiled and nodded like I did.

"My apologies for rudely interrupting you girls making sport of me," he said, patting his beard dry with a dish towel. "But have a look at this."

Dad picked up the slick remains of his soap from the dish, held the little piece out, and said, "Looks a bit like Abraham Lincoln, no?"

Mom and I both tilted our heads from side to side to try and see the resemblance.

"Not so much," Mom said. "But I'd say it's definitely a wishable piece of soap you've got there, Douglas.

"So, Cass," she said. "You want to take that wish, or shall I?"

"You go," I said.

"Well, if you insist," she said. "I'll make a big one."

Dad and I both listened like we were going to be quizzed on it later.

"I just wish that I could do more," she said.

"What do you mean?" asked Dad.

"Like, to be everywhere I'm needed all at once, you know?" said Mom. "So I could reach out to someone without having to let go of someone else to do it."

She picked up a piece of mail and fanned her face with it, making her charm bracelet tinkle like crazy.

"Well, you never know, Toodi, this may be the day your wish comes true," Dad said. "I've got a special something to reveal to you ladies at the party today."

"What? You mean surprises galore are outside that door?" said Mom. "That's mighty unlike you to keep a secret, hon."

"Yep," he said. "And it's the kind of something that will let all three of us do more for people . . . *together*."

Judging by the unchanged look on her face, I guessed

Mom was less than captivated by Dad's hint. But to my relief, she slapped the envelope onto the table and said, "So, what are we waiting for? How about we go on next door before Syd starts to hang Funyuns off his nose?"

"You two go on. I'll be over in a minute," Dad said, rummaging through the cabinets. "First I'm going to find some kind of smell-good to sprinkle in these shoes."

Poor Dad is *so* not the cheese, I thought as Mom and I stood to leave.

four

Cumulonimbus

Mom's hand felt smooth as butter when I grabbed hold for the walk next door. After all, a ten-year-old can do that when it's just a one-Mississippi, two-Mississippi thing. I had to take a double-stride to stay alongside her, which made my phone squeeze up and right over the edge of my back pocket. The phone bounced with a *crack-crack-crack* down onto the concrete steps, but I didn't even care to see where it landed. Then Mom and I went separate ways around the Castanea dentata tree, stretching our arms till her lotiony hand slipped right out of mine.

"Toodi Bleu Nordenhauer, you are a vision!" Aunt Jo called out as she poked toothpicks into rows of Vienna sausages.

"You two are like a magnolia and her brightest bloom," said Uncle Clay.

"More like a magnolia blossom and some stinkweed," said Syd, with a ring of yellow crumbs around his lips.

"Good one, crustache," I said.

"There's that lucky brother of mine." Uncle Clay popped a cough drop into his mouth. When he plans on talking a lot, he always sucks on a Sucrets to smooth out his words a bit.

"Well, Douglas, you think you might have over-seasoned the tootsies a bit?" Mom snickered as Dad walked up with little brown clouds puffing from his shoes with every step.

"Yeah, I guess cinnamon may have been a poor choice for a shoe deodorizer," he said.

Syd snorted as Aunt Jo slapped at Dad's shoes with a dish towel to dust them off.

Uncle Clay pretended not to notice. "That was some mighty fine bird-trapping you did this morning, Douglas. Fine, fine work," he said.

"Thanks, brother." With a gentle pat to Uncle Clay's back, my dad took his usual spot on a folding chair next to the recliner. Uncle Clay tapped a flat carpenter's pencil on the metal part of his arm brace. "Now that we're all here, I'd like to say a few words," he began. "Toodi, we don't like when you leave. But we know that when you do, you're making the darkest day brighter for countless others more needy than us."

His hand trembled as he held the bamboo stick out.

"As a welcome-home gesture, please accept this custom creation of mine."

"Thank you, Clay," said my mom, taking Ye Olde Piñata Whacker and studying the letters carved into its length. "I assume that cumulonimbus dangling over there is in need of some whacking."

I couldn't wait to see what would fall out of that cloud. There was never any predicting what was hidden inside of Uncle Clay's piñatas. Popcorn, cashews, paper clips, but almost never candy. Just whatever was within reach at the time of creation.

"Rubber bands," Syd whispered his guess in my direction.

I thought marshmallows.

"How about I test this thing out after we eat?" Mom said, leaning the Whacker against the fan and making her way to the table, with Syd and me fighting for next in line behind her.

Once everyone had piled food onto their plates and found a place to sit on the porch, we took turns asking Mom questions, so our words wouldn't all blurt out at the same time. Mom always came back from storm trips with the best stories. Chickens stuck on telephone poles. Double rainbows. Toilets in the road.

There on the porch swing, she sat with her toes pointed in at each other, so that her knees were close enough to balance a flimsy paper plate on her lap. Even with a glub of onion dip sliding down her plate, she was graceful.

"Toodi, what was the strangest thing you saw this time?" Aunt Jo asked.

"Whew, that's a tough one," Mom said, damming up the dip with a deviled egg. "But I'd have to say it was this poor old lady hanging on to a church steeple for dear life. My whole team tried to peel her off of it into the rescue boat, but she was so scared of the water around her, she just wouldn't budge. We had to remove her and the cross together, and she held it all the way to the first-aid station."

The way Mom described the lady and the cross was so vivid, I imagined the whole scene depicted in stained glass.

"Did you ever have to bust through a window to rescue anyone?" asked Syd.

"No," Mom said. "But I did see a wall with the shape of a fire hydrant broken through it."

"Cool," he said, and went back to throwing peanut shells at the box fan.

After a while, I noticed that each time the question-asking would make its way around the porch, my dad would always be doing something that distracted him right out of his turn. Clapping the bottoms of his shoes together to knock off the excess cinnamon. Removing his ball cap and scratching at his sweaty head. Jangling the mix of keys and change in his pockets.

"Hey, what's with your dad?" Syd asked me. "He looks like a baseball pitcher doing signals or something."

"I think he's all nerved out," I said. Which was odd, because my dad's edginess is usually pretty smoothed by the time Mom has unpacked. It was like someone forgot to tell his clappers, scratchers, and janglers that Mom had arrived. Or maybe the surprise he had yet to reveal was giving him the same twitch inside as it was giving me.

"Douglas, you've been mighty quiet all afternoon," Uncle Clay said, with a nudge to my dad's side. "Don't you have a question for Toodi?"

Everyone else's questions had just rolled right out like

gum balls, but Dad must have really had to dig for one. He didn't even look up from his lap when he said, "So . . . where'd you get all those beachy charms?"

The tan on Mom's face pinkened.

"Oh these," she said, tinkling the bracelet with her finger like tiny wind chimes. "I just picked these up in honor of some people near and dear to my heart."

Feeling pretty certain that Dad and I were the nearest and dearest to Mom's heart, I couldn't figure what all that beachiness had to do with us.

"I wonder where you'll go next, Aunt Toodi," said Syd. "It better not be Hawaii. I'd be ultra jeal."

I wanted to tell Syd that "ultra jeal" sounded more like a brand of hair goop than a clever phrase, but Aunt Jo handled things even better.

"Can it, Syd," she said. "Toodi's home to stay for a while now, and we're not even going to *think* about her leaving again anytime soon."

"Well, I don't know about all that, Jo," my mom said, flicking at the edges of her plate with her thumbnails. "I suppose this is as good a time as any to tell you all about my summer plans."

In an instant, I ran through ten possible definitions of Mom's "summer plans" in my head, making sure all of them included a ten-year-old girl.

"My next trip, that is," Mom said, staring down at her knees. "I'm afraid it's going to be sooner rather than later."

Dad quit his jangling.

"What do you mean, Toodi?" said Uncle Clay.

"You guys remember that big hurricane that hit the coast of Florida last year?" she said.

"The one where you saw a swordfish poked through a mailbox?" asked Syd.

"That very one," Mom said. "Well, a few of the people I met when I was there last summer . . . a few of the orphans . . ." She began to cry again, so I ran to the table to find her something to dab with. Talk of storm orphans always meant a napkin for my mom.

"Thank you, sweetheart," she said. "The thing is, those kids are in need of someone in a bad way. Someone to help them rebuild their lives after all that devastation."

"Oh, Toodi," said Aunt Jo, getting a little damp around the eyes herself.

"When will you go?" said Uncle Clay.

"I need to leave for Florida in two weeks," Mom said, pausing long enough for the napkin to soak up her tears and for me to soak up her words. I saw a blanket of worry cover my dad's face as he got still for the first time all afternoon. And it was big enough worry for him and me both. *Did she say two weeks?*

I suddenly found myself wondering if it was ever appropriate to be mad at orphans, because being mad at orphans felt icky as Twinkies filled with toothpaste.

"I heard they've got crawfish big as cats in Florida," said Syd.

"Seriously, Syd," said Aunt Jo. "Oh, Toodi, that's so soon. Why the rush?"

"There's simply no one else who can do it," said Mom.

"Wow, talk about things taking a turn for the not-so-awes," Syd leaned and whispered to me. "Your mom's about to leave again, and you're not even trained to rescue a mouse from a trap."

I looked to the paper cloud to try and find that silver lining I hear people talk about.

"Two weeks is more than enough time for training," I whispered back sharply, giving Syd the *shut up dot com* look he deserved, and feeling fairly certain that two weeks wasn't even enough time to begin.

"Well then, forget asking your dad about some puny crawfish," he said. "You better bring me back one of those jumbo Florida ones."

"How noble of you to help those children, Toodi," said Aunt Jo. "But it hurts our hearts to see you go again so soon."

"Ditto," said Uncle Clay, giving my dad a *Go on, do it!* nod that jump-started Dad's fidgets instantly. I could tell without a doubt that Dad was mustering something. Maybe words. Maybe courage. Maybe both. I hoped he'd muster a little extra for me while he was at it.

five

Heart-Shaped Lemon

"Sakes alive, I sure know how to kill a mood, huh?" said Mom, patting her cheeks with the crumpled napkin. "Now, let's see what I can do to fix that." She stood to shake the crumbs from her sundress and made her way to the dangling paper cloud. Grabbing up the Whacker and raising it high in the air, she said, "I'd like to propose a toast."

She waved the stick all around without even touching the piñata once, and said, "Here's to home sweet home . . . to family . . . and in particular, to the Southern Mobile Aid Response Team's youngest future volunteer, Castanea Dentata Nordenhauer."

Mom shot me a twinkly smile. My spirits flared up fast as a struck match.

"And here's to doing more," she said, holding the Whacker firm with both hands and rearing back for a big try at the cloud.

"Wait! Toodi! Wait!" My dad yelled out so loud, he seemed as startled by his own volume level as the rest of us. His mid-swing holler scared Mom into launching the Whacker clean out of her fists, and it landed with *thwunk!* onto the roof of Syd's house.

"Whoa, Nellie!" said Uncle Clay.

"You don't mean it," said Aunt Jo.

"Awes toss!" said Syd.

We all gazed hopelessly at the far-flung whacker, until Dad cleared his throat in a big dramatic way.

"I'll go fetch that later," he said, bringing our attention back to earth. "But first, I too have a presentation to make."

A hush filled the little porch. I couldn't imagine what Dad was going to say.

"Toodi, do you remember when Cass was a baby and you made a wish on that heart-shaped lemon? That maybe someday we could all go sweeten the world together as a family?"

"Mmm-hmmm, I sure do," she said.

"Well . . ." said Dad, aiming his hand across the way, toward the old covered motor home in our backyard. "Folks, may I direct your attention to what's behind, or better yet, what's *under* curtain number one." All six of us gazed at The Roast, big and stuck as ever.

"Happy fifteenth anniversary, Toodi," Dad belted out. "I know she's not so easy on the eyes, and she don't exactly run like the wind, so I won't uncover her just yet. But underneath that plastic over yonder is a circa 1991 Roadstar Deluxe that I like to call The Roast."

Mom's eyes widened, and I hoped hard that Dad's speech would get better from there. Thankfully, it did.

"Or maybe we should call her a wish come true," he continued. "Just imagine, if you will, Toodi. You, me, and Cass. Out there on the road together in that RV . . . helping people. Like our own little storm rescue team."

I found myself instantly wowed by Dad's words. Rough around the edges as it might be, his plan set off a pinball game of possibilities in my head. Unfortunately, though, Mom's version of *wow* looked more like she'd just bitten into a heart-shaped lemon.

"You mean the three of us," she said. "Living in *there*?"

Dad gave her a slow unsure nod.

"Together," he said.

"And you plan on getting that thing ready in the next two weeks?"

"Well, you did throw me for a loop with this Florida announcement," said Dad. "But if I work on her every night, I believe The Roast could be roadworthy just in time."

Mom crossed her arms. "Just how in the world do you plan to pay for this trip, Douglas?"

Dad sat on the edge of the workbench, pulled off his cap, and wiped the sweat from his brow.

"I've been putting aside a few bucks here and there," he said. "A family can save a lot on bulk cereal, homemade haircuts, and potpies, you know."

Dad recapped himself.

"Besides, frozen meat travels well," he added. "I can borrow a freezer and sell on the road. That'll pay for our gas and food. And we'll be sleeping in The Roast."

I looked from Dad to Mom to The Roast, picturing my family as yams squished together in a dented can, but it was okay. Dented cans are bad, but yams are good. And *together* is even better.

Dad shrugged his shoulders and smiled.

"So what do my ladies think?" He said it kind of practiced and clumsy, like it was his one line in the school play.

Mom's blank expression was as hard to read as a wet newspaper.

"Don't you see, Toodi?" Dad said. "I know that you want to do more. This is how we can all do more *and* be together as a family. We can all help those kids in Florida."

Yes, yes, what Dad said! I thought, trying hard to hide my reaction until I could see how Mom was going to respond. It took tremendous control to not shoot Dad a toothy grin, like a dog must feel wagging only the tip of its tail. But then, all too quickly, Mom crossed her arms and added the period to the end of Dad's speech.

"Douglas, I'm sorry," she said. "I just don't know if that's going to work out. Can we maybe discuss this a little later?"

Then, for what seemed like forever, Mom and Dad looked to be having a no-blink contest.

Okay, well, maybe what Mom said, I thought. Perhaps she just has to think it all through before she says yes. No big deal. Even so, I still felt like wagging just the tip of my tail.

"Sure, Toodi," Dad said, breaking the silence to dig a

Dr Pepper from the cooler and press it to his flustery face. "We can discuss things later, I suppose."

And that's when I realized that feeling embarrassed for someone else can make you twice as squirmy as feeling embarrassed for yourself.

"Whoa," Syd whispered to me. "He totally got shot down in flames."

Looking at the stunned faces around the porch, I had to agree that it had been a very short trip from awes to *awk*.

"Bro, I believe you have really outdone yourself this time," said Uncle Clay, like he was trying to chase the weirdness from the air with some kind words.

"Yes, Douglas, I think that is all just terribly exciting," said Aunt Jo. "Looks like everyone just has to let the idea soak in a bit. In the meantime, why don't we all get cozy and do some more catching up?"

And that's just what most of us did for the rest of the afternoon. Aunt Jo, Mom, and I squeezed together onto the porch swing, and with my head on Mom's lap, I listened to the hum of their conversation until the lightning bugs came on duty. Looking mostly deflated, my dad sat at Uncle Clay's workbench, crushing one can after another in the vise. Uncle Clay kept him company until he slumped over the edge of his recliner in a snooze. And Syd spent the rest of his day throwing rocks, big and small, trying to knock Ye Olde Piñata Whacker off the roof. With every run of her long nails across my neck, Mom tickled away most of the pity I'd felt for Dad when his surprise fizzled. My head became filled with images of sitting on a beach after a long day of heroics, sorting through seashells under a chartreuse-and-goldenrod umbrella.

"Aunt Toodi, you're like a lady version of Fearless Fenwick," Syd said, dissolving my dreaming as he lobbed a broken brick for one final attempt at the Whacker.

"Syd Nordenhauer, you break a window and you'll be scrubbing the bathroom tomorrow," snapped Aunt Jo. "And with no help from Fearless Fenwick."

"I think that's our cue," Mom said. "Jo, Syd. Thank you for a darling celebration. Please give Clay my thanks as well."

She hung her sandals off her thumbs, so I hung my tennies off mine. We tiptoed together through the grass while Dad and Aunt Jo helped Uncle Clay into the house.

My mind flickered in as many directions as there were sands on the seashore as I considered how to go about talking Mom into taking a ten-year-old amateur rescuer with her to Florida, whether in a tin-can RV or not. And how if I didn't convince her tonight, I would never hear the end of Syd making that *buh-gert!* chicken noise he does when I bail out of something.

Mom and I *ooch-ooch*ed barefoot across the sharp driveway rocks.

"You never whacked your storm cloud," I said to her.

"It's okay, honey," she said. "That cloud will still be there tomorrow."

six
Buh-gert!

On the nights when Dad tucks me in, he usually gives me air hugs, because his callousy hands tend to catch on my satin jammies. But that night, I knew Mom and her creamy skin would make for my first snagless tuck-in in months. As she searched around my bedroom for the perfect spot to store our airbrushed tank top, I felt a mix of tired and excited that was like Z's and exclamation points floating all around me. My words crouched down and waited to pounce on the first opportunity to steer the conversation all the way to Florida, to convince Mom to invite me to be her rescue assistant sooner rather than later. I'd decided that the indirect approach was best, because blurting my plans out might very well get the same reaction Dad had gotten. His total strikeout had left me feeling way too *buh-gert* to blurt.

Mom draped the shirt across the back of my homework chair and began a little tour of all the sames and differents in my room.

"You guys have added some more of these," Mom said, perusing the collection of pipe-cleaner rescue scenes on my bookshelf. There was still plenty of space left for three or four sculptures of people I would rescue some-day. Maybe even more if they were small orphans.

"Do you think I would like Florida?" I asked.

Mom came and sat on the edge of my bed with the smallest of the pipe-cleaner girls still in her hand.

"Florida is an amazing place, Cass," she said. "The wind and the waves can change their course on a whim, you know? One day busting a house to bits, and the very next, gently depositing a perfect sand dollar on the shore."

Mom sounded just like the narrator on a nature show, and for a moment while she spoke, I was sure I heard the whooshing sound of actual ocean waves in the background. Until I realized it was just my dad's feet shuffling as he paced up and down the hallway outside my bedroom.

"Cass, I'm truly sorry about all that weirdness at the party today," Mom said in a hush when she heard him. "I'm just not real keen on the idea of us all living in that RV . . . What does your dad call that thing?"

"The Roast."

"Yeah, well, I'm just not big on the thought of us sleeping, bathing, eating, and meat-selling in The Roast for months on end."

"And rescuing," I said. "Remember? All of us together?"

Mom puffed out a big sigh and took me by the hand.

"Please don't think me insensitive, Cass, but that's just the thing I wouldn't expect you to understand," she

45

said. "It would be mighty hard to do storm rescue while traveling the way your dad is suggesting."

She rose to her feet and looked out my window at The Roast. Even from under its cover, the ugliness shone through somehow.

"Who knows, but that beast could blow right over, in the wrong circumstances," she said, turning to me with a serious look. "What I mean is that dependable, fast transportation is an absolute must at the scene of a disaster."

"Like your car?" I said.

"The Rabbit has proved trustworthy in times of need," said Mom. "The problem is, it's not really a family road trip kind of vehicle."

"But it'll hold two people," I said.

Me, Mom. One, two. Things were suddenly not looking good for Dad.

"True," Mom said, glancing out the window once more at the ramshackle motor home. Her agreement was sweet music to me.

"It sounds like your dad is dead set on us roaming about in that old thing," she said. "But that sure would be a rickety kind of together, Cass."

"That's okay," I told her. "I'm not really big on Dad's idea either."

After all, Dad would be okay if both his girls went to Florida. He might very well be nervous enough to smear butter on everything but the toast, but he could learn how to play solitary Scrabble or something. I just needed to convince Mom that I was qualified to work alongside her.

"There's an orphan in my class at school," I said. "I showed her how to open her locker once."

I didn't feel the need to mention that she was really a former orphan and that I opened her locker accidentally, thinking it was mine.

"How sweet, Cass," Mom said as she sat on the bed next to me and pushed the hair from my eyes. "You've definitely got your mother's compassion. Which I must say, can be a blessing and a curse."

Having your mom's same chin or eyes or nose is one thing, but having her gift for helping people has to be even better, even if she did just happen to call it a curse.

"But how could helping people ever be bad?" I asked.

Standing the curly pipe-cleaner girl on my dresser, Mom drew in a slow deep breath. "I can tell you this, baby. It's only a curse when you're not strong enough to stand back up when you've fallen."

"Like if the wind knocks you down?" I said.

"Like that," she said.

"I'm good at holding on," I said.

Mom put her arm around me and gave me a squeeze. "Know what, Cass? Then someday you are going to be a real hero indeed."

"Soon?" I said.

"Maybe so." She smiled.

My heart took that as enough of an invitation to Florida to settle my gut, even though my mind knew we were only halfway there.

"You know what else?" she said. "I bet they'll even make a statue in your honor."

"For real?" I said. "Will they make a statue of you too?"

"Aw hon, I sure enough doubt that," Mom said.

"Yeah they will, Mom," I said. "I bet they will. They'll make a big one of you with writing at the bottom and everything."

Mom lay down beside me and put her head on the pillow next to mine.

"You think so, huh?" she said, staring up at my bumpy ceiling. "And just what exactly do you think my inscription would say?"

"I don't know," I said. "Maybe your name and when you were born and—"

"Oh! I've got a name for it!" Mom interrupted. "How do you feel about Toodi Bleu *Skies*?"

I felt great about Toodi Bleu Skies. It was like Toodi Bleu Skies drifted above us in airplane smoke letters.

"So what would my inscription say?" I asked.

"Hmmm, let's see," she began, and then her voice got squeaky with inspiration. "How about this one?" She made her hands into a rectangle-shaped plaque above us. "Castanea Dentata . . . She's off-the-chart SMART . . . with compassion in her heart!"

Mom propped herself on an elbow to see my reaction and almost rolled off the bed. Honestly, I thought her idea was a little hokey, but who really cares what the inscription says when you have a statue of yourself? A monument so famous, some kid might even try to finger-string it someday.

"It's perfect," I said, and with a puff of satisfaction,

Mom situated herself back into her sitting spot while I fumbled under the bed for my little pile of string. Placing the tangly nest next to her, I asked, "Will you show me how to do the Eiffel Tower?"

"Sure I will," she said. "If I can even remember how."

She shook the tangles out and began stringing, mumbling the steps to the tune of "Frère Jacques."

"Hang a left loop. Hang a right loop," she sang.

An enormous stringy-mom-hands shadow filled the whole wall in front of my bed.

"Pick up left. Pick up right."

I watched carefully, trying to memorize as she went.

"Reach the thumb over and pick up the far string."

Then she paused mid-pickup.

"I've been wondering," she said.

If your dad will let me take you to Florida is how I wanted to finish her sentence for her. But instead Mom said, "When are you planning to show me that Book of In-Betweens?"

Quick as a whip and thrilled by her request, I dangled off the edge of the bed and grabbed the binder from the floor. Then I hoisted myself back up just as quick, stood the binder on its spine in the middle of my bedspread, and let it fall open.

"Read some to me," Mom said, getting desperately tangled in string.

And so I began, telling her about a handful of highlights and lowlights from the months she was gone. Like how on February 12th, I filled a whole roll of toilet paper full of drawings and Dad made us roll it back up and use it so we wouldn't waste the paper. Or how on May 3rd, Dad put bleach in with all our brown thrift-store towels and made them look like giraffe skin. After reading a few more yesterdays, I opened to today's page, the one I'd worked on half the night before, decorating it edge to edge with swirls and stars and just one word . . . a big "fun" in parentheses right in the middle.

"You do have a knack for that gorgeous scribbling," Mom said, her thumbs knotted to the point of turning purple. "But my dear, you mustn't ever put *fun* in parentheses."

"It's *noodling*," I said, flipping to the next week's pages, swallowing hard, and saying, "And all these blank pages are for the SMART stuff we'll do in Flor—"

And just when I was about to share my plans to fill up future blank pages with all things girly and heroic, Dad knocked at the door and poked his head right in, unaware that there was half of Florida hovering in the air. If there were ever a statue created in honor of my dad, it would be made out of mud and meat, and the inscription would have to say, "In Honor of Mr. Ground Beef."

"Toodi, we need to talk," he said, stuffing our fun right back into its parentheses. "Is now a good time?"

No way, no how, not now, I thought.

"I suppose it's as good a time as any," Mom said.

"Hold that SMART thought, Cass," she whispered close, tossing the half-Eiffel in a lump onto my bed. "It sounds like your dad's gotten himself in a knot too."

Following him into the hall, Mom sent me a finger-kiss over her shoulder. "Good night, Castanea," she said as she glided away into the next room.

"Good night, Toodi Bleu Skies," I said, clutching my ball of string, which wasn't any more French than it had been ten minutes ago, and maybe even a little more snagged.

And just like Mom said, I did indeed hold that SMART thought. In fact, had I known how very long I would be holding that thought in my head, I might have held it a little looser, so it wouldn't leave such an ache in my brain.

seven

Wrength

I have this thing I call my front-and-back-of-forever prayer. Usually I begin with asking for good things for my whole family, from the beginning of the past to the end of the future, as I picture each person passing by me like a big parade in my head. First come the ones dressed in animal skins chewing on bones, then the surly-looking pioneer ones with long skirts and almost-as-long beards. And finally, the ones who will have their silver boots shined by robots someday.

If I'm not asleep before then, I invite all of my family's friends, and if I'm not asleep before then, I bring in the families of the people my mom helps and all of their friends. Together, they all gather and mingle at the foot of a magnificent Castanea dentata tree, one that's as wide as it is tall and reaching out toward each of them at once.

On the nights I can get through the entire front-and-back-of-forever prayer, I figure it covers just about the whole world. But that night, right about the time I imagined Toodi and Cass drifting by with Douglas lagging behind, my forever was interrupted by the unmistakable sound of arguing in the backyard. From the other side of The Roast, two voices floated through my window, which was still open from Syd's morning dive. I moved closer to the opening, to aim an ear in my parents' direction.

"Toodi, what exactly happened on this last trip?" My dad said, with each word coming out as the same note. I thought it was really weird of him to ask, since Mom had just spent all day telling us all about that very thing.

"And what's with this Florida nonsense you dumped on us today?" he said right after, like he didn't even really want an answer to the first question.

"What does one thing have to do with the other?" Mom said. "And I'd hardly call helping kids nonsense, Douglas."

"Okay, well then, what's with you dropkicking my surprise across the yard?" he said, followed by what sounded like a kick to the side of The Roast. "I mean, I know this thing is nothing fancy, but I don't recall you being so fancy either. Up until today, that is."

"Douglas, keep it down," Mom said. "Cass is going to hear you."

"No she won't," snapped Dad. "And you know why? Because I guarantee you that little girl is sound asleep, plum exhausted from the thrill of having her family back together. I just wish I could say her mom felt the same way."

Dad paused, I thought surely to spit out an apology for being so cross.

"Toodi, I guess what I want to know is, what all of a sudden is so unpleasant about me, you, and Cass venturing out as a team like we always wanted?"

Because she's just taking *me*, I thought. The Rabbit only holds two people. I wondered how Mom would break that news to him. I hoped she planned to be gentle. I also hoped that Dad hadn't dented The Roast, since he might be wanting to sell it soon.

"You see, that's the problem, Douglas," Mom said. "Maybe it's not about the *we*." She said *we* like it was a cuss word. "Maybe *we* are not what they need."

"Well, who exactly do you mean by *they*?" Dad said *they* like it was an even cussier word.

"Douglas." Mom mixed his name in with a sigh. "There's just no easy way for me to say this."

"Well then, say it the hard way."

"We won't be taking this motor home to Florida. We won't be sleeping in this thing, eating in this thing, or selling meat in this thing." Mom spilled it in one-breath, like Syd doing the Belch of Allegiance, and she wasn't half as gentle as I'd hoped.

"The deal is . . ." she began.

And then, behind that wall of motor home, the gap between words was unbearably long and deafeningly quiet. Every eyebrow-tug I made was loud in comparison. *Say it, say it, say it*, went my pulse.

"The deal is, I'm going alone," Mom finally said. "Just me. Not we."

It was her worst rhyme ever.

But . . . I thought.

"But . . ." my dad said.

"That's the plan." Mom trampled our *but*s. "Me, alone, in Florida."

"You alone, huh?" said Dad, the energy draining from his voice. "This isn't about orphans at all, is it, Toodi?"

With that, this sickly stillness washed over everything, and I couldn't tell if it came from outside or within me. It was like this thing I'd heard about called "the calm before the storm," when the sky gets eerie-green and even the crickets have an intermission. From the midst of that terrible calm, I heard my mom let out a little sob.

"I hoped we could avoid this conversation for a couple of weeks," she said, all hushed and blubbery. I waited for her crying to be muffled by my dad offering his shoulder to her, but it stayed very much unmuffled.

"I hoped we could avoid this conversation for a whole lifetime," said Dad, sounding like he could use a shoulder himself.

"So go ahead," he said. "Tell me his name."

"Douglas, don't. . . ." said Mom.

"The least you can do is tell me his name." Dad said it like his back teeth were pressed together.

"Ken," she finally answered, and for such a tiny word, it sure was heavy. Just saying it made my mom cry even harder. While she did, I desperately searched all my memories for a Ken, but couldn't find one. Could Ken be the guy who ran the orphanage? Was there a Kenneth, Missouri? Couldn't there, oh please, couldn't there have somewhere been a Hurricane Kenneth?

And then there came a storm so fast and scary, like when a wall of rain overtakes you on the playground. The green sky cracked right in two as a tornado of awful words whipped up beyond The Roast. A twister of whispers with words like *cheat* and *how* and *betrayal* and *lies* all spun up with ones like *intentions* and *loss* and *needs* and *boring*. But no shred of a *sorry* or a *stay*. It was more vicious than raccoons fighting over garbage, and it gave me a bellyache worse than bad mayonnaise ever could.

As the storm raged on, I heard my mom say, "What about Cass?" sobbing my name into three syllables. "What do we tell her?"

My dad answered with the terrible words, "Toodi, maybe *we* are not what she needs. . . . It sounds to me like there is no more *we*."

Hearing that, I figured I had a choice to make, and quick. I could pull out enough eyebrow hairs to grant an army of wishes. I could crawl into the bathtub and drag a mattress over myself until it all blew over. Or I could run right out there and perform my first-ever storm rescue. Before I knew it, I'd jerked a fistful of blank pages from my journal and was headed for the door, planning first to tell them both to *Can it!* and then to tell Mom all the amazing things she and I could fill those pages with. Things that had nothing to do with anyone named Ken.

I dashed outside so fast I didn't even notice the abandoned cell phone that sat there waiting for revenge. Tripping over the phone and skinning my hands and knees on the gravel, I watched the blank pages swirl in the gust stirred up from my mom's car as it squealed out of the driveway. Her taillights shrank away to nothing at the end of our street, and my dad just sat like a lump on the front bumper of The Roast.

"Where's she going?" I said. "What did you say to her?"

While Dad perched there noiseless with his head bowed, Toodi Bleu Skies took off for the ocean, without even one piddly wave to spare for me.

eight

Nothing Good
Left to Find

I should have crawled into the bathtub and drug a mattress over myself.

Oh please, won't some kind of superhero fly around the globe so fast that it'll spin in reverse and make time skip back? That's what I was thinking as I limped all the way to my bed, where I wrapped up tight in my blanket and tried hard to drown out my thoughts with the whistling in my nose. Not even a minute later my dad crept into the room. Looking much like a ripe tomato, his eyes all swollen in the red glow of my alarm clock, he laid a crumpled pile of journal pages and that stupid beat-up phone on my dresser.

"You okay, Cass?" he said. "Are you hurt?"

He should have known the answer to that. It was as dumb as asking *Are you a girl?*

"Where did she go?" I asked, hoping he'd say that Mom was just testing out the new tire or getting some fresh air.

"Florida," Dad said, using his *Uncle Clay's in the hospital* voice. "She's gone to Florida."

I tried to remind myself that Mom had been gone and come home many times before, but something in Dad's voice made this one sound different. Like the superglue version of gone.

"Truth is, I've had a bad feeling about things for weeks," he said.

"So why didn't you tell me?" I said.

"Because I just kept praying that I was imagining things," Dad said.

"Who's Ken?" I said.

"You heard us?"

"Some."

Dad sighed what seemed like four lungs' worth of air.

"Ken is a man who lost his wife. And your mom, well . . . I guess sometimes compassion can lead you down the wrong street, Cass."

And thus began the worst bedtime story ever told. No frilly princesses, no white horses, no pointy castles. Just a Storm Rescue Barbie who wants to help a Storm Victim Ken rebuild his life without the help of her boring other family. While Dad talked, I stared at my bedroom wall, watching the shadows of the pipe cleaner people grow.

"But why'd you make her go?" I asked.

"She was going anyway, Cass. She only wanted the two weeks to pack all her things and to . . ." He stopped short.

"To tell *me*?" I said. "Why didn't you let her tell me?"

"Cass, you need to understand—"

"I could have changed her mind," I said.

"You need to understand that your mom's mind has made some real bad choices," he said. "And she's likely to keep on piling them up."

"But what about the orphans?" I asked.

Another even bigger sigh from Dad. "I think this Ken has kids who lost their mom. I guess that's who she was talking about."

Suddenly, the long thin shadows of my pipe-cleaner people turned scary, stretching up the wall like they were trying to tear it down.

"But she'll just be with them until they find their own new mom, right?" I said. "Right? I mean, isn't there an end to every rescue?"

Dad took half of forever to answer.

"Cass, there's something pulling on your mom real hard right now," he said. "It's like she's gotten herself all tangled in the fresh start of a new place and new people. Like she's gotten addicted to being Toodi Bleu Skies."

"How did you know about her statue name?"

"I heard you two talking."

"And you still busted in before I even got to ask her," I said.

"Ask her what?" said Dad.

"Nothing."

That's about all I could stand to hear from Dad, and I think it was just about all he could stand to say. Short of stopping time and dragging my bed to Syd's storm cellar, faking sleep seemed the best way to avoid any more awfulness that night, so I breathed in and out so deep and so regular I made myself woozy. My dad sat wedged in my purple papasan chair with his face in his hands for hours, while I stayed low under the covers to avoid catching glimpses of a sniffly man in my dresser mirror.

When Sunday morning arrived without the *Whew, it was only a nightmare* wake-up I'd hoped for, I peeled the sheet unstuck from the scab on my knee. Dad was stretching awake, still curled up in the toppled chair. I had to step over him on my way to the hallway, where I found one of Mom's framed awards lying on the floor with its glass cracked in half. I picked it up and propped it against the wall before going to the kitchen for a breakfast of baby sweet pickles. While I ate them straight from the jar, a big fat fly stomped around in a drip of sweet on the table.

"You going to eat that last one?" Dad said, groggily stumbling over the laundry basket and catching himself on the edge of a chair.

"You can have it." It was a shrively brown pickle anyway.

Dad sat down and rubbed his face. We both stared at a bottle of Tabasco. The fly rubbed its feet together.

"Did you know I was your mom's first-ever rescue attempt?" Dad said, thumping crumbs across the table.

"Really?" I said.

"Yep, I turned my head to get a look at her and stumbled into a puddle deep as my shins," he continued. "She came all the way across the road, took me by the hand, and helped me to my feet. I remember that the first thing she ever said to me rhymed. 'I'll help you out of this crunch in exchange for some lunch,' I think it was. They had to mop up the mud at the Burger King after our first date."

Dad ricocheted an old Cheerio off the fridge and said, "So, to answer your question, Cass . . . maybe there is an end to every rescue after all."

"That one doesn't count," I said. "That wasn't even a real rescue."

I hated how he was talking about Mom like she had vanished into thin air. Like we were as powerless as a couple of poopy pansies to get her back again. I looked Dad square in the eyes for the first time since yesterday.

"You broke her certificate," I said.

"What?" he said. "That wasn't on purpose, Cass. I knocked it off running in to check on you."

"So then why didn't you run after *her*?"

"Because car-chasing is best left to dogs," he snapped. "And mainly because your mom made it real clear she didn't want that."

Dad waved the fly off the jar lid.

"But she was going to teach me to rescue," I said. "And now she's gone, and I'll never get to go to wherever and help anybody. And I'll for sure never ever have a statue."

Sure enough, my summer suddenly felt like it had become a hidden-pictures puzzle in a magazine. One that some kid had already made into a circled-up mess. Like there was nothing good left to find. That there'd *never* be anything permanent in my whole life that was worth noodling on a wall.

With that thought, another cry came squeezing at my throat.

"Why couldn't you guys just put it all in the storm

cellar?" I said. "Why couldn't you just *can it*?"

But Dad only made a sad little snicker at my suggestion.

"Because, Cass," he said. "It seems you can't really can a Ken."

The deflated *I give up* tone in his voice made my anger swell up high inside me. From the overflow came just two mumbled words.

"Thanks, Dad."

"For what?" he said.

"For ruining my chance of ever being a hero because I'm stuck here in my own shoes eating other people's stupid potpies forever."

I scooted my chair back so hard it went up on two legs.

"And you *did* knock it off the wall on purpose!" I shouted with all the volume I could muster, turning to run from the room. But Dad grabbed me by the elbow just in time.

"Now listen up, Cass," he said, sounding like something might be squeezing at his throat too. "Do you remember that time your hair got spun up in that minifan and I had to cut you free?"

Of course I did. I remembered him singing every Gordon Lightfoot song he knew to try and calm me while he snipped off half my ponytail bit by bit with a pair of nail scissors. I remembered Syd turning purple with the laugh he was holding in. I remembered thinking I'd look like a haystack forever.

"No," I said.

"Well, I know this all seems sudden and scary and

hopeless," Dad said, his words slow and deliberate. "But I promise I'll get you out of this terribleness too."

With that, he smashed the fly so hard with his palm, it made the little wooden letters leap off the Scrabble board, and sent a mean splash of pickle juice straight into my eye.

nine

(fun)k

Dad got up to wash his hands as I made a squinty dash to the bathroom, where an unexpected discovery totally distracted me from my stinging eye. The pink plastic beauty box. I couldn't believe Mom hadn't taken it with her. And gut-wrenching as it was to find it there, in a weird way it was also kind of comforting to have a little box of momness left behind. So I immediately ran to my room to bury it under a stack of old stuffed animals at the bottom of my closet. Then, after the burial was complete, there was nothing left to do but flop onto my bed and lie there for hours, switching positions only when my hair started to hurt.

Every time I rolled onto on my side, I could see my dad standing on a chair in the backyard, his bottom half sticking out from under the hood of The Roast. To me, the motor home had become as unappealing as a milk jug left in the garbage too long, and I hoped hard that Dad was getting the useless old thing ready to be recycled. What if Dad hadn't upset Mom with his bad plan? I would have had two whole weeks to change her mind about leaving.

All day long I lay there and wondered. Wondered if maybe she'd left behind a long red finger-string for me to follow. Or a trail of cotton balls. Or at least an unused wish or two.

I didn't even remember getting the phone off my dresser, but I found myself holding it, smushing the MOM button again and again, like I needed to report to her that my head had fallen off my shoulders. The cracked phone just sat there dead in my hand, so I clicked it onto the charger just in case it could maybe be revived. In the shuffled stack of in-between pages Dad had salvaged and left on my dresser, I found the torn entry from the day before. I grabbed a pen, and for the first time ever, couldn't come up with a single noodle.

At dinnertime, from the other side of the wall, I heard my dad searching for the Beefaroni pan as if he were juggling everything metal in the kitchen. My head throbbed with every clank. Minutes later, when the smoke alarm sounded, I rubbed my temples like grown-ups do when they're plain old fed up.

"Hey! Psssssst! Cass!" All I could see of Syd were his eyes and nose above my windowsill.

"Syd, I'm really not in the mood."

Truth is, I was a little glad to see Syd in the window, the scene being like a repeat of life as I knew it yesterday. I just didn't want to have to tell him how the scene ended.

"What was all that fussing about last night?" he said.

"And what in the world is that noise?"

Syd's bull's-eye questions meant there was no putting it off. Jagged and painful as my words were going to be, they had to come on out.

"My mom is gone," I said. "And burned Beefaroni."

Syd raised up on his elbows. "Get out dot com!" he said. "What do you mean Aunt Toodi is gone?"

"I mean *gone*," I said. "She went to live with another family for a while."

Just saying it out loud made things more sickeningly real.

"You . . . don't . . . mean . . . it," he said.

"Yeah, well, my dad said sometimes compassion can take you down the wrong street," I said, trying to sound like I remotely understood how doing good for people could turn so bad. Syd was silent so long, I thought he'd passed out standing up.

"That's weird," he said. "Compassion comes with a *compass* right there in it. Shouldn't compassion always lead you in the right direction, then?"

Syd's unwelcome opinion made my ears itch like crazy.

"Besides, can you already have a family *and* get another one?" he said.

"Can you be nosy *and* obnoxious?" I tugged hard at my earlobe.

"I mean, isn't that like having a new heart installed and forgetting to take the old rotten one out?" he said.

"Are you calling me a rotten heart?"

"Sorry," he said, and then got quiet again. "You staying in bed all day?"

"Maybe all week," I said.

Syd looked like he was searching his mind top to bottom for something suitable to say.

"Hey, you know what, Cass? I heard about this guy in Miami that got all shark-bit," he said. "They kept him asleep for a month until his body could handle the pain."

"Sharks aren't the worst thing in Florida," I told him.

The smoke alarm went off a second time.

"What do you mean by that?" he asked.

Fighting back tears and befuddled by the alarm, I took a deep breath.

"Look, Syd," I said. "Thank you for checking on me and all, but it's real hard to talk about this right now, okay? I mean, let's just say that there was a whole ocean-ful of wrength at my house last night."

Syd got all squirmy with speechlessness. I could tell I'd pushed him beyond the level of tenderness that a twelve-year-old boy is comfortable with.

"Well, all I know is, you better not lay around all week while I'm sitting in summer school," he fussed. "That would be big-time unfair."

"Can it, Syd." I rolled over and faced the dresser, try-ing to pretend I couldn't see my cousin's sun-speckled face in the mirror as he stood there and watched me like I might just fade away.

Just then, there came a buzzing that was so weak and so hard to hear over the blaring smoke alarm, I thought I was imagining it. That is, until Syd's reflection said, "Well? Are you going to answer that?"

I didn't have the time or the presence of mind to tell Syd how glad I was he'd stayed in the window. Instead, I bunched my bedspread and sheet into a pile on the floor, trying to get at the cell phone to answer it.

"Mom?"

"Cass? Baby?"

Crackly as it was, the sound of her voice gave me such a dizzying relief, I sank to the floor in the corner of my room. My thoughts raced. *She's sorry. She's coming back. She's turning around.*

"Mom! I can barely hear you."

Through the open window, Syd gave me a double okay sign, and I shooed him away.

"Mom, where are you?"

I shooed Syd again.

"Cass, baby, listen to me good, okay?" she began. "Your dad won't let me talk to you on the other line, so I thought I'd try this one real quick.

"Listen, baby, there are things so hard to explain . . . like how some people need rescuing more than others," she said with sobs filling in the gaps between the words. "But Cass, you can make a difference, and you will make a difference. Will you remember that? And someday I will visit *your* statue, okay?"

With all the figuring I could muster, I couldn't make much sense of the things she said. They sounded more like pieces of a late-night TV movie you hear when you're half asleep than a Mom thinking about coming home.

"But when—" I said, when a big *schlak!* came from the kitchen, followed by the sound of batteries rolling across the linoleum.

"What, Cass?" she said.

"When are you coming back?" I said, super loud. "And what do you mean *I'll* make a difference?"

"Cass, you talking to me?" Dad hollered through the wall.

"No!" I yelled back.

"What?" he said.

"No! Sir!"

"Cass, I'm so sorry, baby, but I have to go," Mom said, her voice trailing off.

Dad came stomping down the hall. Syd finally shooed.

"I love you," she said. And when she hung up, there was total silence. No alarm, no Syd, no breathing. Just silence.

Dad opened my bedroom door to find me pressing the phone to my face, like maybe I could smell her through it.

"Was that your mom?"

"Yeah, and she said you wouldn't let her talk to me."

Dad didn't even offer an excuse.

"Did she say where she was calling from?" he asked.

"How come?" I said. "Do you want to go get her?"

"What did she say?"

"That she loves . . . *us*."

"Really? Was that it?"

"And that this is just an in-between." I took the liberty of filling in a few of the blanks for Mom. Dad rubbed his face hard.

"So are we going to?" I asked.

"Going to what?"

"Go find her."

Dad reached down and took the phone from my grip,

70

like I was a baby who'd gotten hold of a chocolate bar and now he was going to go hide it from me.

"Try to get some sleep, Cass. We'll talk tomorrow."

Soon as Dad's footsteps faded, I ran to the open window and looked for Syd, but he was gone. I stood there alone and gazed at the part of the night that wasn't hidden by a big nasty RV, and I tried again and again to begin my front-and-back-of-forever prayer, but not one person would show up for the parade in my head.

ten

Goo Grief

The first Monday morning of summer break brought the smell of scorched coffee under my bedroom door. I went to the kitchen to find the coffeemaker turned on, but nothing but a circle of burned blackness in the bottom of the pot. Through the window above the sink, I could see my dad stepping high over the dew-soaked weeds of the backyard.

I poured myself a bowl of cereal, wedged my fingers into the sugar bowl trying to get at the last few clumps, and then searched the drawer for a spoon that hadn't been chewed up by the garbage disposal. The only smooth one I found was too big to fit in the sugar bowl, but I did catch a glimpse of my upside-down self reflected in it, and my upside-down self said to me, *So, why in the world aren't you finding that cell phone and calling your mom?* I also happened to notice that upside-down me looked about as puffy-eyed and ugly as right-side-up me was feeling.

I ran straight to Dad's bedroom and stood on a flipped-over laundry basket to search the shelf at the top of his closet, his one-and-only place for hiding things my whole life. Sure enough, among dusty papers and an old hunting knife, the phone sat right there, so I snatched it and ran to my own closet. Taking my first real breath of the day, I put the phone up to my ear and pressed MOM one more time. I don't know what in the world I'd planned on saying, but the voice on the other end sure enough decided for me when it said, "Your prepaid minute balance has expired. Please purchase a refill." I immediately pictured Dad calling dumb things like dial-a-joke over and over again just to let the minutes leak out of the phone, and it made my heart feel tight like a sunburn.

On the way out of the closet, I got poked in the foot by the corner of the pink plastic beauty box. Peeking out from underneath a layer of mangy Beanie Babies, the box offered no help for my heart, but at least maybe a fix for my eyes. I nestled back into the closet floor in a dusty strip of sunlight and carefully unfolded the box's levels, one by one, until I found a big jar labeled *Goin' Undercover*. The stuff inside was probably too tan for my skin, but I spread it on good and thick under both eyes, all the while thinking about what Mom might say, like, *If sad is what you feel, use this to conceal!* And when I was done, my eyes did look sort of okay in the little beauty box lid mirror. Okay for a darkish closet, that is.

"Cass! I need your help!" my dad yelled. Dad never rhymed, not even by accident.

I closed up the beauty box, the cell phone still inside,

and headed outside to find Dad trying to yank the blue cover off The Roast. He was already in a sweat.

"I thought I could do it in one grab," he said, pulling off his T-shirt to wipe his face. The contrast between Dad's tan arms and his white chest made him look like he was wearing another shirt underneath. His curly brown hair was fluffed out like he'd run his fingers through it a million times. Even his beard was all mussed up.

"Want a sip?" Dad grabbed a bottle of Yoo-hoo from off a lawn chair and twisted it open.

It made me even madder at him that he would drink something as cheerful-sounding as Yoo-hoo on such a sad day.

"No thanks," I said.

As he gave it a guzzle, the morning sun lit up the gray-brown flecks in his eyes.

"You mind helping me uncover this thing?" he said.

"Okay," I said. "But . . . why?"

"So we can clean it up," he said. "Now, you take that corner, and I'll get this one."

As I reluctantly grabbed a handful of cover while trying to avoid blotches of mildew and bird blech, the thought crossed my mind to be glad that Dad might very well be planning to sell the beast; but it crossed my mind real fast, because my mind was a busy street full of other bigger thoughts. Like how I could figure out a way to talk to Mom again. To steal her back away from Ken and the not-really orphans. How when she waved good-bye to them, her little Cass silhouette charm would ting in the Florida sunshine. Then she'd come make things right with Dad, and press the unpause button on all my plans.

And until that day, how in the world was Aunt Jo's storm cellar going to hold all the bads in my head, including the one that was about to jump out of my mouth.

"Did you let the minutes run out on purpose?"

"Excuse me?" he said.

An angry itch spread beyond my ears and into my whole face.

"Why'd you have to hide the phone from me? Why won't you let me talk to Mom?"

Dad dropped his corner to the ground.

"Two words," he said. "Surplus suffering."

"What?"

"It's kind of like that time you wanted to play storm rescue and put on a whole box of Band-Aids at once," he explained.

"But you told me no."

"Exactly, because I knew they'd pull all the fuzz out of your arms and make you hurt more than what a Dad should ever allow his daughter to go through."

He picked up his corner again.

"And frankly, Cass, you talking to your mom right now is what I would call surplus suffering."

Dad crumpled the blue plastic in his fists and said, "Now pull!"

We both grunted and snorted as we yank-yank-yanked the cover into a pile, sending a puff of shower-curtain smell all around us. Then Dad grabbed the half-empty Yoo-hoo bottle, held it by the tip, and waved it in the air, saying, "It's no sparkling grape juice, but fit for a christening such as this."

"Christening?" I said.

"You know, like sending a ship off on its first journey," he said, and smacked The Roast three solid times before the Yoo-hoo bottle shattered against it, spattering the side with watery chocolate.

"What journey?"

The lift in his voice sure didn't sound like he was talking about a journey to the junkyard.

"Didn't I promise I'd get you out of this terribleness?" Dad said, tossing the jagged Yoo-hoo neck toward the garbage and missing, landing it in the grass. "Well, three days from now, we'll be blasting off, Casstronaut. Just you, me, and The Roast," he announced, trying to hug an arm around my shoulder. But I backed away just out of reach.

"You. Me. The Roast. Three days?" I stammered.

"Yep," he said. "I figure if I work nonstop, that'll be plenty of time to get her ready to travel."

"Travel where?" I said. "To Florida?"

"Not to Florida," Dad said abrubtly. "Maybe everywhere *but* there."

"But what about Mom?" I asked.

Dad looked like I'd just licked my fingers and pinched out his flame with a *tsssss*. "Your mom's already made her own travel arrangements."

"I know," I said. "But what if she changes her mind?"

Dad knelt in front of me. "Look, Cass, you're just going to have to trust me on this one. I know I'm feeling my way around in the dark right now, but I figure an adventure together might just bring some much-needed inspiration into our lives. I've saved us up a little money, and who knows? Maybe I've a bit of excitement tucked up my sleeve too. Maybe you'll find that your dad's not a total bore after all."

Yeah, and bologna potpie might be delicious, I thought.

"But what if I made other plans?" I said.

"Well, one thing I do know for sure is that you and I are going on this trip regardless," he said. "And we're going to have us some fun, even if it takes us weeks."

"Did you say a week?"

"Nope. I said week-*suh*."

One thing *I* knew for sure was there wasn't enough goo in that beauty box to conceal the disappointment on my face.

"Come on and help me shine this baby up," he said.

Perhaps not enough goo in the world.

eleven

Rategy-stay

I spent the rest of the morning scrubbing bug guts off The Roast and imagining what it was going to be like to spend weeks trapped in a RV with my dad instead of waiting at home for Mom. What if I spent the whole summer living in that box, missing her miserably, having to be a meat-seller's assistant to the man who refused to even try and get her back?

As I stooped to pry one last gluey moth wing from a taillight, Syd wandered up behind us.

"Looking good, Uncle Douglas!" he said, giving the motor home a slow *fwoooeeet-fwoo* whistle. "Wish I could buy this thing. I'd totally live in it."

"Sorry, Syd. She's not for sale," said my dad.

"How come you're home so early?" I asked Syd, sounding only a tenth as happy to see him as I felt.

"Because I asked my English teacher if vegetarians had to speak Fig Latin instead of Pig Latin," he explained.

"And then the whole class talked Pig Latin and wouldn't quit. I told her I was eally-ray orry-say, but I still got sent home.

"Yikes!" said Syd when he saw my eyes. "What's up with your face? You got peanut butter smeared on there?"

"Butt a stump, Syd."

I must have looked all sorts of miserable.

"Whoa. Are you okay?" he mouthed.

"No!" I mouthed back, motioning him over to the storm cellar. While my dad admired the transformation The Roast had undergone, from dull-stained beige to shiny-stained beige, Syd and I raced to the shelter, where we sat on the edge and swung our legs down into the opening.

"Why's he still working on that thing?" asked Syd.

"Because he's taking me on a trip."

"A trip? To where?"

"I don't know." I shrugged. "Wherever they need steaks other than Florida, I guess."

"For how long?"

"Could be weeks, Dad says."

"So why are you so ajorly-may ummed-bay?" Syd sounded confused. "You've always wanted to see new places, right?"

"Yeah, but I wanted to see them in a Mom way, all heroic and exciting and stuff," I told him. "Not all funky and junky like *that*."

We looked back over our shoulders just in time to see my dad trying to re-aim The Roast's cross-eyed headlights.

"I kind of see your point," said Syd.

"And not just that," I said, "but Dad's been talking about Mom like she just poofed into the air, and now he wants us to go spend every moment together pretending there was nothing we could do to stop her from going."

When Dad turned and made his way toward Uncle Clay's porch, Syd and I bypassed the steps and leapt all the way down into the dim shelter, where the family's fortune-size worries filled jars all around us. Syd pulled the doors shut over us and tugged a dangling lightbulb on.

"Did you tell him you don't want to go?" he asked.

"Yeah, but he said we're leaving in three days no matter what."

I drew circles on the dusty floor with my finger.

"How're you going to work on your big wall doodling in that crusty RV?" he said.

"Noodling," I said, rubbing the circles gone. "And don't worry. There's not going to be anything permanent worth drawing in my future anyway."

Syd and I both looked to the lightbulb and watched till it quit its swinging.

"So what did Aunt Toodi say to you on the phone?" he said.

His question put a lump in my throat the size of a hush puppy.

"That this is only an in-between," I said.

"What's that supposed to mean?"

"It means I need to find a way to tell my mom to C-O-M-E B-A-C-K other than dropping eight Scrabble letters into an envelope."

"Excuse me?"

"It means that I just need to *talk* to her again. To convince her to come on back."

"Yeah right," said Syd. "You couldn't convince a wad of gum to stick to your shoe. Besides, I'd be mad too if I were Uncle Douglas. My mom said Aunt Toodi really did a number on you guys."

"Well, she didn't mean to," I said. "She's just gotten a little carried away with her job is all. And she's going to come back when those kids get their own new mom and don't need her anymore."

"Whatevs," he said. "Do you really believe that?"

I hated the way I had to pause to check if I *did* believe that.

"It's not about what I believe, Syd. It's about what I know. She's *my* mom, and I know *my* mom loves me too much to stay gone."

Syd picked at a callus on his palm. I wanted to shake him by the shoulders.

"Besides, there's an end to every rescue, you know."

I was beginning to think I needed to airbrush *There's an end to every rescue* on the back of the tank top. Folks around here sure needed some reminding.

Uncle Clay's wheelchair made squeaks above the cellar as he rolled out to greet my dad. I scooted close and looked Syd right in the face.

"Syd, it is crucial that I be home when she comes back," I said. "If I'm not here, she just might leave again."

"All right, all right," said Syd, his big knobby giraffe knees bumping my little ones as we both sat crisscross on

81

the shelter floor. "Then what we need to do is come up with a rategy-stay."

"A what?"

"A strategy. For getting you out of this trip," he said. "All we've got to do is think up a good excuse for you not to go."

From above, there came some garbly mumbling. I could have sworn Uncle Clay said the word *strategy* too.

"They must have heard us," whispered Syd. "Keep it down."

I studied the shelves, trying to read just one of the folded messages inside a jar, while Syd worked up a thinking sweat. The lightbulb over his head made him look like a shadowy mad scientist. I could tell what he was thinking. *What would Fearless Fenwick do?* And boy, was I ever right.

"I've got it!" he said, packing a yell into a whisper. "How do you feel about Fake Tetanus?"

"Fake Tetanus?"

All I knew about tetanus was that Mean Maritucker Mentz down the street got it once from stepping on a nail and couldn't shake a fist or call anyone a *dweemus* for a whole week because of her twitchy arms and her lockjaw.

"It's easy," he said. "All you need is a fake injury and some ketchup for blood."

"Syd, I'll try to put this in a way you'll appreciate," I said. "That idea is totally *ridic*. Besides, didn't Maritucker have to get a shot for her tetanus?"

"Yeah. I think she did."

"And didn't she say the needle was big as a toilet paper tube?" I said.

Syd just stood there and burped. After that, we spent practically the whole day ping-ponging plans, writing each and every one down, and then crossing the stupid ones out.

Hide in the storm cellar for a month
Volunteer to go to summer school
Fake leprosy (Syd's idea, of course.)
Catch a bus to Wherever, Florida

When Aunt Jo opened the cellar door to hand us down a tray of sandwiches, Syd crumpled up the evidence of our scheming and tossed it over his shoulder.

"Take what you want and pass it back up," she said. "I gotta feed the menfolk too."

On the corner of the tray was a little manicure kit.

"What's that doing on there?" asked Syd.

"Your guess is as good as mine," Aunt Jo said. "Uncle Douglas said they needed it."

While Syd picked potato chips from his back teeth, I stood on the ladder to take one more look at The Roast. The late afternoon sun sent a gleam of inspiration right into my eyes.

"I've got an idea!" I said, thinking about Mom's flat tire and how Dad should have left it that way.

"What?" Syd squeezed in beside me on the ladder.

"There's no spare tire on the back of The Roast," I said.

"What?"

I pointed Syd's head toward a big chunk of broken Yoo-hoo bottle in our backyard.

"See that broken bottle?" I explained. "Just to delay the trip a while, what if I—"

"Syd Nordenhauer!" called Aunt Jo. "Come on in and do your homework, boy."

"Wrengthapalooza," said Syd. "I gotta go."

"It's okay," I told him. "I've got to go too. You just be here right after school tomorrow."

I climbed out of the shelter behind Syd. Once we'd parted ways, I watched the tops of Dad's and Uncle Clay's heads through The Roast's little side windows to make sure they weren't looking out. I could see Uncle Clay wheeling around wearing a top hat and my dad laughing at him.

When the coast was clear, I grabbed a stick and picked up the neck of the Yoo-hoo bottle with the tip of it. Then I crept up to The Roast and placed the broken neck ever so gently, jagged edge up, underneath the right front tire. I'd never felt so criminal as I did squatting there waiting for my chance to bolt unseen to the house. I could totally hear Dad and Uncle Clay talking loud and clear inside the RV.

"This is really great stuff," said Uncle Clay. "I wish we could have done this when we were kids."

"Yeah, she's going to wig when she sees all this," said Dad.

"We Nordenhauers do have immeasurable power," said Uncle Clay.

"And immeasurable potential," said Dad.

Overwhelmed by a prickly mix of guilt and curiosity, I wriggled the stick back into the neck of the broken bottle and flung it far as I could out from under that tire.

The dads silenced their talking when the bottle clanked against a rock, and I darted in a stooped position to my house, replaying their words and wondering who exactly it was that was going to wig when she saw what. I spent the rest of the night wishing that the immeasurable Nordenhauer power they'd spoken of included long-distance eavesdropping skills.

twelve

Sabo

Tuesday morning, I found a note attached to a sausage biscuit on the kitchen counter. It said: "Cass—Sorry so busy. Getting things shipshape for the big trip. Just 2 minutes in the microwave for the biscuit, and just 2 days till we hit the road!"

The two-minute countdown was time enough to become thoroughly disgusted with Dad for thinking that this lousy trip could cover up all the heartache he'd caused, like some goop on a zeeyut. And not to mention, for making all these plans without even asking me. And, while we were at it, for using an exclamation point at a time like this.

I accidentally cooked the note with the biscuit, setting the corners on fire a little, and had to blow on it all the way to the storm shelter. Syd arrived less than an hour later and totally busted me trying to open one of their jars to stuff the note in.

"Okay. Forget the tetanus," he said. "I've got an idea."

"Syd, you scared me! Why aren't you at summer school?"

"Because I put a sign on the guidance counselor's door that said 'Guy-Dunce' and got sent home," he said. "But I did grab you this while I was there."

Syd unfolded a brochure with a little Snoopy dancing on the front. It said CAMP GOOD GRIEF in chunky red letters.

"I think it's mostly for when somebody dies," said Syd, "but it says it's for broken homes too. You could tell your dad you want to go there instead of on a trip."

Until that moment, I'd always thought of broken homes as the buildings Mom pulled people out of.

"My home's not broken, Syd," I said. "It's just a little bendy in the middle is all."

I used the corner of the brochure to scratch my ear, and then threw it on the ground.

"All right, so tell me *your* plan, genius," he said.

I was sure that what I'd done would impress Syd. He didn't have to know right away that I'd bailed on it.

"Well, last night," I told him, "I thought about my mom's tire and how she couldn't have gone with it flattened and . . . I kind of put that broken bottle underneath the front wheel of The Roast."

"You *kind of* put it, or you *did* put it?" he asked.

"*Did* put it."

"Hmmm, sounds like some good sabo to me," said Syd.

"Sabo?"

"As in sabotage. As in making the RV the one who can't go on the trip," he said. "You think it'll really bust that big tire?"

"Probably not," I said, the truth wriggling free. "I took the bottle right back out."

"*Buhgert!*" Syd made his chicken noise.

"I wasn't chicken," I said. "It's just that I heard them talking about stuff, and, I don't know, we just might want to wait a little before we do anything drastic."

"*Buhgert* again!" said Syd. "You don't have time to wait if you want to get out of this trip, Cass. I think it's time we approach things in a Fearless Fenwick kind of way. Like pour something sticky in the gas tank or something. As Aunt Toodi might say, *The Roast is toast.*"

"Yikes, Syd. When you put it all that way, it sounds really mean."

"You're the one who put a broken bottle under the tire!" he huffed.

"Yeah, but I took it right back out!"

"Well, what's your big idea, then, genius?"

"I don't know. What if we just maybe spy on them a little and see what they're up to," I said. "Then we can decide what to do."

"Why don't you just *ask* your dad what they're up to?" Syd rolled his eyes.

"I did ask," I said. "He wouldn't tell me anything. He just keeps saying 'Trust me.'"

"Do you trust him?"

"That's a dumb question, Syd."

"Well, do you?"

Syd didn't even wait for my answer, which was a good thing, because I wasn't totally sure what it would have been. He was already lifting the cellar door with the top of his head to take a peek across the yard.

"Check it out," he said. "Good timing . . . it looks like the side door is opening."

Syd and I climbed out into the daylight and hid on the side porch while Dad rolled Uncle Clay down the ramp and into our backyard. He pushed Uncle Clay's wheelchair with one hand and pulled my old red wagon with the other.

As the two of them made their way slowly up our street, Syd and I zigzagged from tree trunk to tree trunk a safe distance behind them. We did this until the big trees ran out, two blocks from my house. That's when the dads disappeared around the corner, headed toward the shopping part of town.

While we waited for them to come back our way, Syd and I hid behind a garbage can, speculating about what in the world the two of them might be doing.

"I've barely seen my dad for two days," said Syd. "I don't even think he came in to bed last night."

"Same here," I said. "All I know is, Dad's been leaving me these weird little notes that don't explain any of it. And get this: last night I smelled some spray paint fumes coming in my window. And not just that, but I thought I heard something jangle, like an instrument, maybe."

"Oh, come on," said Syd. "Now you're imagining things."

"Then Dad woke me up with his banging around in

the attic this morning," I went on. "He must have been getting that old red wagon. Maybe they're using it to load the meat or something."

"Speaking of meat," said Syd. "I've been meaning to ask you . . . if your dad has access to all those steaks, then how come you guys eat Beefaroni and church potpies all the time?"

"I don't know," I said. "I guess steaks are for people with stuff to celebrate."

Syd reached up to shield his face from the afternoon sun, looking in the direction of our missing dads. When he did, I caught sight of an empty cicada shell clinging to the sleeve of his shirt.

"Looks like you've picked up a hitchhiker there," I said, expecting Syd to tweeze the little carcass off with his fingers and flick it at me. Instead, he was fast overcome by a major case of the heebie-jeebies.

"Ugh! Get it off!" he yelped, dancing all over the sidewalk and flailing so fast it looked like he had twenty arms and legs. He shook so wildly, and I laughed so uncontrollably, we didn't even notice when Dad and Uncle Clay rounded the corner and wheeled up on us.

"You gonna be all right, son?" said Uncle Clay. Dad just smiled and gave me a wink. Syd turned ten shades of embarrassed.

"Um, yeah," he said, regaining his composure enough to say, "We were just taking a little walk."

"Yeah, us too," said my dad. I noticed that they looked just as tense about running into us as we were them. My dad tried to stand between us and our view of the wagon while Uncle Clay tied all their Then Again Thrift Store bags shut. After that, the four of us headed home, no one mentioning cicadas or garbage cans or wagonfuls of who-knows-what, which made for the longest walk back down the street ever.

When we reached the driveway, Dad said, "There's still some work to be done, kiddos. You guys check in with Aunt Jo if you need snacks."

Syd and I stood and watched as Dad and Uncle Clay rolled their pile of things into The Roast and shut the door behind them.

"I suppose they'll be in there the rest of the day, huh?" I said.

"Yeah, I suppose," said Syd. "They had an awful lot of stuff on that wagon. Maybe they got everything they—"

"Wait! Listen!" I interrupted Syd with a shush. "There goes that jangly noise again. The one I was telling you about."

Syd heard it, too. "What in the world? Have our dads gone loopy or what?"

"I'm going to watch and listen out the window in my room for a while," I said. "See you tomorrow?"

"See you tomorrow," he said.

That night, the curtains remained shut in The Roast, but when its lights came on, I watched my dad's shadow move back and forth across the length of the RV. I went to sleep trying to remember the only secrets I'd ever known Dad to keep from me before this week. Little stuff, like surprise birthday cupcakes and Easter candy. All I knew was it sure did seem like a lousy time for him to graduate to the big secrets now.

On Wednesday morning, I found my frozen biscuit on top of the Scrabble board, with the words BIG FUN SOON spelled out next to it, as if little wooden letters could make everything right.

The microwave stunk of smoke from my minifire the day before, so I took my frosty sausage biscuit and made my way back to the cellar, to find Syd already there waiting for me.

"Syd, did you skip school?"

He had a sheepish look. "I told my mom you've been acting kind of screwy and needed some help," he said, doing his hands on the sides of his face like cuckoo clock doors. "But never mind that. Can I have half your biscuit?"

"You don't want it," I said. "It's still hard in the middle."

Syd gave my breakfast a poke like he didn't believe me. "You come up with a good plan for staying yet?"

"Nope," I said, because, truth be told, the reasons for *going* were starting to pile up, mainly in the form of little bits of mystery. So, together, my confusion and Syd's lack of inspiration settled around us in a haze of awkwardness that lasted most of the morning. To pass the time, I spun my half-thawed sausage patty like a coin across the floor. Then suddenly its wobbly twirl gave me a little spark of an idea.

"Hey," I said. "The other day, my dad said something about borrowing a freezer to keep all that meat in, right?"

"Right."

"So that means he's probably already put a freezer in the RV, right?"

"Yeah."

"And maybe it's full of meat by now, right?"

"So?"

"So, I say we . . ."

"Snip the cord!" Syd cut at the air with his fingers.

"No, Syd, we just unplug the thing. Then it will all be thawed by the time we're ready to leave. And if the meat is unfrozen, we got nothing to sell, right?"

"Whoa, that beats the Fearless Fenwick approach by a mile," said Syd, biscuit crumbles flying off his lips. "Plus, then we'll have some good eats around here for days!"

I didn't find it necessary to mention that I'd also thought of the reverse plan of plugging the freezer right back in, if necessary. And how I planned to have a good look around The Roast before I made a final decision.

"That settles it, then," said Syd. "You and me, midnight tonight, we break in to The Roast!"

"Break in?" I said.

"What? You scared or something?" said Syd. "'Cause you know I'm not."

This from the same Syd who once got both pinkies jammed into a Chinese finger torture at the flea market and panicked so hard he ripped the thing right in two.

"Whatever, Syd."

"Great," he said, with a thumbs-up. "Now, let's split up for the day. We've got tools to gather, dark clothes to find, and alarm clocks to set. Plus, I have to make a fake Syd for my bed."

"A fake Syd?" I laughed. "Can I keep him as my cousin instead?"

Syd rolled his eyes. "See you at midnight."

I climbed up onto the grass, feeling a little twinge of nervousness when Syd whispered behind me, "Be sure to wear some gloves tonight . . . in case we have to eak-bray an indow-way!"

thirteen

Schwickity-flack

When Real Syd came tapping at my window at 11:59 p.m., I was beyond prepared.

Dark purple sweat suit, for camouflage. Check.

Old fuzzy slippers, for their tight fit and quiet sneak-ability. Check.

Dad watching *Bonanza* rerun way too loud in other room. Check.

Cousin wearing an old Batman costume. Check.

I scrambled out my bedroom window to find Syd wearing a tool belt cinched around his plastic cape. One pocket held a long black flashlight, another held Uncle Clay's big wrench, and the rest were filled with pistachios.

"Hey, Batboy, you think you could have brought a quieter snack?" I whispered. Syd rushed at me to thump my arm but couldn't follow through without nutshells tumbling to the ground. We stood side by side surveying the dark tallness of The Roast, its shadow looming large and spooky.

"So which window's gonna bite the dust?" asked Syd, whap-whap-whapping the wrench into his palm.

"Shouldn't we at least try the doors first?" I asked.

"If you want to waste time," he said.

Just to aggravate him, I strolled over slow as I could and checked the driver door. Locked. I checked the passenger door. Locked. I checked the middle door. *Un*locked.

"Dang," said Syd, holstering his wrench.

I pulled the door open, slow and quiet. There was so much darkness inside, it spilled right out, all mixed with the smell of spray paint and cough drops. My goose bumps came together with second thoughts about the whole midnight plan.

"We're going to need your flashlight," I said.

Syd handed over the light. He had a scared, *You go on in and I'll stand watch out here* look on his face.

"You go on in. I'll stand watch out here," he said, standing stiff with the wrench squeezed tight in his hand. "Just let me know if you need backup."

"Come on, Syd," I said. "This was half your idea in the first place."

"I know." He shrugged. "But what if there are ghosts of past owners hanging out in there?"

"What in the world?" I said.

"Like old dead robbers who were shot by police. Or old dead spies who were shot by the FBI. Or old dead robbers who spied on the old dead spies who robbed them?"

"Syd, you're not making any sense," I said. "Besides, I'm sure they'd all run at the sight of a handyman in a cape."

Syd made a cross-armed pout and secured the wrench in his pocket. I stepped up into the darkness of The Roast by myself, holding Syd's flashlight out at full arm's length. I'd never walked into something with so little idea of what to expect. It felt like landing on a whole other planet.

Just then, the flashlight faded to half strength, and I was forced to take things in just one bit at a time, shining my way item by item through the front of The Roast. At first, my weak beam of light revealed a scattering of very Dad-ish things. A Swiss Army knife with all the tiny tools fanned out like a little sunshine of gadgets. A half bag of stale candy corn. A caseless, scuffed-up CD of *Gordon Lightfoot—Complete Greatest Hits*. The middle section of the motor home simply held a gray velour sofa on the right and a rolltop desk with a folding chair to my left. Nothing much mysterious about all that.

It wasn't until I lit my way farther to the back that things became not so predictable. The entire rear section of The Roast seemed to be separated off from the rest by a tablecloth covered in faded poinsettias. The tablecloth hung from the ceiling like a curtain, tied back with one of my old ponytail ribbons. Inside the little area behind the curtain, filling most of the space, sat a wooden box long as a bathtub and tall as my hip. On the front of the box, I noticed there was a plate-size hole, just big enough for me to stick my face into and regret it when I got a noseful of dirty-sock smell. I couldn't see inside the box through the hole, but I sure wasn't about to put my hand inside, scared it could very well be holding the ghost socks of dead robber-spies.

On top of the wooden box was a stack of familiar items mixed in with some unfamiliar. I recognized the cushion from Syd's den couch laid all the way across the lid. Folded neatly on that was the yellow afghan that Aunt Jo made me years ago, the one I'd retired because my long middle toe used to get caught in it. The next level up was a small blue pillow of worn velvet, and balanced on that was a fresh box of colored pencils, newly sharpened and great for noodling. A little red sharpener sat on top of the pencils like a cherry.

Above all that, out the back window, Syd's head popped up as he jumped for a peek. "Freezer?" he said on his first jump. He'd nearly startled the soul right out of my body.

"No freezer!" I said on his second jump.

"Meat?" he said on his third.

"I don't see any!" I said on his fourth.

I ignored the fifth, sixth, and seventh jumps, and waved the light around for more discoveries. There was "CASS" written in glitter in Uncle Clay's jagged handwriting on the back side of the curtain, a poster showing the construction of the Eiffel Tower in six different black-and-white photos thumbtacked to a wall that had been freshly painted white, and a stack of old wrinkly magazines on the floor. So this is what they were doing in here, I thought. Setting all this stuff up.

At church they call it having your conscience pricked when you suddenly feel like some of your rights may have been wrongs in disguise. Like sabotaging something that could very well have been designed with your own happiness in mind. I made my way to the gray couch and squished down into its softness to soak everything in. As I leaned back, my heel bumped something tucked up under there. It was a worn leather suitcase I had never seen my dad carry before, and on it were faded gold non-Dad initials that read *MBM*. I sure couldn't think of any MBM's that we knew. Then, as I fiddled with the lock on the suitcase, another odd detail caught my eye. Straight ahead of me and parked under the rolltop desk was that old wagon of mine, with a shoehorn wedged under to keep the wheels from rolling. As the wagon sparkled in the shine of my flashlight, I could have sworn it was freshly covered in glitter paint.

Suddenly I felt The Roast shaking, and heard a muffled voice from below.

"Hey!" said Syd. "Check it out! Raiders of the Lost Roast!"

Please tell me he is not holding on underneath, I thought.

"I'm holding on underneath!" he said. "I'm a stowaway!"

As the batteries in the flashlight gave out, I pushed the suitcase back under the sofa and rose to feel my way to the exit. Then, no more than two seconds after the last whimper of light, I felt myself step right smack-dab into the middle of the most bizarre thing thus far inside The Roast. The thing was jangly and tight on my foot, and my biggest problem was, I couldn't seem to step out of it. An icy wave of remorse flowed all through me as I considered the possibilities. Was this an alarm of some sort? A booby trap set for spying kids?

Of course, my best option at this point would have

been to simply sit still, but sometimes when you're scared, best options get mixed up in your head. So instead, I scrambled out the door and across the carport, running like I'd been caught in a bear trap. My foot sent up a rowdy *schwickity-flack! Schwickity-flack!*

It wasn't until I found a chunk of moonlight that I looked back to see ribbons, colorful and long as a peacock's tail, trailing behind me. The ribbons were attached to the fanciest tambourine ever, wedged stubbornly onto my own left foot. It seemed the more I shook, the less the tambourine budged and the louder it got. And then I saw a light come on in the kitchen.

"Let's get out of here!" I shouted, making a dive for my bedroom window.

Syd slid mechanic-in-a-panic style out from underneath the motor home, letting out a yowl as he scraped across the concrete. And while my *buh-gert* cousin ran all the way home with a fresh hole flapping in the back of his costume, I closed my window just in time, almost pinching the trail of ribbons under it. The tambourine was jammed so tight on my trembling foot that I squeezed my muscles desperately to not rattle it. I sucked in a breath and almost choked on my own spit.

"Cass? Cass? You okay?" my dad called from the hallway.

"Um, yeah, Dad. I just, um, sort of tripped is all."

"All right," he said. "Well, good night in there. Get some good rest so you can be ready for our big bon voyajee in the morning." Dad slipped his words under the door quiet and careful, like he was sneaking bits of food to a trapped animal.

"I'll be ready," I said, surprised to hear the rise in my own voice, like my mouth had forgotten to consult my heartache first.

After Dad was gone, I found my fattest pillow and pressed it down over my foot to silence the racket of trying to wrestle the tambourine loose. As I tug-tug-tugged with my free hand, I wondered, if I had found a freezer in The Roast, would I have unplugged it?

The tambourine finally came off. I combed its tangled ribbons with my fingers as best I could, realizing that any plan that would make a meat salesman acquire something as silly as this might very well be worth giving a chance.

Nope, I thought. I definitely would *not* have unplugged it.

fourteen

Bon Voyajee

On Thursday morning, The Roast *rrr-rrr*-rumbled to life right on schedule, signaling the start of a journey that fake disease, crackpot plans, and one concerned ousin-cay couldn't delay. While Dad waited outside, I ping-ponged around the house, gathering my things.

First, I packed the most important stuff: cell phone, red string, the injured Book of In-Betweens. And then came the *well, you never know* category, which included the Sharpies and the pink plastic beauty box. And finally the regular stuff, like clothes, toothbrush, and flip-flops. As I grabbed a handful of underwear from my drawer, the little fortune-size Castanea dentata tree tag came out with them and fell at my foot. I stuffed it into my pocket to remind myself to ask Syd to water the tree while I'd be gone. After that, I found that the airbrushed tank top made for a good undershirt, with a light hoodie thrown on over it to help me sneak the tambourine back into The Roast.

Then there was just one more thing I needed to do, in case Mom returned while we were gone. I yanked a blank page loose from my Book of In-Betweens and wrote:

Dear Toodi Bleu Skies,
   In case Dad didn't tell you, we've gone on a trip in The Roast (bleh).
   I know you didn't mean to leave without saying good-bye, and I know you've been trying to call too. My phone ran out of minutes, but I'm going to try to fix that as soon as I can. And I guess if you're reading this note, it means that you're home. Just pllllllease stay here and wait for me.
                    Love,
                    Castanea Dentata Nordenhauer
(Oh, and P.S. I took the beauty box with me.)

I wanted to add my first noodling in days to the page, but before I could finish even one little raindrop next to my name, I was interrupted by the jarring honk of The Roast's horn. So I left the good-enough note on the bathroom counter, grabbed my backpack, and went outside, where Uncle Clay, Aunt Jo, and Syd were on their side porch, ready to say their good-byes. When Dad saw me, he slid out from the driver's seat slow enough to only slosh his coffee a little. He crunched his way over the pistachio shells on the ground, and Aunt Jo gave Syd an irritated glance, like she knew he'd been involved in some kind of nutty scheme.

I stood right next to Syd, who shook his whole body in rhythm with the grumble-hum of The Roast. To prevent the tambourine under my sweatshirt from speaking up, or worse yet, dropping out and rolling across the driveway, I had to dedicate one whole arm to pressing my tummy.

"They let you stay home again?" I asked Syd, out the side of my mouth.

"Nope," he said. "Suspended. For skipping yesterday."

"Sorry."

"No bigs. So what was the inside of The Roast like?" he whispered.

"Truly?" I said. "Kind of wackadoo."

"Good wackadoo or bad wackadoo?"

"Not sure. Some neato things, but definitely some weirdness."

"Don't worry," said Syd. "Maybe it's just stuff left over from the dead-robber-spies."

"Thanks," I said, with a small kick to Syd's shin. "You're a big help."

Dad stood between Uncle Clay and Aunt Jo and licked the coffee from his thumb.

"Well, I suppose it's time for some see-ya-laters," he said. "You all keep an eye on the abode, if you will, while Cass and I are out broadening our horizons."

"You two take care of each other," Aunt Jo said to Dad mid-hug.

Uncle Clay grabbed my dad by the hand. "Clean start," he said, squeezing his fist real tight. "Clean start."

"I appreciate all the help this week, bro," Dad said.

"Thanks for trying to get me out of this," I whispered to Syd.

"No prob."

"Oh, and one more thing," I said to him. "Water the Castanea dentata tree while I'm gone? Please?"

Syd rolled his eyes. "Sure, and I might as well feed some dead squirrels while I'm at it."

"Come on."

"Okay, okay," he said. "I'll squirt the twig. . . . Now, come here, I made something for you." He pulled me by my elbow just a few steps over and dug something from his pocket.

"Since I can't be a stowaway on The Roast *and* go to summer school," he said. Then he handed over a Sucrets box with the words CAN IT! scribbled in black marker on the lid.

"Cass, I'm real sorry Aunt Toodi went. And I'm real sorry you have to go. But maybe when you're on the road, you can put all the thoughts you can't live with in this, and we'll store them in the cellar when you get back."

Syd's momentary sweetness made me smile inside. That side of him would have made a great stowaway.

"I'll try," I said, thinking I'd probably be needing a container much bigger than a Sucrets box. "And hey, will you please watch for Mom while we're gone? If she does come back, tell her I need to talk to her right away.

"And promise you won't bust the cloud piñata," I added.

"Come on," said Syd.

"Promise!" I said. "And don't let Fake Syd bust it either."

"I promise," he said, and gave my belly a jangly wallop. "Nice tambourine, by the way."

I silenced my gut with a press of an arm as Dad and I crossed the yard to The Roast. It was really about to happen. Me, Dad, and all his secrets were about to hit the road to anywhere-but-Florida. The notion to run in the other direction passed through my mind, but the thought was quickly chased off by a rolling boulder of curiosity.

Dad gave me a little boost through the driver's side, and once he'd shut the door hard behind us, he turned to me and said, "Welcome aboard, traveling partner. Shall we begin our tour of The Roast and its amenities?"

"I guess so," I said.

"I'll admit it's more Ritz cracker than Ritz-Carlton," said Dad. "But here goes."

As he began, I scanned the space and made my best *Wow, I've never seen all this stuff before, and especially not last night when I snuck in here* face.

"Directly to your right," he said, "you'll see our general living area, which will double as my bedroom when necessary."

The squishy gray couch was loaded up with my dad's pillow and faded quilt. In front of the couch on a plastic coffee table, his duffel bag sat, with a corner of the Scrabble box poking out through the busted zipper. On the floor next to the couch, the strange MBM suitcase was still pushed up under the driver's seat.

"Dad, who's MBM, and what's in that suitcase?" I asked.

"Oh, all that will be revealed soon enough," he said, with a slight double-lift of his eyebrows.

"And just beyond the living area is our food pantry,

which I've stocked with some sustenance for the road," he continued, opening the cabinet door to reveal a selection of canned meals that would have made Chef Boyardee himself proud. On the side of the pantry that faced the big couch, there was a hook with a suit bag hanging from it. The suit bag was puffed out full, like there could very well be a gorilla costume inside.

"Now, on the left, you'll find our little bathroom, which I affectionately refer to as the knee-bumper," he said.

I stuck my head into a room so small, a girl could sit on the toilet and wash her hands and take a shower all at once.

"And this space just past the knee-bumper, I've deemed our thinking area."

Dad pointed to the scuffed rolltop desk that was bolted down to the floor. On a shelf above the desk was a collection of frayed encyclopedias, two old sets shuffled together. Half of them were labeled 1987, the other half 1998. From beneath the desk, that old wagon of mine still sat and sparkled, like the night before.

"Why'd you bring the wagon?" I said. "Is that on the will-be-revealed-soon list too?"

"You bet," said Dad, looking pleased that I had noticed.

"And last, but hopefully not least," he said, squeezing around me to just beyond the desk and sweeping the poinsettia tablecloth-curtain to the side. "Your own custom space."

He did that part in a weird TV voice, like when you

watch an old game show rerun and the announcer is seriously excited about the prize, even though it's just a big ol' seventies microwave.

"Check out that big box under there," he said. "I found it at the Then Again. It's an old magician's trick box."

"Yick. Like where the lady gets sawed in two?"

"Well, yeah, but not for real sawed," he said. "And check this out. A special something from your Uncle Clay."

Dad pulled the curtain shut and said from the other side, "You like?"

I had to admit that seeing my name that big and in glitter in the daylight was a cool thing, especially the way the glitters fluttered to the floor each time the curtain moved.

"I know it'll take a while for all this to sink in," Dad said. "So you just do your best to make yourself at home, Cassoline. We've got one stop to make before the adventure begins."

As I unloaded my things from the backpack, wedging them all into the few storage crevices I could find, I noticed that the mystery smell still crept from the hole in the big wooden box.

"Oh, and sorry about the aroma," Dad said, like he could read my nose's mind. "I considered sprinkling some cinnamon back there, but I sure knew better than that. I'll see what I can do when we gas up."

"Thank you," my nose had me say.

I released the tambourine from my shirt, sending it bouncing across the floor like an air hockey puck. Then I peeked around the curtain to see Dad, seemingly unaware of the noise, buckling himself in and adjusting all the things around him like a pilot might do. That is, if a pilot's controls consisted of cold coffee, Kleenex, and a lime-wedge air freshener. Clipped to the visor over my dad's head was a photo of baby him and toddler Uncle Clay eating from the same bucket of dirt. When Dad flipped the visor up, I saw grown-up Uncle Clay through the windshield, wearing the same grin on his face, the cloud piñata dangling all scruffy in the distance over his head. Dad popped the Gordon Lightfoot CD into the dashboard and began to sing kind of quiet and shaky-voiced, "'Carefree highway . . . let me slip away, slip away on you. . . .'"

We made the turn from the backyard onto our own driveway, The Roast lurching back and forth like a dog about to be sick. I scrambled up onto my box-bed and looked out the back window just in time to see Syd, Aunt Jo, and Uncle Clay with openmouthed, surprised faces that made them look like carolers on a Christmas card. My dad had just run clean over the Castanea dentata, without the slightest clue what he'd done. There weren't even any remains left behind, like the tree had just disintegrated under the weight of The Roast. As we bumped off the driveway, I saw *You don't mean it* form slow on Aunt Jo's lips.

fifteen

Rules of
The Roast

I pulled the crumpled tree tag from my pocket and crammed it into the CAN IT! box.

While Dad and Gordon Lightfoot and I rolled slowly past the all-too-familiar sights of Olyn, I planted myself in the desk chair and opened to a blank page in the Book of In-Betweens. On it, I fast-noodled a fitting tribute, a skull and crossbones made out of a leaf and two twigs. I was just fixing to wonder if a Castanea dentata tree was even capable of growing stately and strong at all, when my dad turned in to the gas station so dramatically, my pencils rolled right off the desk and onto the floor with all manner of The Roast's loose doodads joining them there.

As he backed up and inched forward at least five times to line up with the gas pump, Dad said, "Cass, I have a feeling it's time to establish some Rules of The Roast."

When we finally squeaked to a stop, he said, "Ever hear of holding down the fort?"

Well, of course I had. All the times Mom had gone rescuing, it was the last thing she would say to me. All but this last time, that is. She'd say, "Be my little fort-holder, Castanea."

"Here's the thing," said Dad. "Apparently The Roast, well, she likes to make some wide turns, which are more than a little unsettling to her innards. So we'll call this Rule of The Roast Number One: *A big turn is your concern.*"

It was the first rhyme I'd ever heard him do, like he was trying to be all Toodi Bleu Part Two or something.

"From now on," he said, "when we take us a swerve, you'll have the ever-so-vital job of securing anything that you are long-armed and stretchy-legged enough to reach. The last thing I want is for you to be knocked silly by a flying book."

"Okay," I said.

"You willing and able?" he asked.

"Able," I said.

"Care to practice?"

"Sure."

"All right, let's see here," he said. "Our signal to activate wide-turn-stuff-securing mode will be as follows . . .

"Biiiiiiiiiiiiiiig Riiiiiiiiiiiiiiiiiiight!" My dad made such a holler, I chomped the edge of my tongue. And when I didn't jump into action, he did it again. "Biiiiiiiiiiiiiiig Leeeeeeeeeeeeft!"

If for no other reason than to avoid one more holler, I practiced my part of the plan, discovering that if I stretched hard enough, I could secure small desk items with one hand, keep the coffee table from tumping with my left foot, block the wagon from rolling out from under the desk with my other foot, and finally, with my right forearm, I could hold all but one encyclopedia volume on the shelf above. I decided that, in the event of a real flying encyclopedia emergency, X-Y-Z could be sacrificed. Xylophones, yo-yos, and zebras had nothing to do with storm rescue research anyway.

"Excellent first effort," said Dad. "I'm going to fill 'er up and run inside for a few items. Want to come along?"

"No, thanks. I'll just hang out."

"Okay by me," he said. "But sit up here in the passenger seat so I can have an eye on you."

While Dad got the gas glugging into The Roast, I caught sight of our own little church, which was right across the street from the station. The sign in front said, *Triumph is just UMPH added to TRY!* Brother Edge was replacing the exclamation point that had fallen off. In my side mirror, I watched Dad hook the gas nozzle back on the pump. Then, all quick and nonchalant, he yanked a chunk of Castanea dentata tree from under the back bumper and stuffed it into the garbage can. Dad shouted a hello to Brother Edge and waved to him on the way into the store.

Next door to the gas station was the Best Yet Discount Foods, which Syd calls the Best Yet Disco, because Aunt Jo did a slippy dance on a smushed avocado there once while "Stayin' Alive" played overhead. I noticed a nest wedged into the Y of the big Best Yet sign. In it, a bunch of baby birds bobbed their rubbery heads while their mother made trips back and forth to a packet of french fries spilled on the ground. I imagined a Toodi Bleu Bird flying off to another nest in Florida, with my little rubber baby bird butt stuck down in the letter Y.

Y us.

Y this.

Y now.

Sighing, I gave a little stir to the pile of things in the center console—various gum, ancient peppermints, ball-point pens, and a toothpick or two. In the midst of it all was a small piece of paper, a gum wrapper with a name and address written down.

Kenneth Brandt, 42 Wintergarden Street,
Fort Napaco, FL

Suddenly, that one address landed heavy as a whole phone book on my brain. Could that be *the* Ken? It had to be *the* Ken. We didn't know any other Kens. I considered swiping the wrapper, but thought, What if Dad is taking us there to get Mom, and needs it? So real quick, I wrote myself a copy on another wrapper, just in case I might need it too.

When I leaned to put the address in my back pocket, something beneath me rubbed my ankle in a most irritating way. It was a big piece of paper rolled up like a scroll in the floorboard. I tried to unwedge it and take a quick peek as Dad rounded the back of the RV. Before I could get it loose, though, both Dad and his jumbo bag of teriyaki beef jerky had already climbed in.

"Sorry if you saw any of that tree carnage back there,"

he said sadly. "Some landscaper I turned out to be, huh?"

I pretended I didn't even know what he was talking about. After all, if he didn't already know that tree was important to me, I sure wasn't going to tell him about it or any other important things now. Dad was developing quite a knack for making important things disappear.

"Did you get some smell-good stuff?" I asked.

"Yeah. Hopefully these guys will do the trick," he said, producing an air freshener from behind the jerky bag. It was a bonus double pack of two little cardboard pizza slices with arms and legs and faces that winked at me. One was a mister with a mustache, and the other a missus with red smoochy lips. Dad busted the seal on his beef jerky and it smelled almost as bad as my box-bed. I couldn't get those fresheners opened fast enough.

"Look at ol' Brother Edge over there," he said. "I bet he'll fix that sign a dozen times this week. When your Uncle Clay and I saw him the other day, he was in a stir trying to knock a hornets' nest from the awning before the church swap meet, but check it out. He still found the time to gather us a little something for our trip."

Dad leaned toward me and opened the glove compartment, bumping my knees a little with the door. Inside was a stash of CDs, each case with the word *Encouragement* written in orange on the spine. Dad's *It's a dirty job* ball cap sat upside down next to the collection.

"Some of his best sermons to go," said Dad. "The ones with the most *UMPH* in them, I guess. On Sundays, we'll take a rest from our work and give a listen."

Dad tried to slam the glove compartment shut eight times before it stuck.

"Speaking of work," I said. "Where's the meat?"

"In the church parking lot, like always," Dad said.

"Not the swap meet. The M-E-A-T."

He aimed the bag of jerky my way.

"No," I said. "The *meat*. That we're supposed to sell this summer."

"Oh that," Dad said. "I thought you'd never ask." He squinted one eye and looked down into the bag. "Cass, have you ever looked at, I mean really studied, the number eleven?"

"Um, not really."

"Look here." He pulled two long matching pieces of jerky out of the bag and dangled them side by side in front of me. "Now, pretend this is the number eleven, albeit a teriyaki-flavored eleven."

"All right."

"See how the left and the right of the number eleven are in perfect balance with one another? Ignoring the lumps and bumps of the beef jerkiness, of course."

"Uh-huh."

"Well, that there is a good demonstration of what's so great about being almost eleven years old, Cass. On one side, you're old enough to gain knowledge about certain unexplained secrets of this our tiny mobile world, and on the other side, you're still young enough to appreciate the magic of them. It's the perfect balance."

Dad leaned in, bit off half a 1, and gave me the other 1. I took a nibble, finding the taste way less bizarre than his little speech.

"Regarding the meat," Dad continued. "You just don't even need to worry about that. We're about to have a summer beefy with new places, new faces, and some lumps of wonder mixed in along the way."

"Florida would be a lump of wonder," I said, bracing inside for the scowl I expected from Dad.

"I've got forty-nine better ideas than Florida, Cass."

As soon as he said those words, I wanted to crumple them up and stuff them right back into his mouth.

"Then why do you have Ken's address written down?"

Dad almost urped his jerky.

"Well, now that you mention it, I've been wondering the same thing myself, Cass. I looked the address up, I guess out of some kind of morbid curiosity. But it occurs to me that that little piece of knowledge may well cause us some surplus suffering."

He picked up the gum wrapper and crammed it into the plastic quick-mart bag. I was so glad I'd made a copy.

"How come we can't just try?" I said. "Maybe go and see her? I bet both of us talking to her will help. We could stay there until she changes her mind."

"It won't do any good, Cass."

"It might."

"It won't."

"So then, where *are* we going?" I said. "Do we even have a map?"

Dad peered over a pair of convenience-store sunglasses that were already so stretched they scooted down his nose.

"I see that you are ready for Rule of The Roast Number Two," he said. "And that is: *Maps are for saps.*"

"Then how will we know where to go?"

"Go lift the lid on that magician's box back there," Dad said.

"My bed?"

"Yep. Go on back there and have a look inside."

Arming myself with the new air fresheners, I made my way to the back and lifted the pile of things off the box. I opened the latch to find a small collection of old shoes inside. There was a clog, a dress shoe, a hiking boot, and a loafer. One almost new, one almost crumbling, all of them dirty, and none of them matching.

"Whose are these?" I asked.

"Don't know. Uncle Clay and I found them while we were running errands this week. On the side of the road. In the middle of the road. One about to fall into a sewer drain.

"Which brings us to Rule of The Roast Number Three," he said. *"It's the shoes what choose."*

Again with the rhyming. Who is this man, I wondered. And what has he done with my dad?

"The shoes choose what?" I said.

"Choose where we go. What I mean is, that there is our map," Dad said. "You and I are going to drive until we find a deserted shoe in the road, whatever kind of shoe it may be, and then we'll stop to work in the nearest town thereafter."

I started having that strange other-planet feeling again.

"But why shoes?" I asked.

"Because," he said, "I heard a certain someone once mention how exciting it would be to not know where she's going next, and to have to be ready for anything. I thought of the shoe thing when Clay and I found all those the other day. They were like a sign."

He started the engine.

117

"I'll admit it's an unconventional way to see what life is like in someone else's shoes. But frankly, I felt like you and I needed some *why not* on this trip, and it just seems to me like a good *why not* thing to try."

Lowering the box lid slowly, so as not to puff out a blast of stink, I watched Dad's face in his rearview mirror for some sign of *Ha-ha, just kidding about the shoe thing*. A twitch, a wink, anything. But he was serious as he could be.

"And we're not coming home until we find a matching pair," he said.

I dropped the lid of the box right onto my thumb.

"What?" I said. "You mean two alike?"

"Two alike."

"Together?"

"Not necessarily."

My stomach got a little twisty. "But that could take forever!" I said, feeling certain that forever wackadoo would not qualify as a good permanent.

"Yeah, well, the way I see it, Cass, if we find something good out here on the road, then forever might not be such a bad thing."

My thumb still throbbing, I knotted Mr. and Mrs. Winky Pizza onto the latch of my big metal shoe-box bed. Within seconds, the scent of oregano replaced the foot smell in my space, but I still took my little velvet pillow and crammed it into the hole just in case. Once my nose was totally satisfied, I made my way back to the passenger seat and buckled in.

"Sorry," said Dad sheepishly. "I seemed to have

overlooked the stink factor. We can shove those shoes in a bag if you'd like."

"It's okay for now," I said. "I think I sealed them up good."

Besides, I had bigger concerns than my nose for the moment.

"Dad, are you okay?"

"Will be," he said, chewing so hard I could hear his jaw pop. "And you will be too."

He nodded toward the big roll of paper on my floorboard.

"Careful not to squish that with your feet," he said.

"Why? What is it?" I said.

He smiled. "We find a shoe, and you find out."

The Reacher

It was a hypnotizing afternoon of scanning the road ahead of us for just one abandoned shoe. We were on a west-bound highway, and just about anyone knows you can't get to Florida driving west, so I found myself counting the white dashes of the center line and imagining that each one represented a day that would pass before we'd ever find two shoes that matched each other. Three hundred and seventy-four dashes had gone by before Dad stirred me from my daze.

"What rhymes with *suds*?" he asked.

"I don't know," I said. "*Floods*?"

Dad looked at me like, *Now what did you have to go all weather on me for.*

"Maybe *cruds*?" I said. "Or *duds*."

"*Duds.* That's a good one," he said. "What about *bubble*? What all rhymes with bubble?"

"Why are you asking?"

"Just humor me," he said. "Is *flubble* a word?"

"I'm pretty sure not," I said. "How about *stubble*? Or *rubble*? Or *trouble*?"

"That's it! *Trouble* it is."

And trouble it was indeed. The way I saw it, not only had my mom gone away, but now my dad may very well have gone nutty. Fortunately, I remembered Aunt Jo telling Syd again and again to *Leave trouble well enough alone*. So that's exactly what I did. I excused myself back to my little room and immediately put Ken's address in my CAN IT! box, alongside the Castanea dentata tree tag.

For the rest of the afternoon, Dad seemed to drive aimlessly, merging on and off exit ramps and swoopty-loops, passing up towns, small and big. Despite the back-and-forth, I was able to balance pretty well on my knees to keep a steady watch of the sights out the back window. Houses strung with Christmas-in-June lights. Deer families bounding across the road. Shotgun pellet dents in the back of every sign. There were things I'd never seen before that passed across the window, like a mountain of junked-out cars and even a trailer home built into the side of a hill. Neat things. Things that would have even been more enjoyable alongside a mom in a Volkswagen convertible, where I might still notice them despite much wind-whipped hair and girly conversation.

Once my legs and the sunlight gave out, I lay down and thought about how Syd must be spending his day, and hoped that he hadn't busted that cloud piñata with a stick as soon as we'd left. I thought about how it would have been great to have even a fake Syd along for the ride, to tell him about beef jerky and old shoes and a dad talking nonsense like a Cheshire Cat. When The Roast climbed a big hill, a few loose colored pencils rolled under the curtain into my space. So with my hand dangling at the floor, I waited patiently for the next hill and the next delivery. I propped my feet on the wall below the Eiffel Tower poster and lifted the bottom corners of it with my big toes. It sure did look like a good blank canvas for some permanent wall noodling hidden under there. That is, for another kid who had something worth putting there. I figured I'd just have to be satisfied with noodling in my Book of In-Betweens.

Just after another handful of pencils arrived, The Roast took a swerve to the side of the road so sudden, there wasn't even time for a "Biiiiiiiiiiiiiiig Riiiiiiiiiiiiiiiiiight!" to burst out of my dad. All ten encyclopedias came tumbling off the shelf in an avalanche of old information.

"Sorry about that," Dad said. "You in one piece back there?"

Miffed that he'd already forced me to break a Rule of The Roast, I crawled around the floor, gathering as many books as I could into one armload. The Roast came to a stop, and when I got up, there was my dad standing in the weak glow of the ceiling light. He held a fishing pole that looked remarkably familiar.

"Cass, would you like to do the honors?" he said, extending the pole in my direction.

I dropped the books onto the desk and took hold of the handle. If it had been a surgeon's knife in my hand, I couldn't have been less sure of what to do next.

"Allow me to bestow upon you the honor of being the first to ever assume command of Ye Olde Sneaker Reacher," he said.

The pole was only about as tall as my hip and looked like a piece of bamboo with a reel attached and some metal loops with fishing line strung through them. At the end of the line, there was a little silvery hook. I ran my fingers across the pole, feeling the knuckles along its length, and sure enough, it was bamboo. I could also see and feel some rough spots on it, spots in the shapes of little lightnings that someone had tried to sandpaper off.

"This is Mom's piñata whacker," I said.

"It *was* her piñata whacker," said Dad. "Now it's *our* sneaker reacher.

"Climb on up," he added. "I saw some reflector strips flash in the headlights." Dad stood on his knees on the couch and wiped some fog off the side window with his hand. I stepped up onto the cushion next to him, scraping the tip of the rod along the ceiling of The Roast. With a grunt, he slid the window to the side and motioned for me to have a look.

I leaned as much of me as I could out the open window and saw that we were parked well off to the side of a two-lane highway. It was that time of day when the sunset has just left some orangey-pink behind, and the air was still muggy. The only sign of life nearby was a building that had been a gas station, the whole thing rusted and covered in vines. Just a stone's throw up the road, I could already see the WELCOME TO MISSISSIPPI sign, with the loops of its four S's all holding on to each other. There were no headlights other than ours for as far as I could see in either direction.

I turned my attention to the road itself, and sure enough, there it sat, smack in the middle of all that near-nothingness: a shoe on the center line of the highway. One single running shoe, with steam rising all around, like someone had run so fast his foot had just burned right out of it.

Wriggling my upper half back into The Roast, I fumbled around with the bamboo rod. I had imagined many times what the world was like beyond Olyn, but I'd sure never pictured myself parked crooked in an RV on the shoulder of an Alabama highway holding a knobbly fishing pole. I could almost hear Syd doing that *Twilight Zone* theme he does when the electricity flashes on and off.

"Um, Dad, I don't know . . ."

"I see you're feeling uneasy, so I can try it first," he said. "The Reacher, please." He held his hand out, took the pole, and ever so gently, threaded it through the long, rectangular window above the couch. Then he made a slight jerking motion with his wrist.

"Rats," he grumbled.

Then another jerk.

"Shoot."

And another.

"Nuts. That's three strikes for me," he said. "You want to give it a go?"

"Sure," I said reluctantly.

I wrapped both my hands around the handle, dug my tiptoes into the couch, and leaned myself and the pole out the window. Fixing my eyes on the crisscross of the shoe-laces, I gave the Reacher a hard fling, and before I could even see what I had done, my dad wigged out like I'd just won a gold medal.

"You've got it, Cass!" he shouted. "Now reel that sucker in quick, before any cars come!"

I turned and turned the reel until my arm cramped. We both watched the shoe dance backward across the road and then bob right on up the side of the RV. I felt a big *whew* when Dad volunteered to take it off the hook. He stuck his hand right down into that steamy sneaker and said, "You know, I don't think this is what your mom meant by putting yourself in someone else's shoes."

"Yeah, I doubt it," I said, having to bite the insides of my cheeks to make my smile flatten out. I couldn't believe I'd hooked the thing in one throw. I mostly couldn't believe I was actually proud of myself for catching a shoe.

"You know what this means, right?" Dad said, as he pulled open my curtain, unplugged the velvet pillow, and pushed the shoe into the hole in the side of my box-bed. "It means the very next town we see is our first stop."

Dad flicked off the overhead light and fumbled his way back to the front, where he carefully laid Ye Olde Sneaker Reacher across the dashboard before starting the engine. While he coasted us to the first off-ramp in Mississippi, I arranged the encyclopedias back on the shelf as best I could by the glow coming through the domed moonroof.

"Nimble Creek, Exit A, here we come!" Dad called out as I unfolded my afghan, stuffed the little pillow back into its spot, and let loose my little poinsettia curtain,

125

which had already shed so many glitters that the name Cass looked more like "Cuss." We parked for the night in the lot of an abandoned minigolf place, where each hole was decorated to look like a different fairy tale. Crumbling and faded as the displays were, I could still make out Snow White, Rapunzel, and The Princess and the Pea.

After a supper of burritos that stayed cold in the middle despite spinning for thirty minutes in the little microwave, I got myself ready for bed in the tiny bathroom, where my elbow bumped the wall a hundred times during teeth-brushing, and I put both my legs through the same hole of my jammies twice before getting it right. Then I listened to my dad run through his own bedtime routine. There was some gargling and spitting, some rolltop desk top-rolling and page-turning, some general bumping about, a quiet, "Good night, Cass. Big things happening in Nimble Creek tomorrow." And then, nothing but snore.

I balled up one end of the big afghan to use as my new pillow, thankful for my own smarts and to Mr. and Mrs. Winky Pizza that I was no longer the Princess and the P.U. The cushion between me and the world's largest shoe box was pleasantly squishy, but still I had a hard time snoozing under the weight of the weirdness around me. What on earth were we about to do in Nimble Creek? Sell invisible meat? It sure wouldn't make things much weirder, I thought.

It was far too dark to add anything to the Book of In-Betweens, so instead I ate a whole bag of Chex Mix, tugged at my eyebrows a bit, and then totally perfected the Knotty Ball of Failure with my finger string. When all of that failed to lull me to sleep, I tried to make it through my front-and-back-of-forever prayer for the first time in days. As I imagined myself sitting on the bare stump of a Castanea dentata tree, my ancestors and descendants marched by like always, but this time none of them would wave or even smile. Instead, they all just walked past carrying suitcases. Probably going to Florida without me. *Amen.*

M. B. McClean

I woke up the next morning with my ear stuck in an afghan hole. There was so much rustling and commotion behind my curtain wall, I stood up, rubbed my eyes, and peeked around the edge.

If I hadn't seen his long dangly earlobes and the creases on his scruffy neck, I wouldn't have known it was my dad, but there he stood with his back to me, adjusting a yellow top hat in the rearview mirror. The mystery suit bag was crumpled behind him on the floor.

I squeaked out a little gasp that made Dad look back over his shoulder.

"Oh!" he said, turning all sorts of red. "Good morning, Cass."

He swiveled his whole self to face me.

"So what do—" His voice cracked the first time, so he had to start over. "So what do you think?" Dad made some nervous *Ta-da!* arms and pointed to himself.

The afghan fell into a lump at my feet. From head to toe, back to head again, I took in the whole scene. There stood my dad in the yellow top hat, big round green glasses with no glass in them, and a wide-striped, green-and-yellow suit jacket that was a bit snug and buttoned over a crispy white shirt. The jacket had tails in the back and two pockets in the front, one big and one tiny, with a piece of tarnished metal chain looping out of the tiny one. The pants flared at the bottom, and peeking out from the flares were some yellow snakeskin loafers with golden buckles on top. He looked just like the cover of a cheap comic book.

I was utterly flabberwobbled.

"Are you heebed out?" he said. "You're totally heebed out, aren't you?"

It was so quiet you could have heard a jaw drop.

"I realize it leaves a little to be desired in the fit, but check it out," he said. "Two of your new favorite colors."

It was indeed chartreuse and goldenrod, just like Mom's shimmery makeup.

"Did you get all that at the Then Again?" I asked.

"Honestly, Cass," he said. "I know I'm no Toodi Bleu when it comes to fashion, but don't you think I would have picked something a bit more flattering for myself?

"In fact," he added, "I think this is a good time for the brand-new, made-up-on-the-spot Rule of The Roast Number Four. *Don't hate the suit—it came with the loot.*"

Dad tried to bend over to get the old brown suitcase from under the driver's seat, but his pants wouldn't let him.

"Cass, would you mind giving me a hand sliding this thing out?"

I lifted the case with both hands and ran my fingers across the embossed MBM under the handle.

"What do you mean, loot?" I said.

"Gently, gently!" Dad said when I let it drop too hard onto the table. "Delicate stuff inside there."

He wiped the dust off the lid with his cuff.

"This is the loot I speak of," he said. "There's a big family secret inside this case here, Cass, and you and the people of Nimble Creek are about to find out."

"But what kind of secret?" I said. "And who's MBM?"

"He's M. B. McClean," Dad said. "And you're looking right at him."

I thought to myself in my best Aunt Jo voice, *You don't mean it.*

"I realize it's a big transformation," Dad continued, tugging at his jacket sleeves. "But the thing is, Cass, you and I are in possession of something lots more thrilling than plain old Douglas Nordenhauer has the skills to introduce. It's going to take an all-out spokesperson to do this job right.

"Now, be honest," he said, trying to see himself section by section in the rearview mirror. "Are the glasses too silly? No, it's the hat, isn't it? The hat's too much, right?"

Honestly, I figured we'd reached Too Much one green-and-yellow suit ago. My own dad stood before me in someone else's clothes, second-guessing himself and rambling on about a suitcase full of mystery. I wasn't sure if

I should feel excited or worried. "I'll take your silence as a resounding yes," Dad said, tossing the hat onto the couch. "I know the outfit is pretty outrageous. I felt the same way when I found it."

"Found it where?"

"In the attic with the other things," he said, nodding toward the suitcase.

I reached for the brown suitcase immediately and was met with a quick "uh-uh" from my dad.

"Not just yet," he said, pulling a lint roller from his duffel bag.

"Cass, would you mind giving me a good once-over with this? I don't want to make my first appearance as M. B. McClean looking like a ferret herder or something."

I made three passes over his back with the sticky roller and let out four sneezes before saying, "I just don't . . . I don't get it."

"I know," said Dad. "But just trust me on this. It's still me under here."

He took the lint roller and ran it over his pants. By the time he was through, the roller itself could have been mistaken for some kind of critter.

"Bottom line is, you and I are in for some much-needed sparkle today, Cassiopeia," he said. I knew by the nickname that there was indeed some semblance of dadness under all that getup.

"Now, could you get that big roll of paper from the floorboard in the front?" Dad wheeled the glittered wagon from under the rolltop desk with his foot. He loaded the wagon with both the suitcase and the paper.

"And there's just one more thing I need your help with before we start our day, partner," he said. "A folding table that's stored under the couch. Would you mind getting it and carrying it outside with us?"

I scooted the plastic table away from the couch and laid flat on my tummy to reach under. While my hand patted from one dust clump to another, I could see Dad's yellow loafers wandering around The Roast in a circle as he mumbled, "Now, where in the world did I put that tambourine?"

"On the floor under the wagon," I said, remembering that Aunt Jo had once told me to be nice to crazy people because you never know when you might be crazy someday too. And that Mom had mentioned something to me about people being so shocked by a traumatic event, they sometimes act a little weird and unpredictable for a while. Even Uncle Clay wasn't himself for a whole year or so after his stroke. But try as I might, I sure didn't remember Uncle Clay ever wearing a stripy costume.

"Come on out whenever you get ready," Dad said, throwing open the door of The Roast so hard it bounced right back and smacked him in the nose. "The good Nimble Creekians await."

eighteen
Nimble Creek

Half of me considered never getting ready at all, and the other half wanted to break the world's fastest getting-ready record. I made it outside The Roast within minutes, to find Dad-turned–M. B. McClean already setting things up in a big gazebo at the center of a park. It was a bright, sunshiny day in Nimble Creek, Mississippi, and I noticed quickly that my limited view of the minigolf ruins had not done the rest of the town justice. The park had a playground full of shiny modern equipment with kids climbing on every inch of it. Just beyond that was an ice-cream stand with a twirling vanilla cone on top. Throughout the park, there were winding sidewalks of uncracked concrete. Not to mention a towering flagpole that put Olyn, Alabama's to shame. But despite all that, I found the newness of the town to be far less captivating than the newness of my dad. And from the looks of it, Nimble Creek felt the same way too. The park was chock-full of families who slowed their playing to stare curiously in our direction. I took comfort in remembering that today would probably be the first and last time we'd ever see these people.

Dad struggled to unroll one end of the big paper without the other end rolling right back up, so I laid the table on the grass and knelt down to hold one side under my knees. He pressed out the paper all the way, to reveal a banner that said in tall black letters:

TOTALLY FREE! TODAY ONLY!
M. B. McCLEAN AND HIS LOVELY *CASS*ISTANT
BRING *YOU* *SOAP*ERNATURAL WONDERS GALORE!

He tore a couple long pieces of masking tape from the roll on his wrist and put a piece on each of his corners, then tossed the roll to me to do the same.

"*Cass*istant?" I said.

"I wouldn't and couldn't do this without your help," he said, but I was sorely wishing he'd at least tried to.

"Now, hold your side up," Dad said, taping his end of the banner to one gazebo post, before helping me secure my end to another.

"Does that look even to you?" he said.

"Pretty even, I guess. . . . What are *soap*ernatural wonders?"

"Well, assistant, why don't you come have a look for yourself?"

On his left side, Dad set up the wobbly table and carefully placed the brown suitcase on top. When he opened the suitcase slow and easy, I saw what looked like hundreds of old bars of soap that had been used down to little slivers. Heaps of blue, white, pink, and even swirled ones. Some of them were stuck to the lid of the suitcase with thumbtacks. Tons more of them were piled in the bottom. All of the soap slivers had letters, like monograms, carved into them. It may have been just a case full of soap, but it sure had the appearance of being more than just a case full of soap.

"It's just a case full of soap," I said.

"So it would seem," said Dad. "To someone unacquainted with the history of these particular soaps."

I wasn't exactly sure I wanted to be acquainted with the history of a soap, but Dad had a look like it was something way worth hearing.

"What do the letters mean?" I asked, trying to read all the ones I could lay my eyes on.

"The letters indicate who the soaps once belonged to," he said. "Presidents, inventors, artists, explorers, and kings alike. In fact all manner of past heroes are represented in this case."

"No way," I said. "Those people didn't put their initials on their soaps."

"*They* didn't," Dad said. "But the one who first painstakingly gathered this collection did."

"And who was that?"

"Can't say that I know," he said. "I discovered them a while back when going through some old family stuff. This here collection represents a long-lost part of Nordenhauer history, Cass. Turns out, we have us a sudsy legacy. And that's only *half* the story."

135

I reached out cautiously, but Dad stopped me just short of touching one of the soaps.

"No," he said. "Not just yet."

Dad took the handle of the sparkly wagon and bumped it up the steps to the fountain at the center of the gazebo. While I wondered over the pastel rainbow of soaps, he filled the wagon till it sloshed, one doublehanded dip at a time from the fountain. He then parked it a few feet away from the suitcase. It seemed like everything was right where he wanted it, so Dad tugged at his sleeves once more, gave me a *there's no turning back now* look, and slid something from under his jacket in the back.

He lifted the tambourine over his head and gave it a smack that sent out a loud *SHOOKA!* and made the ribbons whip around like crazy. Even people from the ice-cream stand across the way paused their licking to check us out.

"Here," he said. "I brought this for you." Dad tried to hand me the tambourine, but I resisted, resulting in a push-o-war between us.

"How can I be your assistant?" I said. "I don't even know what we're doing out here."

"I'm not sure I know either," he said. "But you make some music, I'll do the talking, and let's just see how the second half of the story unfolds."

"Curious children of Nimble Creek!" Dad shouted as a few families got close enough to form a little crowd. I tried to do my part, but found it to be a lot like that pat-your-head-and-rub-your-tummy thing. It's near impossible to shake a tambourine and watch your dad act a fool at the same time.

136

"Allow us to introduce ourselves!" he said. "My name is M. B. McClean. This here is my able assistant, Cass, and we are here to show you the wonders of the *soap*ernatural."

I gave a slight shrug and a slighter wave to the front row.

"Be the first to witness!" he continued. "We have here in this very case a genuine and rare collection of soap slivers used by actual heroes of history!"

Dad waved his arm over the vast collection of soaps. I found myself so mesmerized by them, I forgot to even shake the tambourine. Instead, I just held it stiffly out to my side like I had me a skunk by the tail.

"Today and today only," he said, "you can wash with one of these slick little treasures and become just as great as these men and women once were!"

A little *woo-hoo* mixed together with a lot of *no way* scattered from my belly button out to my whole body, like when you hear the *click-click-click* on the first big uphill of a roller coaster.

"And it's all free!" Dad went on, chanting louder and louder above the heads of the first rows of perplexed onlookers until even more people were drawn from their seesawing and jungle-gyming. When bikes, skateboards, and roller skates began to appear in the distance, Dad cleared his throat and shouted into the air, "Gather, small ones! Don't be duds! We've got us some magical suds!"

He looked at me as if to ask if the rhyme was decent enough.

Decent enough, I nodded back.

"No more swinging! No more sliding!" he said to the

kids on the playground. "Wouldn't you rather lather?"

Dad shot me a doubtful look, and without him even having to ask, I said, "That one was a little better."

And I clearly wasn't the only one who thought so. Kids came from all directions, pulling moms and dads and uncles and babysitters by the arms.

"Forget your *troubles*! Try these *bubbles*! You can't say *nope* to extraordinary *soap*!"

In a matter of minutes, dozens of noisy children stood in a bunch all around me with their hands in the air, and being a Cassistant felt a tad less embarrassing.

"Do us a good solid smack on that tambourine if you would, Cass," he said. So I gave it my best effort, and the noise immediately silenced the crowd. Everyone, including me, and maybe even including Dad, waited to hear what this M. B. McClean would say next.

I felt a gurgle in my belly and a fluster in my face. Dad must have noticed.

"You up for some more assisting, or would you rather watch and learn this first time around?" he whispered. The crowd made a hushy hum behind me.

"Um . . . watch and learn," I said.

"No worries," he said. "How about a bird's-eye view, then?"

While the fidgety, impatient crowd looked on, my dad, in all his stripy shininess, gave me a boost up the little ladder attached to the back of The Roast, where I found myself a spot to sit crisscross-legged and catch the whole scene.

"Now, let's get down to business!" Dad turned back

to the people. "Remember, any trusting soul can experience the magic himself! So who's going to be our first volunteer?"

Dad scanned the small show of hands.

"You there!" he said to a boy who had brightly colored chalk crammed into his overalls pocket. Dad waved him up the steps, and the boy carefully inspected the soap-filled suitcase. His mom hovered close behind, watching every move.

"I see you are an aspiring artist," Dad said. "Perhaps I can make a suggestion." He pulled out a pink swirly sliver with the initials *V V G* scraped into it.

"This was Vincent van Gogh's actual bar of soap." Dad held the soap up so everyone could get a look. I strained to see the details of the soap, as if I had a clue what the real thing would look like. Then I studied Dad's face, as if I had a clue what him lying to a crowd would look like.

He continued. "Vincent van Gogh's adventurous use of wild colors turned the world of art on its ear, if you will. His painting of a nighttime sky in bright swooshes and blazing stars is his most famous work ever. And not only that, but he painted unbelievably fast, finishing nine hundred paintings in ten years' time."

Dad put the soap in his palm and reached it out to the boy.

"One wash with this sliver, young man, and you yourself can be one of the finest ar-teests in Nimble Creek."

The boy looked ready to snatch it right up, until his mom caught him by the shoulder.

"I don't know, son," she said. "Maybe next time."

"Oh *plllease*, Mom," the boy said. "Let me try it."

"There might not be a next time," Dad said. "And if nothing else, he'll come away with clean hands, right?"

"All right," the mom said. "Go ahead."

Dad guided the boy to the wagon to wash his hands in the water. While the boy scrubbed and splashed, I watched carefully to see what would happen, half expecting from Dad's buildup for there to be paint shooting out of the kid's fingers or something. When the boy was done with his wash, Dad searched all around the gazebo for some semblance of a paper towel before turning around and offering his long coattails for the kid to dry his hands on. The boy looked a little starstruck at the notion of getting to touch the green-and-yellow jacket, like it could be magical too. But despite washing with some so-called Vincent van Gogh soap, he seemed to be just the same kid with the same chalk and the same nervous mom. And besides, I was old enough to know better about this kind of thing anyway.

"Now then, go do your starry thing!" Dad said, nudging the boy down the steps and giving me a wink through his giant green glasses. And that's when something amazing happened. While Dad scanned the group for his next pick, I kept my eyes on the boy, who kneeled right next to The Roast and began the most handsome picture of a brilliant night sky, all vivid and inspired, like he was some kind of born noodler. And a fast noodler he was too, making his way across a universe of chalk within minutes. From directly above the picture, if I squinted, it was like The Roast was sailing through space. Others gathered around and gave their *oohs* and *ahhs*, making the boy's mom puff up with pride. When Dad looked up my way and smiled, I felt a tad bit starstruck myself.

"Cassistant," he called out to me, with a shrug. "Who do you think I should pick next?" That prompted twenty kids to turn and flail their arms in my direction. In the midst of their commotion, I spotted a miserable black-haired girl who seemed to be about my age. She stood next to a kid who looked like the boy version of her. He was ruthlessly and repeatedly poking her in the ribs with an action figure.

"That one," I said, pointing her out to Dad, who then invited the girl to step up to the open suitcase, which suddenly seemed to have a treasure-chest-like appeal, drawing people closer to it.

"Uh, a pink one, please," was her simple request.

"No prob," said Dad. "This one should do the trick." He handed her a pink sliver with *A O* scraped on it in curvy letters. "Annie Oakley's soap," said McClean. "You know who Annie Oakley was, little lady?"

"No, sir . . ." the girl began.

"She don't know diddly!" interrupted her brother.

Dad motioned the girl over and stooped close to her.

"Annie Oakley was the toughest gal in the Old West, and a real sharpshooter," he said. "And you know what? You seem to me like you could be pretty tough, too."

"I do?" she said.

"Certainly!" said Dad. "You've got that serious look in your eye . . . not to mention that water pistol tucked into your belt there."

"But it ain't got water," she said.

"That's an easy problem to fix," he said. "And when it comes to shooting, here's some advice straight from the mouth of Annie Oakley herself. She'd tell a person to simply follow a target with the tip of the gun, just like it was the tip of your pointing finger."

Dad handed the pink sliver over and said, "Ms. Oakley also said to aim high."

The girl took the soap and dipped up to her elbows in the wagon, keeping her back to her brother while he just stood there and rolled his eyes. Unbeknownst to him, she also dipped the water pistol in good and deep and held it there for a bit. When all her washing and filling was done, she spun around on one foot, squinted an eye, and aimed the tip of the purple pistol high. Then she shot a steady stream of soapy water right at her brother's nose, making him squinch his face up and drop his toy into the dirt. After that, the girl shoved the water pistol back into her waistband, and with her brother spitting and snorting behind her, skipped all the way to the swings with her hands drying in the wind.

"Hey, mister! What can you do for a scaredy-cat?" piped up a freckled, tallish girl with a trembly kitten clawed into her shoulder and a slobbery dog growling at her hip. McClean handed her a soap marked *R P* and said, "Here's a soap once used by Rosa Parks, great civil rights leader and a certified expert at standing up to a bully."

The girl dipped the kitten's trembling feet into the soapy water, after which it sprung out of the wagon with a hiss and chased the yelping dog till they were just dots in the distance. The girl beamed with pride and squealed, "Run, Fuzzbucket, run!"

After that, from my perch, the rest of the afternoon passed by in a bubbly blur, the crowd of kids getting smaller and smaller, one satisfied customer at a time. I watched Dad give a Babe Ruth soap to a kid who then took a stick and knocked a rock clear across the park. After that, there was a Paul Revere for a shy boy who ended up riding his scooter around hollering about the things he'd seen. Then there was a Jacques Cousteau to a girl who found tadpoles in the fountain. And last but not least, Orville and Wilbur Wright soaps to a pair of twins whose kites didn't touch ground for an hour afterward. It seemed everyone who wanted a wash got just what they needed, and after each and every one, Dad looked up to check on me, perhaps to make sure I hadn't trickled right off the edge of The Roast into a puddle of wackadoo. But Dad had everything so carefully planned out, it almost seemed too deliberate to be wackadoo. I'd no idea why or how he was carrying on this way, but I had a sense that the whys and the hows were somewhere needing to be found.

As the sun dropped behind the two tallest buildings in downtown Nimble Creek, only one small boy still waited. He stepped up to the suitcase, smacking a Frisbee like a tambourine while his mother fanned herself on the sidewalk.

"Like they always say, last but not least," said Dad. "And who would you like to be today, little fella?"

"You gots any bidey soap?" the boy asked.

143

"Say again?" said Dad.

"Spider-Man," said his grinning mom. "He wants to climb the walls."

I wondered if this would be Dad's first stumper of the day. What on earth would he conjure up for a request like that?

"Errr . . . let's see here," he said, rummaging through the suitcase and grabbing a sliver marked *M* from under the pile. "No Spider-Man soaps in here, little fella, but I tell you what I do have. I've got one Michelangelo left. Michelangelo was super famous for making objects look human by his carving ability. He could take a chunk of almost anything—marble, bronze . . . who knows, maybe even Play-Doh—and make it look like a real person. Pretty amazing, huh?"

The boy stood unimpressed beneath his bowl haircut, giving me a small sinking feeling. That is, until Dad, cool as a cucumber, squatted to the boy's level and sweetened the deal.

"And get this," he said. "Michelangelo was a painter too. And to paint one of his biggest projects, for four years he actually had to hang from the *ceiling*."

"Like Bidey!" said the boy.

"Like Bidey," said Dad.

The kid immediately squeezed the sliver into his chubby fist, tucked the Frisbee between his knees, and waddled up to the wagon. After washing his hands in what was left of the cloudy water, the boy dried them on his shorts and hopped onto his scooter with a "Danks, Mistel McWean!" I couldn't believe I actually felt relief at

144

the thought of my disguised dad being capable of choosing just the right antique soap sliver for a Spider-Man–loving kid.

Once the boy and his mother were gone, all that was left on the gazebo was a wagonful of dirty water, a suitcase with a smaller pile of soap slivers in it, and a man who resembled my dad less and less.

"Let's call it a day," he said as he took off his big green glasses and wiped the nose part with his lapel.

I climbed down from the rooftop, feeling more than a little stunned, my ears buzzing like neon from the electric spaghetti of questions in my head.

nineteen

Grand Ole Soap

"Did I say there'd be some surprises, or did I say there'd be some surprises?" Dad said, sleeve-dabbing the sweat from his forehead. He closed up the suitcase with the tambourine tucked inside, dumped the dirty water out of the wagon, and carefully rolled up the banner. The *sha-sha-sha* of the Nimble Creek street sweeper passed behind us through the park, its spinning brushes turning the little artist's masterpiece into Vincent van Gone. It seemed to me like the whole day might not have actually happened, as if it would just sweep away in a chalky swirl of imagination.

"Cass, would you pick the back end of this thing up?" Dad lifted the front of the loaded wagon into the side door of The Roast. "I promise this will be the last help of the day."

A few clumps of wet glitter from the wagon smeared onto the front of my shirt. M. B. McClean plopped onto the couch and eased his feet out of his shoes. The Douglas

Nordenhauer part of him looked exhausted.

"I think these things must be made from a rubber snake," he said, tossing his loafers aside and rubbing his heels. "I'd have been more comfy in a couple of mismatched shoes from that box back there." He folded the big green glasses and tucked one stem down into his shirt.

"So what did you think?" he said. "I know you must be full of questions."

Full of questions was putting it mildly. It was more like my head was an endless Pez dispenser of mysteries. And my body stood there stiff to match.

"I don't . . . What was . . . How did . . . Dad, why are you doing all this?"

Dad stopped and stared at me kind of flat-mouthed, like he was undecided about his next sentence.

"The question is, why would I *not* do all this?" he said. "Seems to me it would be a shame to turn down an opportunity that one of our Nordenhauer ancestors saw fit to preserve and pass on."

He picked up the yellow top hat, tossed it Frisbee-style all the way to the dashboard, and patted the couch for me to join him.

"You know, Cass, my original plan was to share this family secret with you when you turned the big 1-1, but frankly, due to the turn of events with your mom this past week, I figured you needed an advance on some magic in your life."

"You mean magic like a fake lady being sawed in two, right?" I said, trying to balance my behind on the narrow hard edge of the couch.

"Nope. An entirely different kind of magic."

"So there really is no meat?"

Dad shook his head. "There's no meat, Casstrami."

"No steaks?"

"Not one."

"But you've sold meat before, right? Like to the church people and stuff?"

"Yep," Dad said, mixed in with a groan. "But I'm tired of meat."

I looked all around at the sure-enough no-meatness of the RV.

"So this is all about old soap?" I said.

"Old soap, yes, but not just any old soap," said Dad, his voice brighter. "*Special* old soap."

He pulled the brown suitcase from the wagon and laid it across his lap.

"Cass, ever since you had knuckle dimples, you've been a bright, kind, and curious girl," he said. "That's why I feel like I can trust you with this knowledge at a young age."

Then he suddenly got all hushed.

"Let me tell you about a little something I like to call *Sway*." Dad said it slow, like a teacher calling out a spelling word.

"Sway?" I asked.

"S-W-A-Y," he said.

I thought he meant like when my whole fourth-grade class once had to sway back and forth with our hands in the air while we kazooed "You're a Grand Old Flag."

"You mean like this?" I waved my top half left and

right, nearly swaying myself onto the floor.

"No, no." Dad leaned in close. "*Sway*," he said. "As in *power* . . . As in *influence*."

Despite the thick summer heat of the evening, I felt chills scatter up and down both my arms. I scooted onto the cushiony part of the couch and gave Dad my full attention.

"These here soapy remains, each in its own way, have the power to change the people they come in contact with. Inspiring a person to do more, to be more," he said, drumming his fingers on the top of the suitcase. His promising words echoed bittersweetly in my head. Do more, I thought. Just like Mom.

"How does that happen?" I asked.

"Surprisingly, it's really a simple transaction," he explained. "You wash your hands with one of these here soaps, each one once belonging to a notable historical figure, and *poof!* you begin to take on that person's best qualities. Just like you witnessed from high atop The Roast this very day."

Dad was right. I had just witnessed some pretty nifty things. Even so, I still had a lump of doubt in my throat that felt like I'd gulped down the dry yellow middle part of a boiled egg.

"But van Gogh and Michelangelo . . . didn't they live like hundreds of years ago? How could their soaps be kept for so long and not be all crumbly?"

"By the gentle and careful efforts of those who came before us," said Dad, softly knocking at the case with his knuckles. "Granting us our own unique Nordenhauer way of changing the world, one hand-washing at a time."

"So does it work on grown-ups too?" I asked.

"Of course."

"Have you ever tried one?"

Dad paused for a moment and twisted his mouth from side to side.

"Honestly, Cass, I haven't decided which one I'd want to try first. So many available options make for a tough decision. You see, it's very important to choose the right soap for the right person."

"Then, if you haven't tried one, how'd you know they would work?"

"Let's just say there was some top secret testing done before we left," he said.

I remembered overhearing him and Uncle Clay talking about wishing they had this stuff when they were kids. But then I also remembered how when I was five, Dad used to tell me he could pull his thumb off and put it back on again. How he made it look so real. And besides, I'd never known Dad to use words like *power* and *influence*. Those were Mom words.

"Come on," I said. "How did you *really* make all that happen today?"

Dad set the suitcase on the table in front of him and looked at me real serious.

"Looks like you've given me no choice," he said, fumbling around in his big jacket pocket until he pinched out a teeny brass key.

"I'm going to have to implement Rule of The Roast Number Five: *Keep away from the Sway.*"

Dad struggled to turn the key in the rusty suitcase lock, making me feel like I did the other night when he'd snatched the phone from my hand.

"How come?" I said.

"Because you're not ready."

"But those kids got to try it."

"Because they *believed*," he said. "The power these slivers can have over a believer is strong." Dad looked me in the eye. "Sway is not for doubters, Cass."

"But . . ."

"You'll have your own taste of it when you are good and ready," he said. "When you're feeling more open to the possibilities."

He paused a moment. "Understood?"

"Yes, sir." But it was a *Yes, sir* that was as *No, sir* as a *Yes, sir* could be.

"Until that day," he said. "As we travel, this case will be locked tight. Only when we are working will it be opened."

When he leaned to push the case back under the driver's seat, I saw two damp ovals on the couch where he'd sat on his wet jacket tails. A small part of me wanted to laugh at him, but the rest of me was busy searching my brain for far-fetched things I knew of that had turned out true. Fainting goats. Lizards that spit blood. Babies who can name all the presidents. But magical soap? Could Dad even make all that up? Because making all that up might be the ultimate in wrength.

"We'll hit the road again tomorrow in search of shoe-o numero two-o, and then we'll get to see Sway in action again. And just imagine this: someday soon, you'll be choosing the sliver *you* most want to use. And as my partner, you'll have the pick of the whole collection."

"When will that happen?" I said.

Dad gave a test sniff to his armpit.

"Soon enough," he said. "Now, if you'll excuse me, I've got to air out this sweaty suit." Dad squeezed his way through the bathroom door and turned all sorts of ways to try and get it shut behind him. His changing back into Douglas Nordenhauer sounded like not-so-distant thunder. While I waited, Dad's mention of someday choosing my own soap sliver had me feeling more than a little muddled. I mean, trying the soap could maybe be compared to finally being allowed to open one of Aunt Jo's jars from the storm shelter. Like it would be cool to read all the notes inside there, except for they might end up being nothing but a big bummer.

When Dad came back out in the Roll Tide T-shirt and faded jeans I'd seen so many times before, he warned, "I had to hang the suit from the ceiling light in there. Don't let that lemon-lime scarecrow spook the soul out of you in the middle of the night.

"Now, what do you say we buckle up and find ourselves some supper?" he said. "You starvin' like a Marvin?"

I'd only eaten snacky stuff all day, so I was very much starvin' like three Marvins. Thankfully, by the time I'd even gotten into my seat good, we'd already pulled into a place called Sup 'n' Go. It was one of those restaurants with a flat roof over a drive-up area where people on skates used to bring out the food. Dad thought long and hard about parking up under there with everyone else, but ultimately decided that The Roast was too tall for it. Mainly our bumping the roof with the top of The Roast helped him make that decision. I ate a whole catfish sandwich they called a po-boy, and he had two of the same. With his mouth half full between bites, Dad said, "So be honest, Cassparagus. I know this is a lot to take in all at once, but didn't you think those things you saw out there today were pretty impressive?"

My head and my heart and my gut disagreed on the correct answer to the question. My head knew that I was totally weirded out by new places, new people, and new dad all at the same time. My gut felt pretty excited by it all. And my heart felt like this must be, for whatever unknown reason, something Dad really needed to do. Mom once told me that, in a rescue situation, it is important for the grown-ups to get okay first, so they can then help the kids.

"I'll take your silence as a no," he said. "Who am I kidding thinking I can impress you with that wacky getup, huh?"

"It's just that it was kind of a surprise, I guess," I said. "I mean, have you done all that before?"

"I think it's pretty obvious I haven't," he said. "So maybe at the next stop we'll tone the act down a bit."

I took a long slurp on my Coke, assured that Dad was still Dad, that I had managed to avoid totally crushing his feelings, and soon I would find out more about this mysterious thing called Sway. Surprisingly, my head, my gut, and my heart agreed that for the moment, things were somewhat okay.

"We never saw what the soap did for the Michelangelo kid," I said.

"You know, you're right," said Dad. "But I have heard that sometimes it may take a while for the Sway to have an effect."

Dad and I both chomped on some ice for a minute.

"So does Mom know about all this?" I said.

"Well, no, not so much."

"How come?"

"I guess I didn't want our magical brand of cleanup to totally overshadow the cleanup work that she's done, you know? It just didn't seem right. I thought it could have its debut as a special me-and-you thing, no?"

"But you said it was a *family* secret."

"I said it was a Nordenhauer family secret."

"Mom's a Nordenhauer," I said.

Dad sure did seem to forget that fact. Like he needed to write it on his hand or something.

"Cass, we're not calling her."

I swallowed an ice cube whole and clenched my jaw from the instant brain freeze.

"But . . ."

"Case closed," he said.

Dad stepped down out of The Roast and waved the Sup 'n' Go manager over. While he apologized for the ding in their roof and asked permission to camp in their lot for the night, I retired to my room, where I checked on the cell phone in the bottom of the beauty box and promised myself I'd use it as soon as I was able to buy more minutes. After lint-rolling glitter and fish crumbles from my shirt, plus some leftover Chex Mix bits from my bed, I found the first blank page that hadn't been wrecked in my Book of In-Betweens and noodled a yellow-and-green-striped soap sliver with big ears, a beard, and glasses. Next to it, I drew a brown suitcase with *MBM* scribbled across in gold.

"Hey, Dad!" I said through my curtain. "What's the M. B. stand for?"

"Well, I sure know what it *doesn't* stand for," he said. "Definitely not *Muchos Boring*."

I added a top hat to the sliver.

"And certainly not *Mega Bland*," Dad added.

Perhaps not *Muchos Boring*, I thought. But I wasn't ruling out *Mysterious Buffoon* just yet.

twenty

Sliver War

At sunup the next day, I jerked my curtain open so hard my knuckles cracked on the wall. The first sight to greet me was those big green glasses rocking back and forth on a cord looped around the rearview mirror. Already wearing his M. B. McClean pants and jacket, my dad was in mid-hoist through the driver's door with a top hat full of goodies.

"You tossed and turned something fierce last night," he said, setting a piece of lumpy candy the size of a book on the dash. "I thought you might need some protein."

I wondered even how to begin to eat such a thing, when, with a *whack!*, he chopped the candy with his hand, sending a few bits sticking to the windshield. I noticed that the sugar-speckled view beyond was not the Sup 'n' Go. Instead, we were parked across the way from a little log cabin–style store with a long row of rocking chairs along the front porch. It was just us and two camouflage-painted pickup trucks in the gravel parking lot, and all around the cabin were trees covered in kudzu vines that, if you stared long enough, appeared to have grown into giant animal shapes.

"Where are we?" I asked.

"The other side of Mississippi," Dad said. "My sleep was fitful last night too, so I got us a head start toward our second work stop."

I was pretty sure that meant we were even farther from Florida.

"Here's to the breakfast of champions!" he said, handing me a shard of brownish candy. "The lady in the store says they make enough Nutty Brittle each year to stretch all the way to Tennessee."

Nutty. Brittle. Sounded like a good description of my dad and me.

"Hey, you mind if I ask you something?" Dad asked. "You don't have to answer if you don't want."

"Sure," I said. "But only if we can trade questions. And if I go first."

"Go on," he said.

"When Mom first became a storm rescuer, why didn't you become one too?"

Dad slumped a little shorter in his seat. "Because sometimes when someone chooses a job in which that someone will take off on a moment's notice, the other someone has to stay behind and be ground control. But don't sell your old dad short, now." He paused and smiled. "Once, when I was a boy, I caught a frog by its hind leg to save it from being flushed down the toilet."

"I guess that could maybe count," I said.

"Until he slicked out of my fingers and was slurped away."

"Oh."

I had an inkling to think poorly of Dad for this, until I remembered some of my own failed rescue attempts. Most notably, the frozen butterfly I tried to thaw back to life with a birthday candle when I was eight.

"Seriously, though, Cass," he said. "Have you even begun to consider what we have here? I mean, have you thought about the things that we can do with Sway?"

"You mean like rescue?"

"Who knows?"

Dad dug some brittle from his back teeth.

"Now, how about that question I was promised?" he said. "Is it my turn?"

I wanted to tell him, *Game over. That was two questions already*, but that didn't seem fair.

"Go ahead."

"What all did your mom really say to you on the phone the other night?"

I couldn't believe he'd mentioned Mom. It made me glad I'd allowed one more question.

"I don't know. Just that she loves us and stuff."

His eyes perked up some, despite his voice remaining flat. "Did she ask to talk to me?"

"That's an extra question," I said, glancing down at my knees. Mom had done no such thing, but Dad sure didn't have to know that right then.

"Okay, I get it," he said. "Let's just head on up yonder

dirt road a bit and find our next stop."

"Without a shoe?"

Busted, I thought. Breaking his own rule already.

"I dig your catch-on-itude, my friend," he said. "But have you a look-see in that direction."

I looked out the passenger side window and spotted something lying heavy in the dirt on the road that ran beside the cabin. But it sure didn't strike me as shoe-ish.

My dad stood and slid the Reacher out from the crevice between his seat and the console like it was a sword.

"Feeling lucky?" he asked, reaching so hard to slide open the sunroof, I saw the seam in the armpit of his jacket strain.

Dad stood on tiptoe at the edge of the driver's seat and put the Reacher up through there like an antenna. He cast it out and reeled it back in, over and over, until he was near knocked silly from what he hooked on the fifth try. Then he freed the weighty object from the hook and held it in front of his face like a rusty smile. It was a horseshoe.

"Like catching shoes in a barrel," he said, tossing it across The Roast and landing it right in the hole. "Now, let's go see where that horse was headed."

Dad cranked up The Roast and we drove up that very dirt road, well into a thick forest of cedar trees, which scratched along the roof of the RV. Within just minutes we found a cleared-out place in the woods where what seemed like a hundred pickup trucks were parked every which way. We stopped just past a bearded man in a gray uniform with gold buttons. He was tapping a sign into the mud.

JUNE 8
BATTLE OF HANOVER'S BLUFF
CIVIL WAR REENACTMENT
ADULTS $5
CHILDREN UNDER TWELVE $2
INFANTS FREE
BATTLE BEGINS PROMPTLY AT 11:00 A.M.

The man stooped to pick up a crumpled fast food bag, and tossed it into a garbage can shaped like an owl.

"I guess even a Confederate general's got to multi-task," Dad said with a wink.

"What's a reenactment?" I said, finding the word difficult to even say.

"It's when a bunch of folks get together and act out an old battle," said Dad. "Kind of like a play of sorts."

"But didn't the Civil War split up America and make people fight against their own families? Why would you want to reenact something terrible as that?"

"Well, I've personally never tried it," he said. "But I guess what it means to them is keeping the stories of their ancestors alive, be they tragic or heroic, by reliving them. It's their way of making those stories a part of themselves."

Dad pried bits of brittle off the windshield. "But what it means to *us* is an opportunity to dazzle some folks with our inventory."

"You think these people are going to want old soaps?"

"Cass, this here is a captive audience of people who have a deep appreciation of all things authentic. Our gift ought to be more than welcome here." Something in his voice sounded like he was trying to convince himself as well as me.

A few more brass-buttoned soldiers passed in front of The Roast.

"Plus, it looks likes these folks are no strangers to grown-ups playing dress-up." Dad sucked in hard to button his jacket. "And this makes me look a tad historical, no?"

The taddest of tads, I thought, giving him a nod.

Dad gathered up the rest of his green-and-yellow ensemble while I slipped on my tank top, a T-shirt, and some cutoffs.

"I'm thinking we scale back a little on the setup today, out of respect to our unique audience," he said. "What do you think? Perhaps we should leave the banner behind?"

"Yeah, maybe," I said, finding myself wondering what on earth he planned to rhyme with Civil War.

"Let's get a move on," he said. "I bet they're already setting up in there."

We finished getting dressed and then gathered the wagon, suitcase, tambourine, and fold-up table. It made for a very slow walk across the woods having to yank the loaded wagon free from the forest thicket, and Dad had to help me again and again. When we finally reached the huge clearing that was to be the battle site, we stopped next to some ladies laying out sandwiches and drinks on a huge quilt.

"Morning, ladies," Dad said with a bow. "Mind if my partner and I take a few of those waters off your hands?"

"Be our guests," said one of them.

The women all wore poof-sleeve dresses with tiny waists and long hoopy skirts, one color for every lady. Beyond them, a crowd of men in faded blue and worn gray milled around the big clearing, many on foot, some on horses. I realized I'd seen these people in my prayer before, except for this time, they were cleaning guns, sharpening swords, and shining boots. They looked like a page torn from my fourth-grade history book.

"You mind being the wagon-filler?" Dad said.

That I didn't mind. I was just glad not to be assigned tambourine duty again.

Dad unfolded our table and popped open the MBM suitcase, right between a bigger table of flyers about future Civil War reenactments and a display of dirty, dented relics from various battlegrounds. As I emptied eight bottled waters into the wagon, a few of the soldiers broke away from their duties and made their way toward us. Dad was already sweating hard, maybe from the heat, or maybe from the men with guns and knives headed in our direction.

"Gentlemen in blue and gentlefolk in gray," he greeted them. "The name's M. B. McClean. This here's my daughter-turned-partner, Cass."

The men tipped their hats at me.

"Do forgive the intrusion, if you would, but Cass and I have a suitcase full of something that folks such as yourselves might find more than a little remarkable."

People on either side of us stopped setting up their displays to have a listen.

"You see, we have in this very case a genuine and rare collection of soap slivers used by and passed down by heroes of old!" Dad launched into a medium-quietish version of his speech.

The man with the most medals on his uniform scratched his head.

"For just a quick wash in our wagon with one of these soaps, a part of their greatness can magically become your own," Dad added, tugging at his collar.

I saw him shove the tambourine under the table with his foot. That's when I wondered if we would ever make it out of those woods, or if we'd end up in some haul-the-weirdos-off-to-jail reenactment.

"And did we mention it's all free?" Dad's voice trailed off, and it looked like he might very well melt into a pool of nerves and sweat, when a man with a waxy mustache and a shiny Confederate States belt buckle spoke up from among the silent troops.

"You know, I heard tell of something like this before," he said. "Some sort of Indian legend about wearing the headpiece of a warrior and feeling his strength. . . . But that might very well be a bunch of hoo-ha."

"Well, we've got a hundred shades of military heroism represented in this suitcase, sir," Dad said. "A whole mess of valor, strength, and nobility all literally at your fingertips. It can't hurt to try one, right?"

The man adjusted his holster and put both hands on his hips. "What did you say your name was, fella?" he asked.

"M. B. McClean, sir. And Cass."

"Honorary Captain M. B. McClean and Little Miss Cass," the man said, "I believe I speak for my men as well as for the enemy in saying we are a mite intrigued by what you have to offer."

A few of the troops nodded in agreement. Dad responded with some sort of salute, looking like a great glob of worry had slid right off him.

Then the man took out a brassy pocket watch and stared at it thoughtfully. "The battle begins in fifty-three minutes." His voice rose above us all. "You've got that long to do your thing, Mr. McClean."

"Well, let's waste no time, then," said Dad. "Gather 'round!"

A few representatives from the group stepped forward to take a closer look.

"First off, let me tell you about a couple little gems we have in here," he said, shuffling through the case and lifting high two tiny white soap slivers. "These here represent none other than Ulysses S. Grant and Stonewall Jackson.

"As you folks well know, Grant was a celebrated Union war hero and eighteenth president of our own United States. But did you know this?" he added. "Did you know that in the heat of battle, when his officers were ready to give up, Grant never lost his composure? In fact, his nerves of steel were a marvel to all around him. They say he could write orders while shells burst all around him and never even flinch."

The men in navy blue had begun removing their gloves and tucking them into their belts. Then Dad said something that moved the gray men just as much.

"And speaking of never flinching," he said. "Let's not forget General Stonewall Jackson, bold Confederate commander, who earned his nickname at the Battle of Bull Run for sitting calmly on his horse, staying firm and undaunted like a stone wall throughout the fight."

In an instant, the people crowded around both of us so tight, they bumped and sloshed our water. I had to pull the wagon to safety as Dad began a roll call of slivers thumbtacked to the inside of the suitcase lid. And thus began mine and Dad's work at the Battle of Hanover's Bluff. Of course, Ulysses and Stonewall were the first two soaps to be used up. After that went a wash with Napoleon Bonaparte, the French emperor who was hailed as a military genius. Then someone scrubbed with a Samuel Middleton, the only black officer in the American Revolutionary War. There was even a wash with John Wayne, famous movie star, horse rider, and all-around tough guy. As I led man after man to the water wagon for his turn, I noticed a boy slowly make his way to the front of the line. He was a droopy-shoulder kid who looked to be about my age. He had a pair of drumsticks in the pocket of his cargo shorts and a spotted puppy on a leash.

"Well hello, young man," said Dad. "What can we do for you today?"

"Nothing," said the boy, looking over the brown suitcase with a sulky frown on his face. "I don't want any old soap. I just wanted to see what all the commotion was about."

"Do you have a job in this here battle?" said Dad.

"No, I mainly just stand over there and wait for my dad to die and come back to life."

"Do you really play the drums?" I asked him.

"Whenever I can," he said.

"Well, young man, want it or not, I do have something that would be perfect for you," said Dad, rummaging through the collection and finding a green soap marked *T H*.

"Tommy Hubler was rumored to be the youngest member of the Union Army," he explained. "A fine, brave drummer boy he was, alerting troops of their movement orders, sounding retreat in the midst of heavy enemy fire, and standing by ready to lay down the drum and help an injured man if necessary."

"Um, no thanks," said the boy. The puppy whimpered and squirmed.

"You sure? My assistant can hold your pup while you wash," Dad said.

"You mean this stuff really works?" the boy whispered to me. Both he and Dad waited for my response. In place of an answer, I just did a little shrug-nod.

"Hold up," Dad said, finding yet another soap, this one with just an *S* on it. "And speaking of that there pup, who could forget Stubby, possibly the bravest-ever soldier dog, who accompanied soldiers in seventeen battles during World War I, providing comfort, companionship, and the occasional biting of an enemy behind."

"If you say so," said the boy, handing me the puppy and squatting to wash his hands in the wagon. I knelt next to him to hold the puppy's front feet in the water while the boy put some Stubby suds on there. The pup wiggled so hard it sent bubbles splashing all over his little licky face.

"This feels kind of goofy," said the boy.

"I know," I mumbled.

"Which one's your dad?" I tried to change the subject. "I'll watch for him today."

"The guy who used the Napoleon soap," he said, taking the dog into his arms and backing away from the wagon with a shy, "Thanks."

After the boy was gone, Dad turned his attention back to the crowd.

"We mustn't neglect the ladies here today," he said. "For you all, we have a very special soap. A Mrs. Clara Barton, nicknamed 'Angel of the Battlefield,' who tirelessly and tenderly nursed the Civil War wounded back to health."

Three of the big-skirted women raised their hands in response, and the rest of the waiting gentlemen let the ladies cut in front of them.

"Not to worry," said Dad. "It's a sizable sliver Clara left behind. More than enough washings to go around."

A woman with a smear of mustard on her cheek was next up to the table.

"I don't do anything on the battlefield," she said. "But I'm in charge of feeding all these folks, so maybe I could use a good hand-washing for more than one reason today."

Dad smiled and said, "I know just what you need."

He rummaged for a minute through the pile of loose

slivers in the bottom of the case for an *A A* soap.

"Abigail Adams," he said. "The very first woman to be called First Lady of the United States. In the late 1700's, she did such a splendid job of hosting visitors at the White House, she was nicknamed Mrs. President."

As Dad handed out soaps one right after another, I found being so close to the collection totally mesmerizing, especially with Clara Barton, a famous rescuer's soap, in the mix. I remembered reading about her in school, how she was the founder of the American Red Cross, one of the groups that had sent Mom a letter of thanks for her work. I reached over to trace my finger in the letters of Clara Barton's sliver before it was handed off to the big-skirts, but I was stopped by Dad making an obnoxious game-show-buzzer noise.

"Remember . . . not till you're ready," he said firmly, before getting back to the business of assigning soaps and directing people one at a time to the washing line.

The layers upon layers of slivers looked like little pastel pieces of bone, and their faint scents all mixed into one, making me wonder how such ancient soaps could still have smell left in them at all. After a while, I noticed a small tear in the silky lining in the lower left corner of the suitcase lid. Peeking from behind the tear was a paper corner, just a hint of something tucked behind the fabric.

"What's that paper sticking out there?" I asked Dad, between customers.

"Oh, none of your concern," he replied in a singsongy way. I expected him to tuck the paper corner back under the fabric, but he didn't.

Instead, Dad got up to turn the wagon in a way that would allow more than one person to wash at once, and I turned my attention to that half-hidden piece of paper, walking my fingers up the edge of the suitcase and behind the rip in the lining. I slid the neatly folded paper out of there, careful not to make the tear any bigger. Then I shoved it up under my arm, excused myself to explore a bit, and wandered just beyond the ladies to a monument of stacked cannonballs. As the people awaiting their turns at the wagon stood still as chess pieces, I balanced on the topmost one of the slick stack of cold cannonballs and gently unfolded the frail document. It was soiled and faded and burned on one edge, and the words were written in nice cursive, like the roster of soldiers' names at the base of the monument. There was the smallest of melted soap slivers stuck to the bottom of the certificate with a piece of purple ribbon smashed under it, like it had been sealed by a king. The document read:

CERTIFICATE OF AUTHENTICITY
LET THE HOLDER OF THIS COLLECTION OF SOAPS REST
IN THE ASSURANCE THAT THE CONTENTS BEQUEATHED
HEREIN ARE NO LESS THAN ONE HUNDRED PERCENT AUTHENTIC,
THEIR POWER AND POTENTIAL
IMMEASURABLE.

The words shot such a fire through me, I near slid off my cannonball. *Authentic. Assurance. Potential. Immeasurable power.* It certainly was fancy enough language to be something handed down for generations. And the paper looked old and worn as the Declaration of Independence.

Across the field, as I watched uniformed men and frilly women, recognizers and appreciators of all things authentic, put their trust in our collection of soaps, I found myself squeezing that certificate so hard I put peanut brittle fingerprints on it. Then suddenly, it felt like someone had struck a match in a shed full of fireworks, each new thought its own whistling explosion of color. Who had written this certificate? And why had *my* family been chosen to receive these soaps? And then I wondered which soap I would choose for myself, and what it would feel like to wash with it. Would it send ghostly coldness all through my veins? Or maybe give a tingle up my arms, like an itty-bitty electrical zing. A *zingle*, perhaps. After all, even the Tommy Hubler boy had said it *felt* weird to wash with one. Maybe that's what he meant.

It was at that moment that I remembered the baby bird I'd seen nested in the letter Y on that sign back home. And then I imagined my own rubbery baby bird self moving out of the Y and into the O.

O me.

O my.

O wow.

Could Sway be *real*?

twenty-one

Bequeathed

A crowd of spectators was fast filling the bleachers on the opposite end of the field, so I crammed the certificate into my back pocket and galloped my way back to Dad. He was leading the last guy in line to take a quick wash with a Robert E. Lee soap in wagon water blackened by gunpowder.

"Where've you been?" Dad asked.

I suddenly felt bad for swiping the certificate, sure that he'd be mad I'd put my sticky fingerprints all over it.

"At the monument," I said.

"Doing what?"

"Counting cannonballs."

He gave me a look like, *Well, how many are there?*

"And um, I think there are a hundred forty-five." No clue if I was even close, but I was relieved that the Robert E. Lee guy didn't care to correct me.

I pulled up a folding chair and took a look at the

soaps piled in the bottom of the case. Now that I'd seen that certificate, the slivers took on a whole new radiance.

"Who all else you got in there?" I said.

"Tons. Have a look."

I saw a creamy-white sliver marked *I N* sitting right on top.

"Who's that?"

"Sir Isaac Newton. The man who discovered gravity."

"And what about that *F M* one?"

"Ferdinand Magellan, the first guy to sail all the way around the earth."

"And that?" I pointed to a blue *L T*.

Dad smiled. "That one might not be of much use to us here today, I'm afraid," he said. "That's Leo Tolstoy, Russian writer famous for being a pacifist. That means he believed in solving conflicts without the use of violence."

Dad tumbled the soaps around gently to refresh my view. When he did, he uncovered a soap that so stood out, it was like it had a little glow around it.

"That *T N* one right there," I said. "Is that a Toodi Nordenhauer?"

Dad picked up the soap to have a closer look, and I feared for a moment he might squish it in his fist.

"Sorry, Cass," he said, with a shake of his head. "But no. This is Thomas Newcomen, inventor of the steam engine."

"Oh . . . well then, do you have any Toodi soap?" I said, knowing full well I should drop the subject. Dad's reddening face suddenly made him seem like he might become the human version of a steam engine. He squeezed the slickified *T N* soap with a *fwit*, right across the table.

"No, Cass, I'm afraid we don't," he said, wiping the Thomas Newcomen residue on his pant legs. "Surely there must be someone else you admire in this big world of ours."

The crowd of battle spectators grew larger and louder in the bleachers.

"But how do you even know who's what?" I asked.

"Say again?"

"How do you know what the initials stand for?"

"Here's how," he said, finding the tear in the lining of the suitcase and sliding his whole hand behind it, making a few of the slivers almost jiggle off their tacks.

Yeeks, I thought. He's looking for the certificate. But then he pulled out a second folded document that looked to be just as old and crusty and official as the other one had. Dad unfolded it and handed it to me. This one was larger than the certificate, but the cursive written on it was so very tiny, and the handwriting unlike any I'd ever seen. It was an alphabetical list of names, hundreds of them, it seemed, each with its corresponding soap initials next to it. But before I could even read beyond Abigail Adams, I was startled by the shrill blast of a bugle from the far corner of the clearing. As it played a rousing song, the men stood stiff in rows. All the ladies rose to their feet, their shoes hidden by billows of fabric. Dad grabbed the list from me, and with a fold-fold-fold-tuck, it was gone.

"I see Tommy Hubler has masterfully commanded everyone's attention," said Dad, pointing across the field.

And sure enough, the young drummer boy stood straight and proud, a perfectly solemn call-to-battle rhythm coming from a drum he'd fashioned from a coffee can. Even the puppy stood still at his feet.

Soon after, the people in uniform took their posts. After the first chilling shot was fired, Dad and I spent the rest of the day sitting on a quilt at the edge of the battlefield, watching men who looked like living monuments charge at each other with swords and shoot one another with invisible bullets from smoky pistols. Throughout the skirmish, I paid special attention to the ones who had washed with our soaps. Stonewall Jackson led the men in gray. Ulysses S. Grant led the men in blue. Each one of them playing his part in such a powerfully real manner, it gave me a fearful stirring inside, as if I'd stepped right inside that schoolbook and was a part of history myself. Like I'd better choose a side quick and hope hard that my side was winning.

The woman who washed with Abigail Adams sent one Clara Barton after another into the field loaded with supplies, be it water, food, or blankets, for every need out there. More than once, a Clara would drag a collapsed man twice her size out of the line of fire. And all the while, Tommy Hubler played on. At one point, I even saw little Stubby bravely bound across the grass and bite the enemy on the ankle, right before the guy who used the John Wayne soap reared his horse up on two legs at the edge of the battlefield and told his men, *"Courage is being scared to death and saddling up anyway!"*

I felt a fresh twinge of sadness for each and every man

who crumpled in a heap on the battlefield, and for each woman who rushed to a wounded soldier's side. As more and more men lay across each other in the clearing, the sadnesses built up so that I could hardly stand to look. By the time the battle ended with a different, sorrowful bugle sound, there wasn't a dry eye among the onlookers. When all was quiet and still, Abigail Adams passed me a tissue and a tuna salad sandwich, and Dad wiped his nose on a napkin.

"Amazing, isn't it?" he said. "How something so pretend can feel so real?"

"Amen to that," Abigail said, with a sniff.

And I guess I must have totally agreed with them, considering the immense relief I felt that the fighting was over. Once the final call of the drum sounded and all the dead had stood and dusted themselves off, I watched the participants mill about and shake hands. Several folks broke away to come thank us as we packed up our things. Dad was locking up the old brown suitcase, and I was kicking our table legs flat, when Napoleon Bonaparte stuffed his hand into the breast pocket of his gray coat and pulled out an old coin.

"It's a genuine relic, worth at least twenty bucks," he said. "A token of my appreciation for the inspiration today, Mr. McClean."

"Thank you." Dad looked pleased and more than a little surprised. In fact, he had a total *Well, whadya know* look about him.

"The suds will rise again!" he hollered out, and the folks around us chuckled.

Then the spectators made their way toward us, spilling their compliments.

"Most passionate reenactment ever. Stirring beyond words!" they said. And I could have sworn I heard Tommy Hubler call it *awes*, while Napoleon gave him a good hair-mussing.

"Land sakes, what a success," said a purple-skirted Clara, her bun unravelings all stuck to the sides of her face. As a dozen civilians collected at the ladies' table to enlist in the next reenactment, she said to me, "Darlin', will you and your daddy be back here again?"

She stretched out her words slow and sweet, just like my mom.

"No, ma'am. I'm not sure where we're going."

Purple Clara's skirt made a *ding-ding* sound.

"Pardon me," she said, digging a cell phone from a side pocket. "That's my daughter texting me from the beach."

Just the mention of the word *beach* made me feel warm inside.

"From Florida?" I said.

"Nope," she said. "Gulfport, Mississippi. I guess I should tell her everyone made it out alive today, huh?" She laughed, thumbing out her message super fast.

"I'm pretty sure Miss Barton never texted LUV YA to anyone," a green-skirted Clara teased, yanking on Purple's apron strings.

"Excuse me," I said, looking over my shoulder to make sure Dad was still packing. "Do you all know how I could add more minutes to a phone? Ours ran out."

"Oh, it's easy," Green Clara said. "Just get your daddy to buy you one of those refill cards. They got 'em at all the quick marts."

"They got what at the quick mart?" Dad asked, sidling up next to us.

"Nothing. Just beef jerky," I said, and more than one lady gave me a funny look. The mention of beef jerky put a hungry twinkle in Dad's eye and a tiny twinge of liar's guilt in my tummy. He gave the ladies one last salute before joining me for the trek back through the woods.

"Let us cross over the river and rest under the shade of the trees!" a soldier shouted to the crowd.

"They say those were Stonewall Jackson's last words," Dad said as we walked with some of the wounded back through the thicket toward The Roast. "Thankfully, these soaps only give people the good stuff."

"So how do you know so much about all those people the soaps belonged to?" I asked.

"Six words," said Dad. "En sigh clo pee dee uh. I've been doing me some studying."

I helped him nudge the back end of the wagon over root after root. With each step stirring up the curiosity inside me, I decided there was no sense in holding back when it came to this thing called Sway. I wanted to know more about that stuff, and right then.

"Dad, what does *bequeathed* mean?" I said.

He grinned. "You found the certificate."

"Yeah, it's in my pocket. I accidentally put some smudges on it."

"Now, don't you go and mess that thing up too much,"

he said. "That has a lot more historical significance than a SMART certificate.

"In fact," he said, reaching out for the paper, "you better let me hang on to that."

Dad and I tilted the wagon to let the last of the war drippings out, and climbed inside The Roast.

"I heard that freezing cold is a good way of preserving important documents," he said, opening the fridge and sliding the folded certificate onto the ice tray shelf.

For someone to do something strange as that, I knew the certificate must be the real deal.

"So what's M. B. stand for?" I asked him.

"That question *uh-gane*?" he said.

The last time I'd heard him pronounce *again* all fancy like that was when he beat me, Syd, and Uncle Clay by fifty points in Scrabble by spelling the word RESCUERS. "Would you look at that? I used all seven letters *uh-gane*," he'd said, all proud.

McClean looked to the ceiling in thought. "Hmmm . . . perhaps the M. B. stands for *Magic Bubbles*."

"Yeah, maybe," I said.

That night, the smell of gunpowder and hot dogs breezed in through our open sunroof as I noodled in my book. A whole page of fiery swirls being shot from a cannon seemed right for the way I felt. Outside, a few of the sort-of soldiers lingered around a portable grill, telling and retelling the events of the day and how there'd been "new life breathed into the battle," which seemed to me like such an odd thing to say. It wasn't long before their talk and Dad's snoring became just background noise to the thoughts hovering between me and the top of The Roast. I still wasn't certain why people would want to relive something as ugly as war again and again. It seemed like the worst kind of permanent to me. Unless, of course, it was just a permanent reminder of how good it feels for a battle to be over.

As Dad made grumbly sleep sounds on the other side of the curtain, I wondered if he had ever really considered what it means to have a suitcase full of immeasurable power. I mean, if Sway was real, then who knew? Maybe it could bring our family back together somehow. Maybe put an end to our own battle.

After a while, the sound of Tommy Hubler's *rata-tat-tats* lulled my wonderings out the roof. I made a list in my head of the days that I would want to reenact if I could. All but one of Mom's homecomings, of course. The day Syd and I caught a chipmunk in the storm cellar. And this day, maybe.

With that thought lingering, I tiptoed into the bathroom, squeezed a blub of toothpaste onto my brush, and whispered just one word to the mirror.

Sway.

Saying it out loud was like recognizing my own face for the first time in a week, like the twinkly-eyed arrival of a million possibilities.

twenty-two

The Mercyssippi

"Don't be late for church, Cass!"

It was our first Sunday in The Roast, and it was just as muggy a Sunday as it would have been back home. Dad already had us out of the woods and back on the Mississippi highway when I tried to take my first-ever RV shower. It might have been difficult to stay balanced in the shower while Dad was driving, if my elbows weren't constantly pressed up against the walls.

As I dabbed myself dry, the empty M. B. McClean suit swung back and forth on its ceiling hook, making one sleeve annoyingly *whush* against my nose. The suit had been airing out all night. It had a lot more freshening to do.

My own airbrushed tank top was also getting pretty foul, so I reluctantly replaced it with my longest T-shirt and belted it like a dress. The outfit seemed appropriate enough for church-on-wheels, so I came out to join Dad in the front pew, which of course was the only pew.

"That was the quickest shower ever," said Dad. He was wearing his least-faded regular dad clothes.

"I ran out of water after like thirty seconds."

"Oh, sorry," he said. "We need to top off our gas anyway, so let's plan on stopping after a while and filling both tanks. In the meantime, why don't you pick us out one of Brother Edge's best?"

I opened the glove compartment and shuffled through the sermon CDs to choose one.

"Have you been thinking uh-gane about which sliver you might be interested in trying out?" he asked, as I tried umpteen times to shut the little door.

"Yeah, I've been thinking some about it," I said, putting both feet on the door and slamming with all my might. Finally it latched.

"So who tested the Sway before we left? Uncle Clay?" I asked, handing Dad the CD marked "Encouragement—Part One."

"Yeah," he said. "Uncle Clay was the guinea pig. He found him a Karl Benz soap last week. Karl Benz invented the gasoline automobile, you know."

"Did the soap work?"

"He helped me get this thing up and running, didn't he?"

"So did he say what it felt like?" I said. "I mean, to wash with it? Did he feel a zingle?"

"A zingle?"

"Like a zingy tingle in his hands."

"You know, Cass, now that I think about it, he did

181

describe something like a zingle. And not just in his good hand . . . but in *both* of them."

I opened and closed my own hands just thinking of that happening to Uncle Clay. What a great moment that must have been. Dad pressed the eject button and sent the Gordon Lightfoot CD shooting out across the console. He made a *What in the world?* look that turned his whiskery chin all dimply like a golf ball. Then he slid the sermon CD in. While we waited for the lesson to begin, I noticed that a daddy longlegs spider clung to the gap between my side mirror and its casing. It looked like he was hunkered in there pretty tight.

Dad, the spider, and I sat still and quiet as Brother Edge began with a verse, like he always does, this one from the book of Matthew. *Blessed are the merciful, for they will be shown mercy.* Brother Edge sounded much better on CD than he did in person. He told us he would be borrowing a phrase from "our French brethren" for the title of his lesson. *Mercy Bo-koops*, he called it. He said it meant, "Lots of forgiveness," or at least it did for his purposes that day. Brother Edge preached at great length about what a wonderful, mending thing forgiveness could be, and how it's like a big pink eraser that can erase any mistake. It was a notion I found very comforting—that of mistakes never being permanent.

Memphis, Tennessee, was the backdrop for most of our mobile church time. During the drive through downtown, I saw brick warehouses covered in graffiti, and trolley cars on wires, and a man pushing a grocery cart full of cans down the street. As Brother Edge wrapped things up by singing a verse of "I'll Fly Away," Dad and I crossed a huge two-humped M bridge over the Mississippi River. It was the first bridge I'd ever been on—the first time I'd ever crossed from here to there over something so big. I decided that I'd forever think of it as the Mercy Bridge.

"Can you see all that?" Dad asked, craning his neck to peer over the side of the bridge to the water below. "There must be a dozen barges down there."

"Did you *hear* all that?" I said, wondering if he'd been moved by the sermon to aim a little mercy in Florida's direction.

"What?"

"Brother Edge says there's no mistake forgiveness can't erase."

Dad could have played a whole song on a trumpet with the air he puffed from his cheeks.

"You ever seen what a bunch of forgiving does to an eraser, Cass? It wears it away into nothing but a little pile of pink crumblets," he said.

Then he bit on his lips for a few seconds.

"What I mean to say is . . . well, I guess there are circumstances that make forgiving just as hard on a person," he said. "For instance, when there's a big apology due to you that you don't expect to get anytime soon. You know, Brother Edge speaks of the necessity of repentance, too, as in doing a U-turn and leaving your mistakes behind."

I imagined Mom and her car both repenting at that very moment and U-turning right back to our empty house. Dad rolled down his window and leaned out for a look at what was below the bridge.

"Check out all those fishing boats way down the river," he said, changing the subject as smooth as pot-holes. "They seem so little from here."

They sure enough did look like you could push one around with your finger. I pictured Syd down there catching catfish with his bare hands.

"So does everybody else know?" I said.

"Does who know what?"

"Syd and Aunt Jo, about the soap stuff."

"Not unless Uncle Clay told them after we left."

"So how did you know it would work for other people too, and not just Uncle Clay?"

"I wasn't sure," he said. "I kind of wanted us to find that out together."

As we crossed under the WELCOME TO ARKANSAS sign, the downtown Memphis skyline filled up my whole side mirror. It was the first time I'd seen tall buildings in a clump like that in real life, tall ones, short ones, even one shaped like a giant pyramid. The spider on the mirror looked like he was standing at the tip-top of that pyramid. And that was something I bet even Mom had never seen.

"Dad?" I said.

"Yes, ma'am."

"Is Sway permanent?"

"You mean will we always have it?"

"Kind of. I mean like when you wash with a sliver, does it help you forever?"

Dad had a look like it was the first time he'd considered that question.

"Sure," he said. "I don't see why it wouldn't."

Once the city had faded out behind us and we were well into rice fields on either side, Dad and I set our attention on shoe-searching. I felt like I needed to see Sway in action again just one more time to make sense of the belief I had brewing up inside me. It did me good to see it changing peoples' situations. It did me even better to think about it changing mine.

By midday, after hours of Arkansas's truck-stop-speckled flatness, I got so impatient to see M. B. McClean in action again that I considered throwing one of my own shoes out onto the road when Dad wasn't looking. But then I remembered that Dad would probably recognize my shoe. So instead, I just focused in and looked even harder.

"There's one!" I shouted.

"Nope, just a possum," said my dad.

"There!"

"Armadillo," he said.

"Biggest shoe ever!"

"Buzzard eating a possum." He sighed.

In between false alarms, I counted all the eighteen-wheelers with words scribbled in the dust on the back of them. And then I counted white Volkswagen Rabbits. There were twelve dirty trucks, and zero white Rabbits. Frustrated with my dad for not sharing my sense of urgency about matters of immeasurable power, I resorted to practicing my string Eiffel Tower, repeating the steps out loud every time, just to annoy him into trying harder to find a shoe. I added a big *Voilà!* at the end every time, but there was never anything voilà about the mess I ended up with. Oh, forget it, I thought finally, abandoning the Eiffel Tower and inventing my very own Memphis-inspired finger-string creation . . . the Spider's Pyramid.

For a while after that, we rode slowly behind a phone company truck that Dad kept almost passing, swerving over and swerving back, until we both noticed the jackpot that sat on the back of the truck. Right there, plain as day, was a pair of work boots, battered brown with red laces, one on either side of a big drink cooler. One of them teetered oh-so-close to the edge, and I wished hard for it to fall right off, concentrating on it like those people who say they can bend forks with their minds. Dad zoomed The Roast up close to the bumper of the truck, like he was going to knock the shoe off or something. Thankfully, the driver didn't notice how close we came. Unfortunately, the boot didn't notice either. It stayed put.

Dad puffed out a frustrated sigh.

"I guess we're just going to have to refuel at the next town and resume our search afterward," he said.

Which was fine with me. My legs were cramping up anyway.

"And lookie there," said Dad, pointing to a green road sign. " 'Tinbottom, Arkansas . . . Rhubarb Capital of the World!' Sounds like the perfect place to gas up, no?"

He geedunked us onto the off-ramp.

"I should probably go ahead and get that suit freshened up while we're here," he said. "Can't be giving away magical suds in malodorous duds."

I noticed that Dad's rhymes had grown more effortless as time passed. On our way to the heart of Tinbottom, we passed under the town's water tower, which was painted like a huge jar of jam. Dad stopped to ask one of the locals where we could find the nearest Laundromat; she pointed us right up the very same road.

"Gather up anything you need washed," Dad said, passing the Done Rite Laundromat twice before finding a parking lot entrance big enough for us to use. On the side of the building, I could tell where someone had painted LANUDRY on there and repainted the right spelling on top of it.

"So much for all mistakes being erasable, huh?" Dad chuckled as we walked in. "At least they haven't forgotten their E's," he added, pointing to the Sav-Mor Mart next door. The possibility of finding some phone minutes at that quick mart made our stop suddenly seem promising.

Dad balanced a pile of green and yellow in his arms, and I gently placed my airbrushed tank on top. It sat there neatly folded, considerably less white, but just as gleaming as the moment Mom had first laid it across my lap. That moment seemed like forever ago to me.

"Promise you won't lose the shirt," I said.

"I promise."

"Or tear it."

"Promise."

"Or shrink it."

"Good grief, Cass."

I watched Dad closely as he crammed our load of clothes into a silver washer with a round window in the front. I still wasn't positive I could trust his unmerciful self with the tank top Mom had given me. I sure didn't want it to become the third important thing he'd ruined in a week.

twenty-three

Sterling Silver
Pork Rinds

"Imagine, Cassafras," Dad said as he dropped some quarters into a detergent dispenser. "There could be Sway vending machines in the future, full of all sorts of little soap slivers dangling in there."

"No way," I said. "Aren't we going to run out of soaps one of these days?"

"You just let me worry about that," said Dad. "There's plenty more where ours came from."

"From the attic?"

"Our inheritance is limitless, Cass. Uh-*gane*, there's no need for you to worry."

Enough dot com with the "uh-gane," I thought. Through the little round window of the washing machine, I could see the suit and the tank doing their foamy swish thing.

The walls of the Done Rite Laundromat were decorated with framed sheets of uncut paper doll clothes.

Behind a desk in the corner, a high-school-looking boy read a comic book and chewed his nails. Next to the desk was an entrance cut through to the Sav-Mor Mart.

"Can I go next door and get a snack?" I said.

"Sure." Dad reached into his pocket. "Here's a couple bucks."

"You got any more?"

"Like how much?"

"Twenty."

"What on earth are you planning to get? Sterling silver pork rinds?"

Comic book boy snorted out a laugh.

"Here's ten," Dad said, handing me a fistful of ones. "And grab me a pack of Powdered Donettes while you're at it."

At the Sav-Mor, I went straight for the section where the phone cards were. There weren't many choices for a kid with a cheapie dad, but thankfully, my brand was one of them. I found a five-dollar Cellular Now refill card that would give me ten minutes talk time. I knew I had to pick at least a couple more items to go with the phone card, mainly because I felt sort of guilty buying it. Like when Syd once bought a newspaper and jar of peanut butter along with some smoke bombs. I wandered around the store for a while, looking for a combo of things I could afford, finally settling on the Donettes, some pretzels, a yellow plastic visor, and a postcard with a picture of a man wearing a rhubarb costume. The postcard would be perfect for Syd.

Once in a while, Dad would come peek into the store

through the wall entrance to check on me, and every time, I'd put all my merchandise down at my side so he couldn't see the phone card. After the third time, my strange behavior brought the little cashier out of hiding. She must have thought I was stealing stuff, because she watched me over the cash register.

"You need some help, hon?"

I had thought the woman was sitting down, but as I approached to lay my things across the counter, I saw that she was actually standing. She must have been a head shorter than me, even. Her gray-blond hair looked like it would clink off onto the floor if you touched it. She wore a red vest with AMBRETTE embroidered on it, and peeking from under the vest was a black T-shirt with the white silhouette of a man bowing his head. I felt like, given the time to study them, I could have found a whole alphabet in the wrinkles on Ambrette's face.

"No thanks," I said. "I found what I needed."

I couldn't help but stare at the man on her shirt. His silhouette reminded me of a big version of the Cass-head charm on Mom's bracelet.

"Is he praying?" I asked.

"That's what I'd like to think," said Ambrette.

"You see this here?" she said, opening her vest a bit. It said POW in big white letters across the black.

"That stands for *prisoner of war*." Ambrette swallowed hard. "My sweet husband went missing forty-one years ago in the Vietnam jungle."

Hearing those words immediately erased my every notion of what to say or even what kind of face to make, so I just stared at my feet and squeezed out a sad "Sorry." I wasn't exactly sure where Vietnam was, but I knew it was a lot farther away than Florida.

"It's okay," said Ambrette. "After all these years apart, I've grown accustomed to the notion that he ain't coming back. The bad thing is that I'm starting to forget the details about our times *together*."

She beeped my items with her scanner, phone card first.

"So who you planning on calling?" she asked.

"My mom," I said. "She's sort of missing too, even though we know where she is."

"I'm sorry to hear that," Ambrette said as she bagged up my things. "That postcard for her?"

She had no clue what an awes idea she'd just given me.

"Yes, ma'am, it's for her," I said.

"Well, here you go, then. This one's on me." Ambrette slid a postage stamp across the counter. "And hang on, I got something else to show you, too."

She reached under the counter and handed me what looked like a coffee can with a wire handle on it. The can had a bunch of tiny holes hammered into it, with a little slumped candle and a pack of matches nestled in the bottom.

"It's called a C-ration can, from the war," she said. "I'm sure it once held baked beans. I turn them into lanterns to light my windows at night, so my sweetie can find his way home."

"Like a *cantern*," I said.

"I like that." She smiled. "You can have a cantern for yourself, if you want."

I stopped my finger at each metal poked-through spot and felt its sharp edges. On one side of the can, I traced the letters H-O-P-E, and on the opposite side, just P-O-W.

"Thanks very much," I said, feeling a bit warmer inside, like someone had lit a little slumped candle inside of me. When I crossed back over into the Done Rite, I found Dad standing there looking more than a little sheepish. I quickly stuffed the phone card into my back pocket before he could see it.

"Don't worry. The tank top is fine," he said. "I just wish I could say the same for the suit."

He held up the jacket in one hand and the pants in the other. The cuffs on both were all frayed out. I mean big-time scarecrow-style fringed.

"I guess a circa 1973 suit wasn't up for the washer and dryer," he said on our way out. "If I only had a brain, I'd have known that."

Inside The Roast, I tossed my bag of things and the cantern onto my bed and handed Dad the stalest Donettes ever.

"I'm going to need some help from you with this suit mess," he said, twisting some of the long loose threads around his finger. "You think the Sav-Mor's got a cheap pair of scissors?"

"I'll go check," I said, suddenly feeling excited to get to see Ambrette again.

"But first," I said, "do you have any soap slivers that belonged to somebody who was good at remembering things?"

"Remembering what kind of things?" he said.

"Like stuff about people."

Dad went flat-mouthed again. "This isn't about your mom, is it?"

"No, I promise. It's just, there's a lady in there who needs help remembering."

Dad slid the suitcase from under his seat and popped it open, rummaging through the collection, gently but determined, like he so didn't want to let me down on my first sliver request ever.

"Let's see. Nope, nope, no not that one. . . . Wait, here's one!"

Dad handed me a pale yellow soap that was extra per-fumey. "Mark Twain, great American storyteller. Packed a lifetime of books full of his own childhood memories."

"But this soap says *S C*."

"That's right," he said. "For Samuel Clemens. That's his real name."

"Perfect!" I snatched the sliver from his fingers and dashed back to the store.

"Don't forget the scissors!" Dad called out.

The front door of the Sav-Mor jangled when I ran in. Ambrette looked up from her crossword. I had to talk between huffs and puffs.

"I know this sounds crazy," I said, nervously flipping the sliver in my palm. "But my dad, well my dad and me, we have this stuff. And I think it just might be magi-cal, I don't know. He calls it Sway, and we have these old soaps that belonged to famous people, and you can wash your hands with one, and well, the Sway, it sort of gives you some of that person's good qualities. Like painting or singing or dancing or something."

I moved the little soap across the counter to her, slow and steady, like I wasn't sure if I wanted to just rewind that whole speech and walk backward out of the store. Ambrette slid the soap from under my hand and studied it carefully.

"Who's S C?" she said. "Santa Claus?"

"No, ma'am. It's Samuel Clemens," I said. "He was a mighty good remember-er-er. What I mean is, he never forgot a thing, and could tell stories about all the things he never forgot."

I wasn't even sure I was making sense. Ambrette gave a puzzled look.

"I just thought that washing with his soap might make you remember stuff too. Maybe if you just try it, we'll— I mean, you'll see.

"And, oh yeah, do you have any scissors?" I added breathlessly.

"The last aisle on the left," she said, keeping her eyes on the soap.

On the way up my aisle, I took at peek at the big round security mirror on the ceiling. Ambrette was already gone, and the ladies' restroom door was closing behind her. When I got back to the front, I had no earthly idea what to expect, whether she would come out of that bathroom and hug me or cuss me. I considered dropping the money on the counter and running, even with scissors, all the way back to The Roast.

Then Ambrette came out. And she hugged me. When

she did, the scent of that little soap wafted off of her strong, as if her hands had absorbed the whole sliver.

"You got a minute for a little story?" she asked. I noticed that her eyes were watery, and I hoped it wasn't because of the soap smell.

"Yes, ma'am."

"Before he went into the army, my husband was an auto mechanic," she said. "On the night of our second date, a customer with a squirrel stuck in his exhaust pipe had kept him after hours, putting him in such a rush to get ready, he'd accidentally splashed on his mother's perfume instead of his aftershave. That date was the first time we ever held hands, and we held tight through an entire showing of *Planet of the Apes*. I went to sleep that night sniffing the soft rosy scent on my palm and dreaming of our future together.

"I'd forgotten how that feeling smelled and how that smell felt, until just now," Ambrette said. "When I washed with your soap, I remembered."

"That's a really nice story," I said.

"Thanks to that . . . that . . . now, what did you call it?"

"Sway."

"Right. Sway." Ambrette put her hand to her face. "You mind if I keep the rest of the soap? I'll consider the scissors an even swap for this maybe-magic."

"Yes, ma'am. You can have it," I told her. "And thanks for the scissors."

When I climbed back into the RV, Dad was waiting anxiously for a report. He handed me my tank top, folded up neat and springy fresh.

"How did it go?" he said.

"She remembered," I said. "She *really* remembered."

"And you and that compassion of yours helped her," he said, looking at me like, *Well am I right or am I right?*

"So," he added, puffing up with pride, "would I be correct in assuming a certain someone might be becoming a believer?"

"Might be," I said. And it sure was a mighty might.

With his spirits lifted to the point of whistling a little tune, Dad set to filling all things empty. It was early afternoon when we found our way back onto the highway, which was bordered on both sides with soybean fields that looked like they'd been groomed with a giant comb. At first I busied myself with cutting the frayed edges of M. B. McClean's cuffs down to a nice neat row of fringe that looked far more on-purpose. Once the jacket and pants were sufficiently trimmed, I spent the next hour with my face leaned against the refreshingly cool glass of the side window, wondering silently to the blackbirds crowded on the telephone wires what on earth had just happened back there with Ambrette. And whether I was a total nut for sort of believing it.

I tried to remember stories about my mom from back before she even started rescuing. Soon I was wishing that I hadn't left the rest of the Samuel Clemens soap behind, because I could have used it to help me remember things, too. At least feeling the hard corners of the phone card in my pocket gave me some comfort that I'd have Mom's actual voice to help me remember, as soon as I could steal away and call her. Then, just about the time I began to

197

wonder when exactly that would be, there came and went a magnificent sight, all blue and crumply, by the side of the road. That's when I shouted so loud, I made Dad cough powdered doughnut sugar all over the steering wheel.

"Stop! Dad! It's a shoe!"

twenty-four
Belfuss

"Shoe! For real!" I hollered again.

Dad wiped his face, swerved over, and threw The Roast into reverse. We beeped as we backed down the shoulder, till the blue shoe was directly in front of us in the gravel. Thankfully, the passing vehicles were few and far between.

"Your turn uh-*gane*," he said, handing me Ye Olde Sneaker Reacher.

I stood on the center console while Dad steadied my knees. That put me outside from the shoulders up, just enough to be able to hold the Reacher out, aim it, and cast it.

I cast and cast, and cast some more, before having to rest my burning arm muscles. A guy in a Doritos truck honked as he blew past us.

"Steady now," said Dad. "Just hold your breath and try it once more."

I did. And it worked. Within seconds, I reeled the blue crumple all the way up the front of The Roast and lowered it and myself back down into the cab. I even volunteered to take the shoe off the hook, and discovered that it was a moccasin, so trampled and worn, it could have belonged to Pocahontas herself. Turquoise and orange beads just barely hung on by their threads. But to me, the shoe was as lovely as Cinderella's slipper.

"Fishin' accomplished," said my dad, blowing the road dust off Ye Olde Sneaker Reacher.

From where we sat on the edge of the road, there was no exit in sight. Just a cluster of painted signs springing up from the ground. Right between FREE DIRT and REPENT NOW, the biggest sign had an arrow drawn across it. It read BELFUSS FAMILY CRAWFISH BOIL.

"Well, Cass, it sounds to me like the Belfusses could use a little hand-washing." Dad pronounced it *Belfusseseses*, like I'd have to thump him to make him stop. "After all, it's the shoes what choose, right?"

He grabbed the newly fringed suit and his duffel bag.

"Cass, you mind if I use your room for changing? My limbs have taken a beating from that little bathroom this week."

"I don't mind, but um, let me get ready first," I said, not quite sure if I'd completely hidden the pink beauty box that was home to a certain cell phone.

"Sure thing." Dad plopped onto the couch with his stuff piled in his lap and waited patiently while I shoved the moccasin into my box-bed, lint-rolled the green-and-yellow thread scraps from all over me, and tucked the phone card alongside the phone inside the top level of the beauty box. Unfortunately, the twinge of guilt I felt for buying the card and fibbing about it couldn't be lint-rolled or stuffed into a box, so I'd be stuck with that feeling for the rest of the day. After all that was done, I put my new yellow visor on and took it off again three times before finally leaving it on. By the time I came out from behind my curtain, M. B. McClean was already in the driver's seat, and was all decked out in his fakeskin shoes and altered suit.

"I couldn't wait," he said, starting the engine.

"What about the hat?" I said.

"I dig it," he said. "You get that at the Sav-Mor?"

"No, I mean *your* hat."

"It's in my duffel."

"And the glasses?"

"They're back there too."

"I'll go ahead and put them in the wagon," I said.

"So," he said with a half smile, "are you saying the partners should go all out today?"

I shrugged out a *maybe* and began looking for the tambourine. At the next intersection, we turned off and followed cardboard arrows down a road so narrow, The Roast filled up both the this-way and the that-way lanes. And then came a moment I'd been dreading.

"Biiiiiiiiiiiiiiig Riiiiiiiiiiiiiiiiiiight!" McClean bellowed, taking a turn so sudden, all I could do was run for the bookshelf, spread my fingers hard, smush the encyclopedias until my nails turned white, and hope for the best while the rest of everything went sliding. The whole time I was thinking, Please don't let that beauty box break open and send that phone bouncing off the walls of the RV. When all was still, and I finally let my breath out, we had arrived.

"Job well done!" M. B. McClean stood and made his top hat do a little fliparoo in the air and land right on his head.

I leaned to peek out the windshield. In the distance, puffs of steam rose up over a whole slew of people who waved us in as if we had "Busfull o' Belfuss" painted on the side of the RV.

M. B. McClean slid his glasses on and grabbed the suitcase. He held his hat to his side as he approached the crowd. I followed close behind, pulling the wagon.

Across the way, there were men assembled around a big pot, pulling out baskets of little red critters from the boiling water. Tables made out of old doors propped on the backs of chairs were scattered around the grove. People of all ages crowded around the tables and stood, ladies in feathers and sequins and heels sinking into the dirt, and men with vests and dress shirts with rolled-up sleeves.

Each door-table was loaded up with a pile of crawfish, a stack of corn on the cob, and a mountain of potatoes, all steaming. Sticks of butter with the paper half torn off were scattered all around for rubbing on the hot corn and potatoes. In the middle of every table, a round hole had been cut, through which the Belfusses tossed crawfish and corn remains into a trash bucket beneath. Children ran in circles around the tables, holding the crawfish and letting them wiggle in the air, boys threatening girls, and girls threatening boys with the pinchy weapons. I wished that Syd could be here to witness all the mudbugs, and then I imagined how great it would be for my own family reunion to be this colorful someday.

It didn't take a genius to notice, however, that despite all the good eats and the bustling of the children, there was something very somber about the folks at the gathering. In fact, none of the grown-ups were really smiling or laughing at all. Instead, the Belfuss Family Crawfish Boil seemed to be a solemn occasion. As soon as McClean and I got close, half the crowd stopped to stare at us. It was obvious by our skin color that we weren't long-lost Belfusses.

"You folks miss your turn?" A man with an elaborately carved cane spoke up. His legs were as twisted as his white beard, and they made him wobble like he was sitting on a one-legged stool.

"Well, sir, it sure smells like we've made the rightest turn of all," said my dad. "The name's M. B. McClean, and this here's my young assistant, Cass. We've come your way to see if the Belfuss family is in need of any of our help in making this celebration complete."

"Not sure I'd exactly call this a celebration," said the man. "You the photographer or somethin'?"

"No, sir. But if you'll grant us the use of this here table, we can show you what we do have to offer."

M. B. McClean swung the suitcase onto an empty table and popped the latch in the same motion. He opened the lid to reveal the dangling soap slivers, still jiggling on their tacks.

"Suffice it to say"—he aimed his voice just over the old man's head and got louder with every word—"where the Belfusses gather, there's magical lather!"

McClean shot me a mighty proud look after that little gem.

"Well, I'll be a skunk's patoot," the man with the cane said. Women in fancy hats peeked from around women in even fancier hats. There was near total silence across a sea of unimpressed faces.

"If you will allow my assistant and me to set up shop in the shade of this here tree, we will elaborate further on our offerings," said M. B. McClean. "Sir, you got any loose water 'round here?"

The man didn't answer, but only pointed his cane to a well on the other side of a sunflower field.

"Cass, why don't you unroll the banner while I take care of this?" McClean called to me as he headed toward the field. "I'll be back in a jiff.

"No troubles in our bubbles!" M. B. McClean said, marching in rhythm on the path and pulling the wagon behind. Once he'd disappeared behind a row of sunflowers, all ears might have been on him, but all eyes were on me. I laid the banner on the soft grass and started to unroll it with a little kick, but shyness got the best of me under the weight of a hundred Belfuss stares, not to mention the beady eyes of a thousand crawfish. For some reason, I'd expected these people to welcome our weirdness with enthusiasm, but instead I'd suddenly found myself alone and up to my elbows in awkwardness. So I found me a bench made from an old brass bed, shoved the banner underneath it, crossed my legs, and pretended to be messing with my foot. It quite simply wasn't going to be a banner day.

"If you got a splinter, I can help out," came a voice from behind me. The voice belonged to a woman in a hat of navy felt—round and fuzzy like a piece of hard candy that's been rolled on the carpet. Chunks of black hair sprigged out from under her rosy red wig. She had a pile of buttery new potatoes stacked on her plate, arranged much like the cannonballs I'd seen the day before.

"I'm Constance," she said, squeezing in close to me on the bench. "But these folks call me Connie."

Connie had one soft arm and one that looked a bit robotish. It had a plastic sleeve that matched my skin but not hers, and a big metal pinch-grabber at the end.

"This here spread of people and provisions is in honor of my late sister, Celeste, the Lord rest her."

Late sister. Lord rest her. Oh no, I thought. We've crashed us a *funeral*.

"Nice to meet you, ma'am. I'm Cass," I said, peering over her shoulder to see if McClean was back, so I could aim some *Tone it down* vibes in his direction. "What happened to your sister?"

"Disease in her bones," Connie said. "The same that's done snuck its way into mine. It took her left arm and my right."

"I'm real sorry," I said, still looking beyond her, but trying to not let her see. "I bet you miss her."

"Don't you know it," she said. "Funny thing is, me and Celeste, we were always fighting over stuff. Who made the best hush puppies. Who could smell the rain sooner. Who got the cuter boyfriend. But you know what? All of that was forgotten when we sat down at the piano together."

"You play music?" I said.

"Only with her," Connie said, just staring at her plate. I noticed that one of the potatoes was shaped funny, like a mini bowling pin. Mom would have made a wish on it.

"You see, Celeste loved music more than life itself, and these gatherings used to be full up with both. But since she passed, seems no one's got any music to spare."

Connie pinched the tail off a crawfish.

"Is that your daddy hollering all that nonsense over there?" she asked.

"Yes, ma'am," I said, oh-so-wishing that wasn't my daddy hollering all that nonsense over there.

"I could tell by the matching hats," she said. "Looks like he's searching for you."

Sure enough, M. B. McClean was back with a wagon-ful of water, and he was scanning the crowd left to right and left again. I stood on a stump to get his attention.

"Ladies and gentlemen of the Belfuss persuasion!" his bigger-than-ever voice boomed. "May I . . . May *we* have just a slice of your attention, please?"

When he said *we*, he waved me over with both arms like he was helping an airplane land.

"My young partner and I have here in this very case a genuine and rare collection of soap slivers used by celebrated heroes of the past," he continued. "It's a potent collection of soaps indeed, each with the power to grant you the good qualities of its historic counterpart. And with a quick dip of your hands in this here water wagon, you can wash up today and become as marvelous as these heroes of old!"

M. B. McClean pinched his hands in the air like a green-and-yellow-striped crawfish, his top hat sliding sideways down his sweaty head. Folks started moving toward our little table to get a closer look at the suitcase. Their whoosh made the older folks wobble.

"In other words," he said, "let's bring this reunion to life!"

I cringed hard.

"Is he for real?" Connie said, fanning herself with a greasy napkin.

"I think so," I said, real small.

"And you're the partner?"

"Um. Yes, ma'am."

"Do you all make a habit of busting in on memorials?"

"Oh, no, ma'am," I said. "We had no idea we were doing that."

And from the looks of things, Dad *still* had no idea. I had to fix this, and fast. For all I knew, the very next words out of M. B. McClean's mouth could get us plum booted right out of that field with our soaps dumped onto our heads. Then these people who needed Sway so badly would never get a chance to have it.

"The thing is," I said to Connie, "my dad and I still might be able to help your family today. You see, we have these soaps, the ones he's up there talking about. And I don't know how to explain it, really, but they have this magic, and all I know is, when you wash with one, something special happens to you."

Connie's plate shifted on her lap and sent a cob of corn rolling down her leg and onto the grass, but she didn't seem to notice at all.

"I didn't believe it at first either," I told her. "But honest, I've seen what the soap can do. I saw it make a lady remember things she had forgotten. And a bunch of kids do some amazing things. And soldiers come to life."

"Soldiers do *what*?" Connie said.

"Never mind," I said. "What I mean is, it makes things better for people. . . . Even rescuing them from trouble sometimes."

When Connie stood up, her toes all bunched out the openings in her shoes. I thought she'd march away in a huff.

"Well, baby girl," she turned to me and said, "those folks over there might be unsure, but I can tell you I don't need any more convincing if you say you've got something that can make this dreary ol' day any better."

I breathed a sigh of relief.

"Hear that far-off thunder?" she said. "Storm's coming soon. You can stay right here if you want, but Connie's not about to miss out on that mystery stuff over yonder."

Connie adjusted her wig, tugged at her skirt, and struggled to make her way through the thickness of uncertain onlookers gathering fast around M. B. McClean.

"We call it Sway!" I said, excusing myself past men, women, and children all the way to the front, where McClean stood suddenly speechless in the midst of a doubtful crowd of Belfusses. To say that they were insulted by his accidental disrespect was like saying the ocean was damp.

I had to crawl under our folding table and yank his pants leg for attention.

"Psst! Dad! I've got to tell you something."

"Tough crowd," McClean said as he squatted to my level, pretending to make adjustments on the wagon. "I've never seen such a solemn family reunion!"

"That's because it's not just a reunion," I whispered back. "It's a funeral!"

twenty-five

It Is Well

The color drained from McClean's face and almost right out of his suit.

"You're kidding me," he said. "A funeral? And I've been up here carrying on like some kind of doof. These people are probably ready to dropkick me to Little Rock." He glanced around like he was looking for an escape route. "Come on. Let's make some apologies and pack up."

"No, Dad, just wait a sec," I whispered. "I think we can help them."

He looked at me warily. "You think so?"

"Yeah, really!" I said. "The thing is, this Celeste, she loved music more than anything. And when Celeste died, their music died. What they need is *music*," I said.

McClean looked like he was catching on.

"And Sway can fix that easy, right?" I said.

Just then a little of McClean's color returned to him.

"You know what?" he said. "I think you may be on to something there, Cassette."

I peered over our table. There was some wind in the leaves and a fair amount of crawfish-cracking, but the Belfusses had stopped most of their talking.

M. B. McClean faced the audience once again.

"Please forgive our little interlude there," he said. "But as I was saying, my partner and I have here in this case a powerful collection of soaps used by actual heroes and heroines of years past. And as I have been rudely slow in acknowledging, I understand that we are here to honor a heroine who has just passed on. . . . I believe her name is Celeste?"

A few of the men and women gave approving nods.

"Well then," McClean said louder, "how about let's make this a true celebration of her life? A quest to honor Celeste, we'll call it."

I saw Connie's felted head bob up a few rows back.

"I understand Celeste was a marvelous lady," he said. "But I never had the pleasure of making her acquaintance. So who in this crowd can tell me something about her?"

Too many seconds ticked by in uncomfortable silence as people looked left and right for someone to speak up.

"She had the voice of an angel!" finally came a shout from the back of the crowd.

A shorter silence passed.

"And the pound cake to match!" someone else said.

"She taught me how to twirl," piped up a little girl wearing a headful of braids and dragging a dingy doll by the foot.

"Well then," McClean said, stooping to the girl's level. "I think we may well have our first washer of the day here.

211

"Young lady, you ever heard of Ginger Rogers?" he asked.

"Mmmm, no," she said shyly, twisting a braid around her finger.

"Well, let me tell you, Ginger Rogers was a great dancer, and we just happen to have one of her old soaps right here."

The little girl backed away, half hiding behind her dad's leg.

"And you know what?" McClean continued. "Ginger Rogers was not only good at dancing on her own, but she was superb at dancing with a partner. And we just happen to have enough soap here for you *and* your doll. Who knows? It just might make you *both* brilliant dancers."

With that, the girl reappeared in a flash.

"Cass, grab me that *G R* resting right on top there, if you would," he said.

"I get to help her?"

McClean gave me a nod.

I led the little girl by the elbow to the wagon and handed her the soap. I expected her to be scared at first, but she wasted no time plunging the sliver into the water all the way to her elbows, swirling her doll's whole self through the wet. When I bent to help her dab dry with a clump of paper towels, I could see the sparkly excitement in her eyes. Or maybe it was the reflection of my own excitement. As the girl twirled herself a path through the crowd, all the way to a dusty stage under a weeping willow, she never let go of her ragamuffin partner, dipping and spinning quite gracefully.

"So here's the main thing Cass and I want to know," said M. B. McClean to the livening crowd. "Would Celeste have stood by and let this couple dance without any music?"

The people shook their heads no, almost in unison.

"I thought not," he said. "So we feel like it is our duty to let you in on the vast array of musical talents represented in this case right here. *Soap*ernatural wonders that are yours for the trying at no cost at all . . . other than your kind hospitality, that is.

"Before we continue, though," said McClean, "I have but one more important question."

The crowd shushed.

"Did Celeste have a favorite style of music?"

A man in a dark blue crispy dress shirt called out, "She loved the big bands!"

"Well then, step up, fine gentleman," said McClean. And let my partner hail you a Cab!"

"I don't know what that means," I whispered.

"It's all right. Just look for a C C in there," he said. It took me some shuffling around, but I found a green swirly that matched the description.

"You, sir, come on over and try you some Cab Calloway. And when you do get sudsy-sudsy-sudsy-so, just listen to the music playing in your head, like each soap bubble is a word to the song."

And the crispy-shirted man did just that, scrubbing up good and drying his hands seconds before being moved to belt out a sound so big, it made my heart forget a beat.

"Hidey Hidey Hidey Hi!" he called.

The other Belfuss men followed suit, singing out after him. *"Hidey Hidey Hidey Hi!"*

"Hodee odey odey oh!"

"Hodee odey odey oh!"

And the song went on and on just as crazy as that.

"What in the world?" I said to McClean, behind my hand.

"Cab Calloway was known as the master of big band scat singing back in the thirties," he said. "He used nonsense words to make his voice into an instrument."

Awesy Awesy Awesy Awes, I thought.

"Now, who else wants to try washing with a twist?" McClean called out for the next Belfuss as soon as the scat was over. "Who wants to feel the magic in their fists?"

For the first time since we'd shown up, there were more folks smiling than not, the smilers giving full credit to the spirit of Celeste for leading me and McClean to their gathering. M. B. McClean gave away soap right and left and up and down as countless Belfusses joined the fun, washing in the likes of country crooner Patsy Cline, composer Wolfgang Amadeus Mozart, and the King of Soul himself, Otis Redding. There was even one Arturo Toscanini, world-famous conductor, given to the wobbly-legged man with the cane. Every time I'd pick up a sliver, I found myself holding it up to the crowd and showing it off like shiny jewelry. And with every new musical talent added into the mix, their celebration only became more lively and melodic.

There was so much commotion going on, at one point,

McClean got a little hoarse and a Belfuss brought him a cup of iced tea. He guzzled it down as the sky began to rumble, steady and loud, all around us. When the tea was gone and his voice was still fading anyway, McClean looked at me kind of fretful.

"It's okay," I said. "I've got something."

"What?" he said, clearing his throat.

"*Thunder* and *wonder* is a good rhyme."

"You bet that's a good one," he said. "You take it from here."

"You mean *me* say it?"

"Why not?" he said.

And truly, I was feeling a little why-not-ish myself.

"Forget the thunder! Try this wonder!" I tried to yell, but it came out all puny.

"Forget the thunder!" It gained some strength the second time.

"Try this wonder!" By the third time, my voice was downright music itself.

McClean gave me a tip of his hat as he chomped on a piece of ice. A small boy holding a thoroughly gnawed-on cob of corn squeezed himself through a maze of legs to the front and cupped his hands to his mouth to shout, "Mister, I want to make some music too!" He tugged at M. B. McClean's jacket.

"You do?" I said to the boy. "Well then, you just need a rinse with a little . . ." I looked to McClean to fill in the blank.

"How about going old school?" he said, stooping to give the kid a tiny *F C* sliver. "Musical genius Frédéric

215

Chopin began giving concerts at the age of seven."

The boy looked both stunned and pleased at that news.

"Well, I'm seven and three-quarters," he said, standing up straight and tall like he was trying to stretch himself all the way to eight.

"Then you're three-quarters of a year more qualified than Chopin to give a concert, aren't you, my man?" said McClean.

With that, the boy held the corn in his mouth while he took the soap and scrubbed till it was all used up, then marched right to the middle of the grove and pretended to play that piece of corn like a blues harmonica, humming a bittersweet tune. I'd never even heard a real harmonica sound that good. A wave of laughter and applause washed over the crowd.

"I do believe Celeste is smiling down upon us," shouted a man in a rust-colored suit.

"Yes, she certainly is," called out someone from behind. I felt a hand on my shoulder. It was Connie.

"Looks like the magic soap business is your true calling," she said. "Now, what you all got in that case of yours for a grieving sister with a troubled soul?"

"Whoa," said M. B. McClean, sounding raspy and looking stumped. "That's a tall order."

I was beginning to think that poor Connie might be both our neediest customer and the first one ever turned away, until McClean lit up and said, "How about some Horatio Spafford for you?"

Horatio Spafford. I recalled that I'd heard that name before in church.

McClean searched through our stash for an old, fragile-looking *H S* soap. "Here you go, ma'am," he said. "Horatio Spafford was a nineteenth-century gentleman who lost half of his family in an accident and yet still found the God-given strength to write one of the most beloved church hymns of all time. He titled it, *'It Is Well With My Soul.'*

"Are you familiar with the song?" McClean asked, presenting her the sliver like it rested on a satin pillow.

"Why yes, I do believe I've heard it a time or two," said Connie with a grin. Then she dunked her one soft hand into the wagon water and twirled the soap around and around. Even as she washed, she began to sing, so quietly I could hardly hear her.

"When peace, like a river, attendeth my way."

Her voice grew stronger as she stood up straight, her arm dripping at her side. Every last Belfuss, Nordenhauer, and crawfish stopped to listen.

"When sorrows like sea billows roll."

Just humming along with her gave me chills all over.

"Whatever my lot, Thou hast taught me to say."

She sang out to the clouds like her voice might very well split them in two.

"It is well, it is well with my soul!"

Connie kept her face to the sky, making her way to the center of the hushed crowd, who struggled to hang on to their hats in the gathering wind. Soon, they joined in singing with her, the white-bearded man raising his cane to lead them.

"This is just what Celeste would want today to be."

Connie gathered herself and smoothed the feathers on her hat. "A sho'nuff revival."

The look of joy on her face was remarkable, as if it really *was* well with Connie's soul.

"Looks like our work here is done," McClean whispered to me. "We best be on our way before what's left of our inventory gets rained on. No telling what kind of magical montage of a mess that would make."

I moved to press the lid down tight, and noticed that, through what was left of the soaps, I could see the bottom of the suitcase for the first time. As McClean dumped the wagon and folded the table, I picked up the tambourine and shook it wild, the colorful ribbons blowing out into straight lines.

After their song, the people unanimously invited us to join in their family photo. As M. B. McClean and I held tight to each other to make room for a hundred Belfusses around us, a man with a camera that spit out the pictures as he took them kept counting to three and snapping the picture on the number two every time. While the little square pictures developed from nothingness to somethingness on a table, big raindrops landed on most of the tiny faces and wiggled them up like a fun-house mirror. Even so, you could tell that every single one of us was smiling.

The photographer handed one print to Connie, and pocketed one for himself.

"Here you go," he said, handing me the third. "You take this as a memento of your time with us Belfusses today. I'd say you've earned a right to keep one."

"Thank you," I said, but just as I began to dab the

picture dry on my shirt, a storm blew into the grove fast, loud, and heavy. The rain came like a curtain closing, and lightning touched down far beyond the sunflower field.

"Come on, Cass!" M. B. McClean shouted, as he made a dash for The Roast with the suitcase balanced on his head and his jacket on top of that.

I ran as fast as I could with the banner coiled around one arm and the wagon dragging behind me, going airborne with every bump. Looking back over my shoulder, I expected to see the Belfuss family taking cover and moving in huddles toward their own cars. But instead, there they remained, drenched and muddied, still singing and laughing. The old man had hooked his cane on a low tree branch and was leading them all around in a line, waving his hands and kicking up dirt. With the wind gusting in its branches, the biggest of the pecan trees masterfully conducted their symphony of joy.

twenty-six
The Up-est

Dad and I boarded The Roast and shook our wetness off like a couple of dogs. He peeled the photo from my shirt and tried to pat it dry without smearing the details out. Then he clipped the picture to the passenger's-side visor and took off his top hat, revealing a smush-ring in his thick brown hair. The air around him smelled like honeysuckle and hot sauce.

"Not too shabby for crashing a party." Dad laid out a layer of napkins to sit his damp self on before navigating us back to the closest on-ramp. The streetlights were just beginning to flicker on, and the rain looked like a million contact lenses on the windshield. Dad leaned to one side and reached under his leg for a napkin to wipe a circle into the foggy glass in front of him.

"It was a lot more of a party when we left than when we got there," I said.

"Thanks to you," said Dad.

For the first time, being his Cassistant gave me kind of a warmish gushy feeling inside.

"And thanks to you too," I said.

From a doggie bag that a kind Belfuss had packed for us, I ate a mini cob of corn and some potatoes while my dad fumbled the same crawfish three times, trying to pinch it open and drive at the same time.

"That was amazing," I said.

"Oh, you like my crawfish juggling, huh?"

"No, I mean back there. The Belfuss thing. That was really something."

"Agreed," said Dad, trying not to touch the steering wheel with his spicy fingertips. "I'd say we just witnessed us some mighty fine Sway."

Dad popped a whole potato into his cheek. By the time he got it totally chewed, he'd found us an Arkansas truck stop to park for the night, and squeezed us in so tight between two trucks, I thought The Roast might scrape along the sides and make sparks.

"Really," he said, unbuckling and swiveling toward me. "Thanks for the help out there today."

"But I was pretty shaky," I said.

"I know. Like fodder, like dodder." Dad did some fake trembling with his red-peppered hands.

"So what are you considering?" he said. "Is there any special request you might have for your own first dip into the Sway? You know, we've still got a Pablo Picasso in there," he said. "And even a Georgia O'Keeffe, I think."

"I have an idea," I said. "But I just need some more time to think."

"Take all the time you need," Dad said, unbuttoning his jacket. "I'm going to shower this cayenne off me before my skin catches fire."

By the time Dad pulled the bathroom door closed, before he'd even turned on the water, I'd already gotten settled in my room and closed the curtain tightly shut. *Now's my chance to call Mom*, a little voice inside me said, again and again. But the bathroom was right next to my space, and I knew there was a good chance Dad would hear me talking through the thin wall. Besides, the little voice inside me was near drowned out by a single, much louder word that was fast filling my whole self. *Sway.* The word itself had stars and paisleys bursting off of it in my brain. So many sparks and colors that I couldn't even contain. It felt noodle-worthy. But bigger than could be noodled on some old journal page. And bigger than colored pencils. Sway felt *permanent*-noodle-worthy.

Assuring myself that there would be plenty of time to call Mom later when Dad was asleep, I went to work. Despite feeling certain that Dad wouldn't be thrilled with the idea of permanent marker on the RV wall, I simply *had* to do something with the fullness I felt inside. So, before the courage could escape me, I pulled the brand-new pack of Sharpies from my backpack, lit my cantern, and hung it from the window latch with my red string. Then, while lifting the Eiffel Tower poster with my left hand, I began to noodle with my right. First, and across the top, went the outline of the word *SWAY* in black, and then came all manner of colored squiggles and stars and lightnings bursting off of it. Then I filled in the *S*, the *W*, the *A*, and the *Y* with stripes and dots and jagged patterns of red, pink, yellow, turquoise, and orange.

When the Sharpie fumes started to give me a little headache, I leaned back and checked out my work, thrilled that it was a perfect mirror of the bright, wiggly way I felt inside. Sway had just become my first permanent noodle ever, and Sway was a really good perm. In fact, it was so good, I made plans for what would go underneath the word on the wall. I could almost see it there already. . . . A field of soap bubbles with a magnificent Castanea dentata tree in the middle. One with great reaching branches and a fat tire swing. Of course, with me dangling off it and dragging my wavy hair through the suds.

That's as far as I'd gotten when Dad spoke up and near scared me to death.

"Hey, Cass," he said, his voice alarmingly close to me and my secret project.

I capped up my marker and pressed the Eiffel Tower poster down over my noodling fast as I could, just in time for my shiny clean dad to pull back my curtain. I expected him to ask me what in the world put such a look of being busted across my face, but instead he reached in and handed something over that only kept the excitement flowing. It was the brown suitcase.

"I thought spending some time with the collection might help you make your decision." He handed the case so close, the gold MBM glowed in the flicker of my cantern. "Here. Take all the time you need," he said. "I left the key in the lock for you."

I couldn't have felt more trusted than I did at that

moment. It was like he'd just asked me to drive.

"For real?" I said.

"For real," said Dad. "Just so long as you handle with care."

I took the case from him slow and easy, to keep it from jiggling, and laid it gently on my bed.

"You can refer to the soap list in there and look up some of the names in the encyclopedias if you need to," Dad said, pulling an armload of volumes down for me. "And just imagine all the possibilities those slivers hold for me and you."

And that I did. In fact, the thoughts of those possibilities piled high as I unpacked the soaps from the suitcase one by one. First, I laid the little pastel ovals across my bed, from biggest to smallest. Then I arranged them by colors: greens, blues, pale yellows, goldens, swirlies, creamish-whites, and white-whites. Then alphabetically. After all, this was not a task to be taken lightly. If there was one thing that watching McClean in action had taught me about Sway, it was that it required some skill and thought to unleash. So, looking back and forth from soap to list to encyclopedia, I set my mind on finding the one most likely to get my family back together, and back together fast. Tough as the decision was, just thinking about its potential made me feel like I'd just landed on the middle of a trampoline and bounced the up-est of ups, like an up that might never be changed back into a down.

twenty-seven

Leon and Teresa

It took me two hours to find just what I needed, but once it was decided, I couldn't wait to tell Dad. I jerked my curtain back quick, shaking a million more pieces of glitter onto the floor. Dad sat squished down into the couch, grinning at me like he'd been expecting my entrance.

"Guess what," I said, holding my closed fist out toward him.

"You chose a sliver," he said.

"I chose a couple."

I sat next to him and set the two soaps side by side on the coffee table.

"I've made you a believer," Dad said, looking all like his gladness might spring a leak. "So I'm dying to know. What'd you pick?"

"Well first, I've chosen this *M T* one. That stands for Mother Teresa."

"Mother Teresa!" Dad said. "Helper of thousands of poor and sick people. What an honorable choice, Cass.

"Now, tell me about this *J P* one," he said.

"That one is Juan Ponce de León."

"Oooh, a fine Spanish explorer," said Dad. "So which one will you use first?"

"Well, the thing is . . ."

My words circled around and around in my head like a dog looking for a comfy spot. And then I finally just came out with it.

"They're not for me."

"Really?" said Dad. "Then who are they for?"

"Well, I read that when Mother Teresa won the Nobel Peace Prize, someone asked her what people could do to make world peace, and she answered, 'Go home and love your family.'

"So I thought we could give that one to Mom," I said. "You know, to help her do the right thing."

"Cass—"

I didn't even give him the chance to argue. "And then that leaves the Juan Ponce de León one for you," I said super quick.

"And why is that?" Dad asked.

"Because he discovered Florida."

After that, there was a silence dead as beef jerky in The Roast. Dad grabbed a *Popular Mechanics* from the top of the magazine stack and flipped through it so fast, he would have to be the speed-reading champion of the world to even catch a word.

I felt a little burgle in my belly. "I was just thinking that maybe we could use the power of Sway to fix *us*," I said.

I pulled hard at both my eyebrows while Dad just flipped and flipped and flipped more pages. Despite the fanned air coming off that magazine, my ears got so hot and itchy I could hardly stand it. How in the world could he be willing to share Sway with a bunch of strangers, but not with his own wife?

"Why can't we talk to her?" I said, glaring holes through him. "I mean *really* why."

"Plain and simple." Dad rolled his magazine tighter and tighter. "Even if we did, she wouldn't listen."

"But I think you're wrong," I said. "I think she *would* listen because we've got good stuff to say. I think she would think Sway is the neatest thing ever."

"If only that were so, Cass."

"Why can't it be so? Maybe she'd even be so excited about it she'd come right on home just to be a part of this summer. A part of *us*, together. Just like you wanted . . . or at least like you *said* you wanted."

Dad looked at me like I'd spit on him.

"Cass, your mom is going to have to decide to come back on her own, okay?" he said. "End of discussion."

"Okay," I said. "Then let's just call her and give her a reason to. Let's tell her all this. Let's tell her about Sway."

I thought of admitting we had refill minutes just waiting to be freed from the beauty box, but he instantly made me glad I didn't.

"There are things you don't understand," Dad said. "Things that have nothing to do with me and you."

"Things you don't even *want* to fix," I said bitterly.

Dad slowly shook his head. "Cass, some words have

been said and some things have been done that make it very hard for me to want to share this summer with your mom. And besides, didn't I say end of discussion?"

Even more burgle inside.

"I heard all that," I said. "But I guess I thought that maybe, just maybe, your M. B. could stand for *Mercy Bo-koops*."

Dad stopped mid-sigh.

"You know," I said. "As in lots of forgiveness."

"Okay, enough." He dug a packet of headache powder from his duffel. "I'll think about it."

My burgle calmed a bit. At least thinking about it was a start. "Good," I said. "Then tomorrow we can—"

"Cass, please. Enough, okay?"

Suddenly, it felt like there was this imaginary long, stretchy accordion part of The Roast, fast pulling Dad and me apart. Then he flopped down on the couch and rolled over to face the back of it, leaving me just standing there like a doofus, like I'd been hung up on, but in a worse way—in an in-person way. Banishing me and my disappointment to hang out together on our end of the RV.

"Fine," I said to the back of his head. "I'm going to bed."

I'd had just about enough of his stubbornness, and besides, I had a certain refill card and phone to introduce to each other. If Dad wasn't going to tell Mom about Sway right away, then I would definitely have to take matters into my own hands.

End of discussion.

twenty-eight
Flipping
the Switch

I thought it would be half past never when Dad quit tossing and turning on the couch that night, so I sat on my bed, super still and quiet, in order to avoid hindering his sleep. It was ridiculously late, an hour of the night I'd hardly ever seen, but I was too stirred up to be tired. I peeked from behind the left side of my curtain to make sure Dad was asleep, and saw him sprawled across the sofa bed with his mouth hanging open, the *Popular Mechanics* covering his eyes, and one leg thrown over the back of the couch. The empty headache powder packet lay on the pillow next to him.

From the pink beauty box, I got both the cell phone and the refill card and held the card up to the light of the cantern to read the instructions on the back. They were easy enough to follow, and before I knew it, I was ready to press the MOM button. And when I did, it felt as promising and exciting as flipping the switch to launch a spaceship.

For the longest time there was no sound at all, and then a muffled ringing. And another ring. And then a man's voice.

"Hello?"

My spirits sank even as my heart raced. *Could this be Ken?* The connection had a crackle to it, like I was talking to someone on the spaceship I'd just launched.

"May I please speak to Toodi?" I said.

The man didn't say a word. I didn't know much about Ken or what Ken sounded like, but being rude sure did seem like a Ken thing to do.

"Toodi Bleu Nordenhauer," I said a little louder, stirring Dad a bit in his sleep. My heart beat even faster.

"She's not available," the man said. "Can I take a message?"

"Um, yeah, please tell her Cass called, and I have something really huge to tell her about."

"Sure thing, Cass," he said. His voice sounded almost smug, like he knew good and well what he'd stolen from me, and had no intention of giving it back.

"Something really magic," I said. I sure wasn't going to share anything more about this magic with Ken.

"Okay," he said, like it didn't even occur to him to ask about it.

"And that I'm going to mail her a present."

"Huge and magic and present," he said. "Will do."

Then he hung up. And it was a good thing for him. He probably sensed that the next words out of my mouth would be *I know exactly who you are and what you've done, and you better give back my mom soon.*

While I waited for Mom to call, I found the rhubarb man postcard, tore two pieces of tape from off the lint roller, and stuck the *M T* sliver good and tight on there. In the small bit of space left behind, I wrote:

Dear Mom,
    Dad and I both really, really miss you. Here's a little present from our trip.

                                        Love, Cass

I fancified the space around the soap with as much teensy noodling as would fit, making a squiggly frame all around. Then I dug the gum wrapper from the CAN IT! box and copied Ken's address on the card. Ambrette's stamp was the final addition.

If I hadn't become so exhausted from our roller coaster of a day, it might have bothered me more that Mom never did call back that night. *Cell phones are like bricks with buttons*, she had once told me when I asked why she didn't call more often from rescue sites. She said they were as unreliable as the weather report.

I tucked the phone back into the beauty box for the night, my only regret being that I'd blown one of my minutes on Ken, who probably didn't even bother to write down my message, anyway. Resolving to call again the next day, I blew out the candle in my cantern and traced my finger along the word HOPE on the side of it until I drifted off to sleep.

twenty-nine

Gwynette, Misery

When morning came, most of my toes were hopelessly tangled in my afghan, which made it tough to lift my poster and see if my supremo noodling had all been a dream. But the noodling was there, better than I even remembered, and looking at that word *SWAY*, in all its permanent vibrance, was like my own little private sunrise.

My phone call had so distracted me the night before that I'd slept in all my clothes, so I shuffled my way straight to the passenger seat, dragging the afghan behind me. Dad was already driving, somewhat slumpy and gazing baggy-eyed at the traffic in front of us.

"The headache medicine was full of caffeine," he said. "Kicked in at about two a.m. So I just thought I'd do some driving."

"Driving and thinking?" I said, hoping that thought might be *Sway plus Nordenhauers equals family reunion*.

"Driving and thinking," said Dad.

In a snitty tone that on any other day would have gotten me in trouble, I said, "Well then, while you drive *and* think, I'll look for a shoe, okay?"

I grabbed the remains of a candy bar from the console and took a bite. Shoe-searching was a great excuse for not talking.

"All right," Dad said, but his pinched scowl made him look all wrong.

The breaks in the highway made rhythmic *da-dunks* under The Roast, and Dad looked frighteningly close to falling asleep. He cranked the air conditioner so high, I had to bunch the afghan around me all the way up to my nose.

It seemed every billboard we passed was an ad for cave-exploring or discount fudge.

"Are we still in Arkansas?" I asked.

"Not anymore. We've crossed over into the Missouri Bootheel."

The Roast groaned its way up a steep mountainside.

"Mom's Missouri?" I asked.

But of course Dad didn't answer.

I left him to his grump and got back to enjoying the sights, which included a muddy mountainside with old white appliances stuck down in it like marshmallows in hot chocolate, goats eating out of an old bathtub, and a COON DOG CEMETERY sign that I thought said CORN DOG CEMETERY. I tried to memorize it all, wondering if Ken had left enough minutes on the phone for me to tell everything to Mom and still give her time to say how much she'd missed me.

"Just what I was hunting for," Dad said as we passed a giant fake moose with giant fake wings on his back, on the lot of a tractor dealership.

"You were hunting for a moose with wings?" I asked. Dad put on his blinker.

"No," he said. "This town. I was so tired, I almost passed it right up."

"But we didn't find a shoe," I reminded him. "And the Missouri Bootheel doesn't count."

"We're not working here," said Dad. "I just want us to drive through."

"How come?"

"Look where we are," said Dad, as we passed a big WELCOME TO GWYNETTE sign.

"Hey! Is this where Mom was?" I said. "Where they had the big flood?"

Dad didn't seem a tenth as excited about the discovery as me. "And the soggy houses? And the boat rescues? And the steeple lady?" I added. Each and every detail I remembered made me feel tingly, like Mom was close by.

"Take a good look around," said Dad, driving us slowly through the town square like we were a one-vehicle parade. The city looked old, but surprisingly well preserved and clean. I immediately felt connected with it, wondering if any of the people going in and out of the hardware store or the library or the grocery still remembered Toodi Bleu. Was somebody talking about her over lunch at that Main Street Café? Maybe already planning a statue in her honor?

As Dad pulled us into the parking lot of a big white church at the top of a hill, I hoped that all that thinking he'd done the night before might have kindled some Toodi-forgiveness inside him. Before he could even stop, I was unbuckling myself. He parked The Roast far from the church building, in a spot where we could see most of Gwynette laid out before us.

"So how do you feel about it?" he said.

"The town?"

"Uh-huh."

"I feel proud," I said. "Of Mom. It makes me want to talk to some of the people. To see if they remember her."

"That's the thing, Cass. I'm afraid none of these people will remember her."

"But this is where she was, right?"

"This is where she *said* she was," he said.

With that, my happy thoughts skidded to a stop. "What do you mean?"

"Cass, do you see any signs of flood damage?"

"Um, I don't know what flood damage looks like."

"Like water stains on buildings, muddied yards, flooded-out cars."

I scanned and rescanned, but the wettest thing I saw was a birdbath on the lawn.

"No, not really."

"How about anything being rebuilt or repaired?"

"No, sir."

"Do you see any church missing a steeple because it had to be cut off when a rescue team couldn't get a lady to let go of it?"

I looked out my side window and saw that the only steeple in town was firmly intact.

"Maybe she just remembered that part wrong," I said.

Dad closed his eyes for a few seconds and lightly bumped his forehead against the steering wheel. "Cass, I'm sorry, but I can't stand to drag this out any longer." He opened the lid on the center console between us. There on top of a pile of paper towels rested a shiny gold crammed-full charm bracelet. *Mom's charm bracelet.*

Dad motioned for me to pick it up.

"I heard you make that call last night," he said. "And I decided it's time for you to hear the truth about some things."

I began to take inventory of the charms. Palm tree, beach ball, seashell.

"There's been no flood in Gwynette," Dad said. "And there's been no Toodi in Gwynette either."

Dad turned toward me and breathed in like he was trying to suck the courage from all the corners of the earth. "Cass, your mom hasn't been a Response Team volunteer for over a year now."

I squeezed the bracelet so hard it hurt.

"She wasn't even in Missouri these last few months," he said. "She was in Florida. The family she said she was helping was really some rich guy who lost his wife."

It felt like Dad had turned over a beautiful rock just to show me all the wriggly grub-worms underneath.

"In the storm?" I said.

"No, in an accident. Years ago."

Uncle Clay says, on the day he was paralyzed, it felt like he was floating above himself watching all the terrible news being given below, and he was trying desperately to wake himself from the nightmare. For the first time ever, I knew just what he meant.

"Mom's been a total fake?" My words came out all shrunken.

"Not always, but for a while now," he said. "I'll be the last one to make excuses for what she's done, Cass, but when that hurricane hit Florida last year, something bad happened to your mom. During a rescue attempt, there was an old man she simply wasn't able to save. He died right there in her arms."

"She never told me that story," I said.

Dad draped his arm across the back of my seat.

"I think because she was afraid it would ruin the way you see her," he said. "She had a hard enough time telling *me* about it. It was like she fell right off this high pedestal we had her on and couldn't get back up.

"I'm pretty sure that's when her life went into a tailspin," Dad went on. "She quit rescuing altogether and went back to Florida to try to face her pain. That's when she met Ken. I guess she must have found it easier to start fresh with a stranger."

"And his kids?"

Dad let his hand fall to my shoulder.

"Just a son who's grown and gone," he said.

"But she came back home," I said.

"Only to get her things and say some sort of good-bye. To ease her conscience, I guess."

I instantly felt like I could be sick all over the whole dry town at the bottom of that hill.

"How did you even know something was wrong?" I asked.

"Two-three-nine," said Dad. "She called me just a few weeks before she came home, and the caller ID showed two-three-nine. It's a Florida area code.

"I confronted her about it that night she came home," he continued. "She spilled her whole story, and then she went nuts when I got upset. She threw the bracelet at my feet just before she left."

I opened my palm and saw a jillion tiny dents from the charms. My hand smelled all metallic and foul, like somebody had shoved a nickel up my nose.

"Dad," I said. "This isn't an in-between, is it?"

"This isn't an in-between," he said. "Honestly, Cass, I'm at a loss for what to call this."

"I know exactly what to call it," I said. *"Wrength."*

"Wrength?"

"Wrongness."

In fact, the way I saw it, Mom had invented a whole new level of wrongness. A bad so bad that *wrength* might not even be capable of describing it. Like maybe I'd be needing a fresh word from Syd to describe what Mom had done.

"Dad, why didn't you tell me all this sooner?" I asked.

"Because I knew how you dreamed of going with her someday and reaching out and helping people like she did," he said. "And I couldn't stand to crush that."

"You knew?"

"Of course I knew," he said. "Why wouldn't you want to do something so noble and exciting?

"Now you see why I wanted to go ahead and tell you about the Sway," he said. "To let you know there was still a good bit of sparkle to be shared by our family."

"Here you go," I said, handing Dad the bracelet,

which was suddenly as shineless as our day.

"I didn't want you to have to find out about your mom like this, Cass. I truly didn't. But I just wanted you to understand me not wanting to chase after her. And especially wasting something as special as our Sway to do it."

Dad put the charm bracelet back into the center console and closed it tight. I felt like an idiot for being relieved that I hadn't found the Cass charm on there, as if there was a molecule of hope that Mom had it tucked away in a secret place because it was the most important thing in the world to her.

"For what it's worth," he said, "this will be the last bad news on our trip. If you'll bear with me for a stretch of road, I've got somewhere special I want to take you next. I know we've both had enough Misery for one day."

On the way out of town, we passed a sign that said, DO COME BACK! Just beyond it in the grass on the side of the road, there sat a baby's shoe, smooth and purple as an Easter egg. A little Mary Jane, not yet scuffed or faded, and certainly not flood-damaged. It was ripe for the hooking, but Dad and I both pretended not to see it. It seemed neither of us wanted to slow our escape from the disaster scene that had just unfolded before us in that town. As we merged onto the freeway, between trucks so fast they nearly blew us off the road, it took everything I had in me to keep my eyes from making the first flood ever to hit Gwynette, Missouri.

thirty
Casstaway

It was Misery all the way to Kentucky.

What my mom had done was terrible, but not just regular villain terrible. It was something that was wonderful turned terrible. Like a teddy bear that grew fangs. Mom didn't *have* to leave us. She *wanted* to leave us. To live in a place that's not Alabama and do something that's not SMART with a man who's not Douglas and a son who's not an orphan. And she was there right then not missing me.

Dad reached over and patted my leg. He must have been talking to me for a while.

"Hey, Cass, you okay?"

"Not really."

"Well, just bear with me until I can locate that special stop I mentioned," he said. "It's a place your mom and I always used to talk about taking you someday. When we bought our little Castanea dentata tree, the man at the nursery told us about it. I think it's not far from here."

How could he bring up my massacred tree at a time like this? I wondered.

"You ran over the Castanea dentata," I said.

Despite being totally aware of the fact that Dad hadn't meant to smash my tree, I still felt like he needed to do some non-surplus suffering for his carelessness.

"I know, and I'm sorry," said Dad. "But this may very well make up for it."

The two words *make up* repeated again and again in my head.

"Just a sec," I said, darting to the back of the RV.

"I'll be here," Dad called out behind me.

I went straight to my room and snatched up the pink plastic beauty box, suddenly seeing it in a new light. No wonder Mom was so foo-foo this last trip home. All tan and flippy-flowy and shimmery. She had made herself that way for a start-over life with her new family. It wasn't just the idea that disgusted me so, but mainly how long it had taken me to realize it.

Without a second thought, I marched right into the tiny bathroom, set the box on the floor, flipped it open, and expanded out the tiers. Then, one by one, I emptied every lotion, puffed out every powder, broke off every lipstick, and crumbled out every shadow right into the toilet. By the time I finally pressed the handle, it looked like I was flushing a melted clown. The bowl was so smeared with bronze goo and flecked with chunks of shimmery chartreuse and goldenrod, it took three flushes to get it all gone. As soon as I stood back up, I caught a good look at my huffy-puffy, beauty-wrecking self in the mirror. And that's when I discovered something that you might call the exclamation point to my day. It was my first-ever *zeeyut*, and boy was it ever red, obnoxious, and shiny. Not only that, but there I stood, with all hope of fixing it getting slurped down the toilet.

Soon, the flushing sound was replaced by the simple humming of the bathroom light and the clang of regret in my brain. The noises filled my head so completely that when I heard a buzzing coming up from the floor, I thought it was just more of the same. That is, until I noticed the green glow of the cell phone screen shining up from the bottom level of the beauty box. I stooped to take a closer look at the phone, which was the only thing that remained in the box at all. When the 239 area code on its little screen made me instantly queasy, I swallowed big and did what I had to do. I pushed the IGNORE button.

By the time Dad and I made it to Overlook, Kentucky, I'd lint-rolled most of the makeup chunks off myself and managed to totally anger the zeeyut with a lot of poking. I'd also wriggled my tank top off of me out from under my T-shirt and stuffed it in the middle tier of the beauty box. Then I skulked up to the front and slid into the passenger seat, scaring myself a little as I caught a glimpse of my red forehead in the side mirror. I saw Dad looking at me from the corner of his eye.

"It's all right," he said. "That's what yellow visors are for."

So I found the visor and stuffed it down onto my head. And Dad was right. Uncomfortable as it was rubbing on my tender skin, it covered the bump just fine.

"Mom called back," I said.

Dad's eyes widened.

"And?" he said.

"And I don't need any surplus suffering."

Dad looked instantly calm again, and after that, things went totally quiet for a while between us. He asked me a couple of times if I wanted some lunch, but I'd kind of forgotten what hunger even felt like, so I just kept shrugging him off.

"Yeah, I've lost my appetite too," he said. "I'll just stop and see if the folks at this greasy spoon can point us the right way."

We stopped at a diner where music-note decals were peeling up off the windows and a cross-stitched sign at the entrance said, *That which doesn't fill us only makes us hunger.* The place had minty toothpicks, red spinning stools, and a cashier who called me "Shoogie." While Dad chatted with her about driving directions, I leaned on the jukebox and scanned the numbered lists of song choices, looking for the one that matched up with that Florida area code. *Two-three-nine.* Whatever the selection might be, good or bad, I would have to play it, and it would forever remind me of Toodi Bleu. I ran my finger across two columns of songs, and then, through the cloudy, yellowed glass, there it was.

239
Take the Long Way Home
Supertramp

I'd never even heard the song before, but the title alone sounded like the story of my life: a girl and her dad take the long way home to try and forget that the girl's mom might never take any way home at all.

thirty-one
Prolific Bearer of Nuts

Just seconds after my quarter plinked against the insides of the jukebox, the song's slow, lonesome beginning made me feel all kinds of miserable.

"Come on, Cass." Dad was standing beside the register, writing directions on a sugar packet. When I walked up next to him, the pen poked right through the paper and spilled a little pile of granules on the counter.

"Good news," he said. "We don't have far to go."

Our next stop was so close, it was no wonder our directions fit on that tiny packet. My toothpick hadn't even lost its minty flavor by the time we reached the place, which was really nothing but a clump of forest, marked by a sign that looked like the words had been burned into it. The one-lane road closed in around The Roast tight like a green sleeve. We passed through a collection of trees that were the tallest I'd ever seen, until we got deeper into the forest and saw some even bigger. One that looked like the great-granddaddy of them all stood over to the right, with an orange rope around it. There was no one else around, so Dad and I stopped right in the middle of the road and got out. The tip of the tree seemed to disappear into the slow-drifting clouds.

"Go ahead. Give it a read," Dad said, pointing to a plaque on the ground between the tree's roots. It said:

The *Castanea dentata* is characterized by the large saw-teeth on the edges of its leaves, as indicated by the scientific name *dentata*, which is Latin for "toothed." Commonly called the American chestnut, the tree is a prolific bearer of nuts, usually with three nuts contained in each spiny green burr. This, the largest surviving *Castanea dentata* tree in Kentucky, measures 32 inches wide and 86 feet tall.

I had no idea a Castanea dentata could even sprout leaves, much less grow to be such a giant. I looked all the way up its trunk until my neck hurt. Like I could have flopped right on over into a backbend just to see it all.

"Wow," I said.

"Really something, huh?" said Dad. He picked one of the loose burrs off the ground and pried it open. "Check this out, Cass. See those three nuts in there?"

"Yeah."

"Well, let's say, hypothetically, of course, that one of those nuts were to go away."

"To Florida?"

"Wherever a misguided nut sees fit to go."

He thumped hard at one of the seeds and sent it bouncing across the forest floor. "I bet even with that one nut gone, we could plant this here burr and grow us a new Castanea dentata that would make this big tall tree look just like your toothpick. Who knows? Maybe it will be the Alabama state champion by the time you and I are both gray-headed. You think?"

"It reaches out so wide," I said.

Dad put his hand on my shoulder real light and cautious, like he expected a static electricity shock.

"And we'll be far-reaching too," he said. "Me and you together."

"We will?"

"Sure we will," he said. "Just us two nuts . . . and some Sway."

And some Sway. His words echoed in my head.

"Let's sit a spell, if you don't mind," said Dad, and we squatted at the base of the tree.

"Think about it, Cass. You and I have something big in that brown suitcase. Something that can help us get past all this heartache and hurt. Maybe not quickly, and maybe not completely, but it's something pretty good we've begun, right?"

"Right."

"I mean, just because your mom stopped helping doesn't mean we have to. I'm sure not ready to call it quits on our adventure, are you?"

"No, sir," I said. "It felt really good to help people . . . like we did with the Belfusses. It was like all that stuff we did for them was really helping *me* too."

"Yeah, I'd kind of like to feel some more of that myself," Dad said, patting me on the knee. "And where there's a will, there's some Sway, no?"

Just the mention of Sway rounded off the sharp-cornered hurt inside me.

"Well, that settles it, then," said Dad. "Let's camp here in the forest for tonight, and first thing tomorrow we'll get on the road and do us a little sole-searching. Unless, of course, you're weary of the shoe thing."

The instant sting of Dad's comment made me realize that in a matter of days I'd become kind of attached to the Sneaker Reacher routine.

"No, it's actually pretty fun," I said, picking at the split in the bottom of my flip-flop. "I mean, a rule is a rule, right?"

"I guess you're right." Dad smiled as he stood and picked the empty burrs from his behind. He held out his hand to help me up, and passed the little green seedy one into my palm. On the way back to The Roast, I held the burr just tight enough to keep it from dropping and from prickling me too much. When we got there, Dad grumbled about the fresh coat of sticky specks along the sides and front of the RV.

"Sappy Castanea dentata," he said.

Sappy Dad, I thought as I wrapped the little seed burr in a tissue and nested it gently into my cup holder.

That night, through my moonroof, I could see a rectangle's worth of Castanea dentata branches silhouetted against the sky. Being that close to my magnificent namesake inspired me so, I lifted the bottom corners of the Eiffel poster and tacked them up with bits of tape torn from the lint roller. Sharpie in hand, I got to work, at first just outlining a simple, fat tree trunk under the big SWAY that was already there. The tree grew as I added twisted roots to the bottom and a scattering of crooked limbs to the top, drawing more feverishly as I considered the distinct possibility that Sway could very well make Cass a far-reaching girl.

Come morning, the canopy of green around us hung dewy and low. With no room to turn The Roast around, Dad backed and beeped us all the way out of those woods. Through the sticky-speckled windshield, I watched the Castanea dentata until nothing was left but its rounded top rising high and lush above the forest. Like nothing in the world could ever bend it.

thirty-two
Patakatish

The drive out of Kentucky took half of forever. Out my window, there was nothing to see other than an arrangement of grass pastures and curved fences that made the landscape look like a lush green puzzle. Determined to keep watch as long as possible for a shoe, I focused on the pavement ahead until I got so bleary-eyed, everything looked like a shoe to me, including the liquid shapes inside my own eyelids.

"The weigh station back there said we're in Patakatish, Tennessee," said Dad, trying four different ways to pronounce *Patakatish*. Shortly after, we passed a rickety gray barn with the words FIREWORKS, FLEA MARKET, and FRUIT painted across what was left of the roofing. Across the road, there was an Econo Lodge, a post office, and a Ford dealership. We must have been in downtown Patakatish.

Dad hung a Biiiiiiiiiiiiiiig Riiiiiiiiiiiiiiiiiight into the gravel lot of Heap Big's Powwow Fireworks Mart, Flea

Market, and Fruit Stand, toppling our coffee table and dealing our stack of old magazines across the floor like cards. He pulled up between a red-and-white-striped tent and a blow-up Indian twice as tall as The Roast. I wasn't sure if it was the fireworks, the fleas, or the fruit Dad was after.

"I've got a hankering for something sweet," said Dad, parking on top of the Indian's air supply and making him sag right across my side of The Roast. "You want something too?"

"Sure," I said.

Then I waited, eye to belly button with the tall Indian until Dad walked back across the lot looking like the top of his head was smoking. He climbed in holding a honeydew half with one lit sparkler sticking out of it.

"The firework came with the food," he said with a shrug, the sparkler smoking up the cab of The Roast until we both coughed. Once we'd fanned the air enough to breathe again, Dad did a fist-rub on his eyes and said, "Cass, are you seeing what I'm seeing?"

He slurped at the edge of an enormous iced coffee.

"What?" I said.

"Just over there," he said. "By that big trash bin."

Dad pointed his long coffee stirrer at a scattering of garbage overflow on the ground, right next to the fireworks tent. Lo and behold, there rested the filthiest, mangiest, one-and-a-half-eared bunny slipper ever.

Uck, was all I could think. I sure enough had wanted to find us a shoe and see what kind of Sway I could brew up that day as McClean's willing and able Cassistant. But still, *uck*.

"Seek the Reacher, Cass! We've got a fluffy one off the port bow." Dad leaned out his own window to fish the slipper in, since mine was blocked by an inflatable Indian belly. It took him five throws to hook the bunny, but the bunny didn't want to come. So, together, Dad and I used all four hands and yanked the Reacher, all curved up under the strain, like we were catching a whale. We both almost fell backward when the thing finally pulled loose and came flying. As Dad dragged the slipper across the parking lot and dangled it up into The Roast, a family with eight kids in matching clothes stood gawking across the way. They snapped pictures of us with throwaway cameras.

With a wince, Dad unhooked the bunny, its fur all matted with paper bits from spent firecrackers. The sour-milk-and-licorice smell of the slipper gave me instant juicy jaws, like when Syd once talked me into trying his Tuna-Cruller Surprise. Soon as Dad looked into its one cloudy eye, what I knew I was thinking and what I thought my dad was thinking were definitely one and the same. *Let's throw this one back.*

"You know," said Dad, sniffing his fingertips, "I don't recall any rule that says we have to *keep* the shoe."

I would have actually said something in agreement if I hadn't had to breathe in to make myself talk. For the moment, a grateful nod would have to do. Then, in one swift motion, Dad lifted the bunny up and out. And I just had to smile inside. Disgusting as our short time together had been, that bunny did mean something sudsy was about to happen.

"So where are we going to take the soaps this time?" I said, chewing on a piece of smoked honeydew.

"Well," Dad said, scanning the surrounding area. "This may very well be all there is to Patakatish. Besides, I see lots of people over there at the flea market, and where there are people, there are problems. I say let's make Sway while the sun shines." He was already up and gathering all things green and yellow.

He grinned at me and said, "That is, if you're ready to stand tall and reach out."

"Almost ready," I said, flipping my mirror down and adjusting my visor into a comfortable zeeyut-covering position.

M. B. McClean buttoned his jacket, licked his thumb, and tried unsuccessfully to bend down and wipe his smudgy golden shoe buckle, before unbuttoning his jacket and going for it a second time. I felt truly glad to see him all suited up uh-*gane*. If there was one thing this M. B. McClean character was good at, it was making me forget heartache for a little while.

"Anything I can help with?" Dad slid out the suitcase and the wagon with a few grunts and snorts.

"Not really," I said, giving up and tossing the visor onto the gear shift. "But it's all right. I'm ready."

Me and M. B. McClean and all our necessities had to come out the driver's side of The Roast. Suitcase, wagon, and tambourine, all present and accounted for. Since we planned on wandering through the crowd, we left the banner and table behind.

The flea market was inside a big metal building in a field behind the fireworks tent and the fruit stand. The afternoon heat sent wavy wigglies rising up off the cars parked on the grass, making the crowd in the distance look all melty.

"How will we fill the wagon?" I said. McClean pretended he was pouring his giant coffee into it.

"The fruit stand has a hose pipe," he said. "The question is, how are we going to display our soaps for people to see?"

"I know," I said. "We could use your belt to make a strap, and I can wear the open suitcase on the front of me."

"Great idea," said McClean. "It's not like I need it to hold these pants up."

"And can I make some soap suggestions for people this time?" I asked. "I did a lot of studying our list the other night."

"Sure thing," he said. "I'll be the wagon-dragger."

Water-gathering and suitcase-strapping made for a slow journey across the long field to the flea market, but I felt energized to be the one in charge of the magic. Once inside the building, M. B. McClean and I wasted no time putting ourselves and what was left of our Sway right out there in the midst of the shoppers. We'd made it just beyond the third booth when we heard someone call out, "Hey! Ol' boy with the top hat! Hold up!"

McClean and I squeezed our way over to the display booth we'd just passed, where a man was barely balancing on a rocking chair to flag us down. The man wore a satiny gold EXHIBITOR ribbon pinned to his shirt. "The name's Roy, of Roy Biddum's Antiques," he said.

"Pleased to meet you, Roy. I'm M. B. McClean, and this is my partner, Cass."

"What you got there in the case?" he said.

"Soap slivers," said McClean.

"*Magic* soap slivers," I added.

"You don't say," said Roy, sounding intrigued.

"Yeah," I said. "They belonged to famous historical people. When you wash your hands with one, you become sort of like that person."

McClean nodded along proudly. Roy Biddum squenched his lips to the side. While he seemed to be eye-balling the old brown suitcase far more than the soaps themselves, I took a moment to peruse his own merchandise. I could tell even from a short distance that his booth was filled with unscratched furniture, Civil War relics that were lots shinier than the real ones I'd seen, and framed, autographed pictures that looked like they'd been torn right out of magazines.

"Historical soap, huh?" he said, pulling a fat roll of dollar bills from his apron. "Tell you what. I'll give you twenty bucks for the whole collection, including the suitcase. I can package them all up real nice as collector's items."

"Oh no, they're not for sale," said McClean.

"Twenty-five bucks, then."

"No, I mean we're not selling them. We're giving them away."

"Well, that makes things simple," said Roy, with a sly smile. "Then I'll just take them off your hands."

He reached for the suitcase, but the suitcase and I took a giant step back.

"Sorry," said McClean. "But we're saving them for people truly in need of their power."

Roy did a snide little snicker. "All right then. So tell me, what's the oldest one you got in there?"

McClean nervously fumbled through the slivers and came up with a bumpy, creamish *A L* soap.

"Well, a lot longer than fourscore and seven years ago, this one was used by Abraham Lincoln." As McClean held the soap in the air, I had a sudden flashback to that day in the kitchen when Dad showed me and Mom the soap that bore Abraham Lincoln's likeness, the one Mom had made a wish on. Before I could take a closer look, though, Roy fwipped that sliver from McClean's grasp and squatted at the water wagon so fast and so close the air tasted like cologne.

"Magic, huh?" He stuck his hands into the water and rubbed and scrubbed with a vengeance.

"Well then, how come there ain't nothin' happening?" he said louder. "How come I don't feel no different at all?"

Roy straightened up, tossed what was left of the sliver into the dirt, and squashed it with his foot. Right away, I felt like shouting and tackling him to the ground, but I mustered just enough sense to leave that job to M. B. McClean. Unfortunately, M. B. McClean just stood there openmouthed and still, reminding me more of my old dad than ever.

"Here's the deal, Mr. Clean," Roy said, flapping his EXHIBITOR ribbon like a little frayed flag. "You guys don't have one of these, and if you don't have one of these, then what you got ain't welcome here."

Roy kicked the remains of the smushed soap under a table.

"And regarding that crud you're calling magic, my

255

green-and-yellow friend, consider it a favor I'm doing you, keeping you from embarrassing yourself today."

I felt sure McClean would at least have something clever to say about that, and maybe even rhyme it, but neither happened.

"Enough said," Dad muttered. "Come on, Cass. Let's be on our way now."

As we bumped and scooted to turn ourselves around in the tight crowd of shoppers that had pressed in around us, all I could think was how in the world an antique dealer with a boothload of counterfeit junk had the guts to tell us that our stuff was crud. How a man selling rusty, dusty fakes for hundreds of dollars could harass us for giving real, powerful antiques away. After all, what had Roy Biddum's ancestors passed down to him? Nothing but a sour face and bitter words.

McClean and I walked through the flea market exit with Roy still calling out behind us, "Hey! I got a soap sliver for you in my own bathtub at home! Belonged to Roy Biddum. You can have it and all the chest hairs stuck to it for only ten cents!"

Neither one of us turned to looked at Mr. Biddum again. The hateful, spitty sound of his voice alone was enough to make me wish we'd never even stopped in Patakatish, Tennessee.

thirty-three

Sugar and Sardines

The Roast was so far away from us, it looked like a toy model of itself, and the walk from the flea market was twice as hot as the walk to it. Especially since Roy Biddum had left me feeling like someone took me by the shoulders and shook me real hard.

Looking straight ahead toward the tiny RV, McClean said, "You know, I believe it was Abe Lincoln who once said, 'It's better to remain silent and be thought a fool than to open one's mouth and remove all doubt.'" Then he turned to me and smiled. "Good advice for our friend Roy, huh?"

"Yeah, I guess the Abraham Lincoln soap really didn't do anything for him," I said.

"You can say that again," he said. "No one would accuse Mr. Biddum of being a statesman, that's for sure." He pinched a mosquito off my arm. "Forget all that back there, Cass. Abe Lincoln might not have been the right soap for Mr. Biddum anyway," he said, flicking the bug to the ground.

"Or maybe it *was* the right one and it's going to kick in later," he continued. "Like when he gets home tonight, he may very well stuff all the family's important papers into his hat, like Lincoln liked to do."

"You mean the soap might work even if he's not a believer?" I said.

"You never know," said McClean. "Maybe Sway is more powerful than we thought."

I held tight to the suitcase so the sun-warmed soaps wouldn't jostle and stick together as we walked.

McClean shed an unnecessary piece of his uniform every minute or so. Glasses, hat, jacket. By halfway across the field, he was looking Dadish again.

"So isn't it a major lie?" I asked. "Saying things are antique when they're really not?"

Dad coughed like he'd inhaled a dandelion fuzz.

"What do you mean?" he said.

"That junk Roy was selling in his booth. You could totally tell he just took some new things and tried to make them look old."

Dad looked at me like he was surprised I'd even noticed.

"Yeah well, it's no secret the guy's a jerk," he said. "But let's give him the benefit of the doubt. Maybe his stuff is genuine. At least some of it."

"Probably not," I said. "And I think it's terrible what he does, tricking folks like that. People like him don't even deserve Sway."

Dad's arms suddenly went all loosey-goosey, and he started dropping one thing after another on the ground as we walked, letting go of one thing every time he bent to pick up another, like something had rattled him good.

"You okay, Dad?"

"Sure I am," he said. "Um . . . just watch where you step. . . . I think I saw some fire ant hills on the ground."

I sure didn't see any anthills, but I still stepped high to avoid them, making every lift of my legs thump the suitcase hard against my ribs. When we finally got back to The Roast, Dad helped me unstrap the suitcase from my shoulders, and we lifted the wagon in through the side door.

"Cass, I'm afraid it's too late in the day to find us another stop before dark," he said. "How about we settle here tonight?"

It was just as well. My legs, my back, and my thoughts were all equally achy.

"Sorry about the disappointing day," he added.

"It's all right." I flopped myself onto the couch. "I'm just sad that we might have missed helping somebody who really needed Sway today."

"That's always a possibility," said Dad. "But look at this past week. You can't let what Sway didn't do take away the importance of what it did. Which reminds me." Dad picked up the open suitcase and laid it on his lap. He reached his hand behind the lid's silky lining and pulled a little something out. "I'm sorry I didn't do this sooner," he said. "Here you go."

"What's that?"

"Something I think you've been holding out for," he said, opening his fist to reveal a pale pink soap with the letters *T B N* written across it.

"Toodi Bleu Nordenhauer," he said.

Hearing him say her name was good and gross all swirled into one. Like sugar and sardines.

"No thanks," I said. "I don't want it anymore."

I tossed the soap into the suitcase.

"And that's precisely why I'm sorry," he said. "The thing is, Cass . . . just like us, your mom had limits too. Limits that made her doubt herself to the point of losing hold of everything.

"The other day on the battlefield," he said. "When you asked me if that *T N* soap was a Toodi one . . . Well, knowing what I knew at the time about your mom, I let myself get all in a knot just thinking about the way you idolized her. I guess what I'd never considered is that, despite her *wrength*, as you would call it, there is still a history of good, honest heroism that she has accomplished in her life."

Dad handed me the sliver once again.

"And I figure that gives a daughter more than enough reasons to want to be like her," he said.

"Thanks, Dad." I held the soap loose so it wouldn't make accidental suds in my sweat.

"But keep this in mind when you wash with it," he said. "It's okay if you don't feel a . . . a . . . now, what did you call it?"

"Zingle?" I said.

"Yeah, a zingle," he said. "Don't worry if you don't

feel a zingle right away. I've heard that sometimes the zingle happens later too."

"Heard from who?" I said.

Dad hesitated for a moment.

"Don't mind that," he said. "Just trust me."

"Okay, Dad."

"That all being said, I anticipate us having a big Sway day tomorrow," Dad said. "Don't you fret. You and I will make a real difference somewhere."

"But we don't have much soap left," I reminded him. "What happens if we run out?"

Dad looked like he'd been put on pause while he searched for an answer. I kind of hoped he'd know that one right off the top of his head.

"Not a problem," he said. "I told you before that our inheritance is limitless, and I meant it. You just let me worry about all that."

"Why? Do you have a secret stash of freshies with us?"

Dad paused again and bit at his bottom lip. "You bet," he said. "Now, you just hang tight. I spotted a Huddle House in the lot of that hotel across the way. I'm going to go fetch us some dinner. Remember, I may be a little while if they're crowded."

I watched Dad wait patiently to cross the highway, his hair blowing from the blast of the passing cars. All the while, I played back the things he'd said about Mom, realizing it was the first time he'd talked sweet about her since before she left. As I felt the buttery smoothness of the pink *T B N* soap in my hand, Dad's words played over and over in my head: *Maybe Sway is more powerful than we thought.*

Without hesitation, I went to my room, stopping only to stash the Toodi soap in the backest back of the top pantry shelf, where I didn't have to look at it. Then I pulled the rhubarb man postcard from under my bed cushion, pleased to find that the Mother Teresa soap was still intact and stuck tight to the card. I had a good feeling it would survive a trip to Florida.

There was no sight of a supper-carrying dad out the side window of The Roast, so I took the opportunity to make my own dash across the road and drop that postcard into what may have been Patakatish, Tennessee's only big blue mailbox. The card fell to the bottom with a hollow-sounding thunk.

I checked to make sure the coast was clear before crossing back over to The Roast. But the coast was not clear at all. In fact, just a stone's throw away stood Dad in the parking lot of the Econo Lodge motel, where he was talking to a woman pushing a maid's cart stacked high with towels. Nervous I'd be caught not holding down the fort, I hid myself behind the mailbox like a spy and watched as the woman handed Dad a plastic bag. Dad nodded a thank-you and walked off, disappearing into the Huddle House.

What in the world was he doing? I waited there wondering that very thing until I could see Dad through the window of the restaurant, waiting in line to pay. Then I ran back to The Roast and got myself all settled at the coffee table, pretend-reading a magazine by the time he opened the door.

"Sorry for the long wait," he said, setting each of us out a plate of everything anyone ever thought of mixing with hash browns. "The Huddle House was standing room only."

He twisted the Econo Lodge bag shut and set it on the floor between his leg and the couch as he sat.

"I bummed us a few mini-shampoos off the maid," he explained, then raised his cup of orange juice to the ceiling, and waited for me to do the same. We clinked our cups together in the best way Styrofoam knows how to clink.

"Here's to making a splash tomorrow," he said, sloshing a little juice over the edge.

"And here's to Sway," I said, trying to make another toast; but Dad, totally preoccupied with shoving the hotel bag under the couch with his heel, left me waiting way too long with my cup in the air.

thirty-four
The Lye

After dinner, within minutes of patting the hash brown grease from his beard, Dad fell asleep sitting straight up. I let him be and retired to my room, where I was thrilled to find an almost full, perfect-for-noodling moon beaming into the little back window of The Roast. Careful to tilt each Sharpie so it wouldn't make a squeak on the wall, I rooted and branched my tree like crazy for almost an hour, until a fresh rustling around from the other side of The Roast startled me so, I dropped my marker cap at my feet. It sounded as if Dad was right there, outside my curtain, rummaging through the rolltop desk for something. I held my marker and my breathing as still as I could to listen.

"Cass? You awake?" he whispered, and in response I made the most realistic sleep noise I could conjure. After Dad stopped calling to me, there wasn't another peep from him, other than a little bit of shuffling around the

RV and some page-turning here and there.

As I carefully pressed the Eiffel Tower flat against the wall and taped the bottom corners onto their spots, I noticed that I'd accidentally noodled beyond the borders of the poster. Pieces of tree crept out from under it in all directions. I'd have to put off making a plan to keep that hidden, though, since capping the Sharpie was the most pressing task at hand. To aid in my search for the missing cap, I dangled upside down off my bed and fumbled around on the floor for a good while, until I was totally distracted by a small spot of light glowing right through my tablecloth curtain. I watched the little light flit to and fro for at least a minute before I talked myself into stepping up onto my box-bed and steadying against the back wall of the RV to have a better look.

I stood teetering on my toes to see over the curtain. There was Dad, in a torn undershirt and some cutoff sweats, sitting quietly at the rolltop desk. On his head he wore a sweatband with a tiny flashlight stuck down through the side, and the light shone down on a lap tray made from our Scrabble box. The rolltop was wide open, and inside it were the scattered tools of a manicure kit. An encyclopedia volume lay stretched open across the desktop.

Dad covered his eyes with his left hand, like he didn't trust himself to just plain old shut them. Then he made his right hand into a fist with one finger pointed, circled it in the air above the book, and lowered it in a mini-twister. When his finger landed on the page, he peeked from behind his hand to see where he had landed. He cocked his head just right, to aim the weak flashlight at the page, and leaned in close to the book. From so high up, I couldn't begin to tell what he was reading, but then I saw his lips say and say again, almost without a sound, " 'Thomas Edison, American inventor, developer of many devices that greatly influenced life around the world, including the phonograph, the motion picture camera, and a long-lasting electric lightbulb.' "

And then he repeated, like he was memorizing for a test, "T E . . . Thomas Edison . . . inventor of the light-bulb . . . T E . . . Thomas Edison."

My legs stuck together as I stood there watching, and sweat beaded on my dad's brow. Closing the book ever so quietly and still saying "T E, T E, T E" to himself, Dad leaned as far and low as he could to grab something from off the floor. He came back up with the plastic Econo Lodge bag, turning it upside down by its corners real slow and careful, like he didn't want the little shampoos to make a racket. But what poured out of that bag was definitely *not* shampoos, and I had to rub my eyes to believe what I was seeing. It was soap, and a whole pile of them, all blank and white as my own face. No way no way no way, I thought. There's got to be a good explanation for this.

Dad grabbed a pair of tweezers from the manicure set, picked a small soap from the pile, and laid it gently on the Scrabble box in his lap. Softly in the background, Gordon Lightfoot sang about feeling like he's winning when he's losing again. My dad laid down the tweezers, grabbed the nail file, and with the edge of it shaved the soap down to a sliver. And right there, in the glow of his tiny spotlight shining down, with the sharp point of the file, Dad scraped the letters *T E* into that soap sliver. When he was done, he blew on the soap, blasting the shavings onto the floor and shoving them beneath the desk with his sock foot. As he stood to carry the box lid over to the couch, my tummy growled and almost gave me away. I squeezed on my gut so tight to shush its growling, baby stars danced in front of my eyes.

I hoped hard that my late-night hunger was making me imagine things. Or maybe that I'd dangled upside down too long looking for the marker cap, and now my mind was playing tricks on me. But when the growling stopped and the stars cleared, I looked again to see my dad pop the latch on the MBM suitcase, open it wide, tilt the Scrabble lid up like a slide, and send the newly carved soap sliver sledding into the case. Suddenly, my hope and my joy and my legs all failed me at the same time, sending me sliding down the back wall of The Roast. As I sunk to the floor, a lightbulb of understanding zutzed on and off above my head, with a different cruel flash of thought each time. *It's all fake. The soaps. The case. The suit. Everything.*

I crumpled myself into a ball next to my bed, in a spot right between the beauty box and my backpack, and right on top of the lost Sharpie cap. Then, from my pack, I felt with my thumb for the sharpest pencil in there, pulled my curtain tight, and poked the biggest hole possible right through it. Sitting with my back to the big shoe box, I watched my dad squint, point, and carve, again and again. Every time, it was the same. He'd grab a fresh encyclopedia, flop it open, and do an eeny-meeny-miny motion until he found a name, any name. Then he'd pick up a blank soap from the desk, shave it down, carve the initials right in, and slide it into the suitcase. When he scraped, some of the soaps would bust in two, and with his fingertips, he crumbled those into tiny crumbs and piled them on one of the napkins.

The whole time I watched, it felt as if I, Dad, The Roast, and everything in it were tumbling down a mountainside, like all things good and nasty deafeningly clanking against each other. All I could imagine were flicker-flashes of the faces of people helped by our so-called magic; memories that had suddenly become tangled in sickening questions. *How could he? How did he? Had he fooled me? Had he fooled us all?*

After closing and shoving the case back into place for the last time, Dad stepped gingerly past the desk and into the bathroom, grabbing the napkin full of broken soaps on the way.

And in one big flush, the crumbles . . . and Sway . . . were no more.

thirty-five

The Other Shoe

"No-good, sticky-fingered, kid-cheatin' con man!"

When I was six, this is what my mom yelled at the ice-cream man as she chased his truck three whole blocks because I'd paid for my push-up pop with a five-dollar bill and come back with no change. She ran on her heels, cotton balls separating her freshly painted toes. I mostly remember having to help her hold a bag of ice on her raw heels while my pop melted in the sink.

Now, in the RV, as Dad snored on the other side of the curtain, I lay across that old trick box that was my bed and realized for the first time ever how miserably uncomfortable it could be. I felt like a magician's assistant being cut in half for real, my insides hurt so bad from the Sway snatched right out of there. I thought about Syd warning me once that if you say a word out loud enough times, it will totally lose its meaning, and how I sure didn't have to do that with Sway now that Dad had just trampled the meaning right out of it for me. Then I considered all the things that M. B. probably really stood for. Like *Major Bunk*. Or *Mister Bull*. Perhaps *Mondo Bamboozler*. Something befitting a no-good, sudsy-fingered, kid-foolin' soap scum.

I closed my eyes tight while all the lies Dad had told elbowed and kicked each other around in my head. The soaps, the suit, the list, the attic, the limitless inheritance. And then I remembered the certificate. *The certificate.* I'd forgotten all about that thing, and I had to see it again right away. Careful not to wake Dad, I reached around the side of my curtain, opened the fridge, and slid the cold paper out from its frosty spot. I unfolded the paper and held it up to my little window, hoping against hope to feel some of the magic again. Like maybe Dad's carving thing was all some kind of weird misunderstanding. I mean, I'd seen with my own eyes what Sway had done for all those people.

But as the full moonlight shone through the document, there, plain as the zeeyut on my face, was something I'd missed before, something very telling in the bottom left corner. On a spot not quite as burned off as the other edges, I recognized the mascot's cartoon foot from the Olyn Middle School stationery. And as if that weren't enough, I could even smell the blackened edges of the paper, which made me instantly picture Dad burning it over the sink with the *flick-flick-flick* of a lighter. That thought alone made me so furious, I folded the paper again and again and stuffed it into the CAN IT! box, which was now far beyond full—paper corners poking out of every side. How dumb could I be for not learning from Mom's SMART certificates that a document doesn't give you authenticity.

Overcome by the realization that I couldn't even trust my own smarts, or my own eyes, for that matter, I began to wonder: Had *every*thing important in my life been nothing more than imaginary? Not just soaps and the comfort they seemed to give people, but maybe even the biggest stuff . . . even my own parents' love for me?

My heavy thoughts and the sobs they squeezed out of me made it harder by the minute to keep silent, even with my face muffled by my pillow. I'd heard from Brother Edge about God not letting people suffer beyond what they can bear, but what I was feeling was surely as close to unbearable as it gets. In three weeks' time I'd been up, down, and all around. And now there was nowhere left to go but *out*.

Dad was so sprawled out across his space, there was no making it to one of the RV doors without getting caught, so I leaned beyond my curtain just far enough to grab the brown suitcase. Then I dragged my bed to the middle of my room, one little jerk at a time, and stood on top of the box, hoping hard that it wouldn't break underneath me.

The bed put me high enough to reach the moonroof, and as I worked to pop open its latch, my hands got all nervous and uncooperative, like they'd never even met each other before. When the door finally gave way, I lifted the suitcase above my head and pushed it out, slow and easy, where I let it rest on the roof to wait for me to join it. After that, I raised my arms and wriggled myself up through the opening. Once my top half was out, I had to slide on my belly along the roof until my legs were free as well. Suitcase in hand, I climbed down the back ladder of The Roast, stepping soft as I could; and as soon as my feet hit the ground, I ran.

I ran harder than I'd ever run before, even in a thousand races against Syd. I ran so hard, the taillights, the weeds growing up through the asphalt, the moist thickness of the air, everything that passed me was a swirly blur of smells and sights and sounds. I ran so hard that a million night bugs flecked me in the face, a whole new one for each terrible thought that passed through my mind. Like how cruel it was for heaven to assign two rotten-hearted parents to one girl. And that paper cuts caused by fake certificates are by far the most painful kind. And how I wished on all the crooked cucumbers in the world that I could dive to the bottom of that blue mailbox and get Mom's stupid, worthless postcard out of there.

When I couldn't move fast enough in my flip-flops, I took them off and carried them. Though a fresh cover of clouds kept the moon's light from guiding me, I felt like I could very well close my eyes and let my fury steer my feet. The loose pavement on the shoulder of the road was warm and smooth enough on my skin, and even smoother when it changed to just hard-packed dirt underneath me.

Even above the noises, which had turned from the *whush* of trucks into the fuss of crickets, I could hear myself panting like a dog, and my right leg itched where the suitcase pounded it with every stride. The blood in my cheeks made me feel like my face would catch fire, and

I was sweating like I hadn't ever sweated before. Even so, it was like my body and soul were hardened and in full agreement, like my legs wouldn't get tired of running and that was okay because my heart didn't want them to anyway. Unfortunately, though, legs can be a lot more wobbly than hearts sometimes. Much like the wobbling my own did right before I came to a dead stop.

The way I saw it, though, my stopping just made for a good opportunity to deal out some revenge. So, best as I could while still holding it, I unlocked the brown suitcase and let the bottom drop open like a trapdoor, sending an avalanche of useless soaps tumbling onto the ground. After that, I took the open case into both hands and summoned what was left of my energy, shaking hard to loosen the stubborn, clingy slivers. In my head, I seemed to imagine a thundering sound that made the perfect companion for the disposal of such a heap of wrength.

Only, the next time the thundering happened, it came with a sharp flash of lightning and a tremble of the earth below me. Then, sudden as spit, the bottom dropped out of the sky, and huge, relentless raindrops smeared my vision. Between the drops, I took a good overdue look at my blurry surroundings.

And that's when I turned scared. *Really* scared.

It seemed in all my muddled rush, I had left our parking lot and even the main highway far behind, and nothing at all was familiar anymore. The night bugs had stopped their attack. Even the road under me was little more than a path, made by who knew what kind of wild Tennessee animal. If I was even in Tennessee anymore. It seemed I'd run so far, I could very well be in California. Only, I had a feeling it didn't rain this hard in California.

Just one yellow light hanging from a splintered pole poorly lit the scene around me. To my right, there was a rickety fence with rusty barbed wire across it. To my left, there was a ditch already filling with water. Behind me was a narrow woodsy clearing growing darker by the second. And the way I'd come from was merely a slick of shiny brown mud. *Or was that even the way I'd come from?* I wanted so bad to turn back, but I didn't for the life of me know how. Starting off in one direction and then the other only made me more confused.

Just when I chose a direction and began to walk that way, something suddenly made me slip and fall hard to my knees. As I struggled to free myself from the soaked overgrowth on the ground, there in the mud all around me floated the melty remains of dozens of little slick soaps that had made their own revenge. When I was finally able to pull myself up by a loose root, the soapsuds clung to a whole mess of scrapes on my shins, making them sting something fierce.

Feeling a braided chain of regret and fear cinch tighter around my gut with every breath I took in, I held fast to the nearest fence post, like an imaginary storm victim clinging to an imaginary church steeple in the midst of a not-so-imaginary flood. And just when it seemed the world didn't have enough oxygen for even one girl, I heard a voice.

"Cass!" Dad screamed, loud as the thunder, from somewhere way too far away. "Castanea!"

I let go of the post and scrambled toward his voice so desperately fast, I fell to my hands and knees again, with no regard for the scrapes and the mud. All I knew was every call of my name was louder and more comforting.

"Cass!"

"Dad!" I yelled, still running toward him.

Then finally, up ahead, the main road came into view.

"Cass!"

"I'm here!" I said.

Within a matter of seconds, The Roast appeared, taking a Biiiiiiiiiiiiiiiiig Leeeeeeeeeft that almost sent it tipping over on its side. When Dad stopped, the RV hung off into the thicket by the side of the road, all leafy and twiggy like it had just busted through a wall of hedges.

I stopped in my tracks and stood firm between the cockeyed headlight beams, waiting for Dad to get out. He tried and tried to fight his way past a branch that slapped through his window, to push what he could of his face out through the leaves. I wondered if he'd be relieved that he'd found me, or mad that he'd had to come looking at all. Then, soon as I caught sight of Dad's face, I silently cursed how very instant tears can be, and how the sudden slowing of the rain sure did make them hard to hide.

"Cass, baby, are you all right?" he said.

"Not really," I answered. "How did you even know I was gone?"

"Your curtain," Dad said, all out of breath like he'd had to power The Roast with his own feet. "It was blowing like crazy from the wind through the moonroof."

"But how did you find me?"

Dad held up a familiar flip-flop. I didn't even realize I had dropped it.

"I found this at the turnoff," he said.

My ears itching like never before, I lifted the other flop up to the light so he could get a good look before I threw it hard on the ground in front of me.

"Well, here's the other one," I said, wrestling back my tears. "Two matching shoes. Now we *have* to go home."

thirty-six
Where the
Heartaches Come

Dad shook the leafy mess from his hair.

"Come on," he said. "Get in."

There was a NO TRESPASSING sign so close to us on my side of the RV, I had to slide up into my seat like a thief between laser beams. Dad found a big towel and draped it across my shoulders, lingering a moment to squeeze me close to him.

"Cass, are you hurt?"

The relieved part of me wanted to turn and hug him back. Even so, the mad part of me won out.

"I'm okay," I said, slowly scanning the insides of the RV. With books and wagon and banner and tambourine all wet from the open moonroof and strewn everywhere, The Roast looked like it was going to a costume ball dressed as a shipwreck. I thought about how, on the day we left for this trip, Uncle Clay had wished us a clean start. And how this didn't feel like a clean start at all, but more like a really dirty finish.

After pulling the moonroof lid shut with the Sneaker Reacher, Dad got back into his seat and squeezed the steering wheel so tight his knuckles turned white.

"*Why*, Cass?" he said. "Why would you do this?"

As I tugged and tugged on what was left of my eyebrows, I felt the words fight their way upstream from my gut to my lips. I knew I needed to confront Dad about what I'd seen. To see what he'd do if given the chance to confess the ugly truth to his daughter, face-to-face. The chance that Mom never got.

"Are you a con man?" I tried to say, but it came out kind of lockjawish.

"Excuse me?" he said.

The rain outside had stopped completely, but inside it suddenly felt like Dad and I were two empty Coke bottles taped together, with a little cyclone swirling between us.

"I said, are you a con man? And is that really why Mom left?"

It was a lot less lockjawish that time, and inspired a total deer-in-headlights look on Dad's face.

"Dad, I *saw* you. Tonight, with the hotel soaps and the encyclopedias. I saw you carving.

"You *lied* to me." My voice got even louder. "You said they were special, that they were part of our heritage, that we could change the world with those things. That's what you said."

Dad put his head in his hands for a few seconds. Then he turned toward me and laid his hand on the armrest of my seat.

"Cass, please just hear me out," he said.

He was shaking a little.

"It's just that . . . The reason I . . . I mean, you need to understand . . ."

Dad began three speeches, but couldn't seem to find the rest of any of them.

"Just go from the beginning," I said.

"All right," he said. "Here's the beginning." He looked at me sheepishly, like he wasn't sure I was prepared for his next words. "I made a wish on Abe Lincoln."

He was right. I wasn't prepared for those words.

"You mean that funny piece of soap we saw in the kitchen with Mom?"

"That very one," he said. "The thing is, Cass, I've always known how much you admired your mom, how you looked up to her for the good she does—well, the good she *did*. And believe it or not, I do understand those feelings. I've worked a lot of years digging holes in the dirt and selling raw meat to make sure she could keep doing that stuff.

"What you and I both have to realize is that your mom's leaving has been brewing for a while, and there wasn't anyone or anything that could stop it. Not you. Not me. Not a trip in a cruddy RV. So the way I saw things, I had no choice but to try and rescue what was left of our family. That day in the kitchen, when your mom made a wish on that silly Abe Lincoln soap sliver, I made my own wish too."

"You did?"

"Yeah, and I knew it was a long shot," he said. "But I wished that I could stop being a total nobody in the eyes of my own daughter."

"But I never thought you were a nobody," I said,

instantly flashing back to a hundred reasons he might have thought that.

"Well, I've sure never been much of a *some*body to you." Dad wiped his face on his sleeve. "I guess I just wanted to come up with something special that you and I could share, something that was just about *us*." He paused. "And that's when I got the soap sliver idea."

I gave Dad a hard, hard look. I wanted to make sure my next words sunk in good.

"You made me believe those soaps were magic."

He drew in a deep breath. "I know. I made *me* believe those soaps were magic too."

"But what about all the people we met?" I said. "The kids, the soldiers, the Belfusses, Ambrette?" A bunch of suckers, I thought. Just like me.

"All believers," he said.

"All lied to," I said.

"But all *helped*."

That one truth plopped on top of the pile of lies made me feel more confused than ever.

"The thing is, Cass," Dad continued, "I think sometimes, *believing* is all the magic you need. Don't you see? They all believed so much, they made their own wishes come true. And didn't we give them a fun way to do it?"

I scooted my arm out from under his hand.

"I just don't understand how you could lie about something like Sway." Even saying the words *lie* and *Sway* in the same sentence made my voice crumble.

When the storm ended, an unbearable first-morning ray of sunlight flashed through the windshield. Dad flipped down his shade visor, and I did the same.

"You're right, Cass," he said. "I did lie about Sway, but not like you think. The thing about Sway is, well, Sway *is* genuine, but as it turns out, not so rare."

Dad took a slow look around the shambly insides of The Roast.

"Think about it this way," he said. "It's like we're all born with our souls real sticky, and we pick a little something up from every person we've known."

"Sticky souls?"

"Yeah, well, a lot like that lint roller we've got back there," he said.

I must have looked as puzzled as I felt.

"I've been thinking hard about this, Cass, and here's what I figure," Dad began. "It's like we all keep a little something from everyone, past or present, who touches our lives. Some of it's as cruddy as beef jerky crumbs. But then there's the sparkly glitter scattered in between all that. That glitter, it's the part you want to keep—the pieces you take from others to help make a better you. *That's* the real Sway."

I felt a rush of relief to hear the words *real* and *Sway* back together again.

"And the soap," he added. "Well, that's just a mighty fun way to make it come to life for people."

His words punched and kicked their way through replayed memories of our entire trip. "Oh," is what I said. *Whoa*, is what I felt.

"Even for a muddy, meaty bore like me," said Dad. Then he puffed his cheeks and let the air out in a slow-leak sigh, aiming his face upward, like you do when you're either trying to stop a sneeze or send some sadness sliding back inside. Just above his head, the photo of baby him and toddler Uncle Clay had slipped and was dangling from his visor by one corner. Peeking out from under it was another picture, one I'd never seen before. It was a shoeless Mom and a beardless Dad hugging on each other, soaking wet, standing in the rain with umbrellas at their sides.

"When's that picture from?" I said.

"The year your mom and I got married," he said, tucking it under like he couldn't bear to look. "Back then, all she knew of storms was that April showers bring May flowers."

From the dashboard, Gordon Lightfoot sang about reaching the part where the heartaches come. Even just the wordless stuff was so sad I could hardly stand it.

"Don't you have any other music?" I asked.

"No, but I guess I ought to find some," Dad said, ejecting the CD. "You know, your mom gave me this thing the very same week that picture was taken, as a first anniversary present. . . . Long before *every*thing went stormy."

As he pushed the photo of him and Uncle Clay back on top of the other one, I thought about how he could have used his own CAN IT! box on this trip too. But he sure couldn't borrow mine. Mine was simply too full.

"May I ask you something?" Dad said.

"Sure."

"When you ran away," he said. "Why did you take the MBM suitcase with you?"

Oh no, I thought. Those poor slivers, they are gone and they are mush. Guilt pricked at my gut again.

"Oh, um, I dumped the soaps out," I said in a small voice.

"And I left the suitcase too," I said in a smaller one.

"Well then, that settles it," Dad said as he cranked the engine. "I guess you're right about going home. We'll just pick us up a map and take the shortest way back to Alabama.

"Unless, of course, you want to go on," he added, with a hint of hope in his voice. But despite how disappointing the thought of us breaking Rule of The Roast Number One and buying a map, I just shook my head *no* to playing assistant to his big hoax anymore.

After that, Dad inched and scratched us along the shoulder of the main road, trying again and again to knock a limb off the windshield with the wipers. As we picked up speed, all manner of prickles and pollens and pine needles blew off The Roast. He didn't even bother to merge back onto the highway, but just stayed on the shoulder until the next exit, where we found the D-Lux Truck Wash just beyond the Ekim, Tennessee, city hall. The wash had a grand-opening sign that looked like it had been there for years.

When it was our turn at the washing station, I watched Dad vigorously squeegee the windshield, my brain doing the same back-and-forth dance. Mostly wondering how everything in my life could be so full of opposites at the same time. Hero, scam. Inspiration, frustration. Truth, lies. For a moment, it seemed that the collection of bad thoughts and good thoughts inside me was as unmixable as oil and water, like maybe I'd have to shake my head to make sense of anything.

Before I even realized Dad had stepped away, he reappeared inside the RV with a folded map of the Southeastern United States, two matching honey buns, two cartons of milk, and a box of Band-Aids. And not the little wimpy kind for paper cuts either. This was a box of wound-worthy Band-Aids.

"Look, Cass," he said, arranging our breakfast on the center console before he took to ripping open three of the extra-large bandages. "I know I might have blown it big-time. And you have every right in the world to be mad at me. But please know that all this pretending—all the silly pretending I've *ever* done—has been done with your happiness in mind."

I wiggled the little side mirror control on my door while Dad leaned over and carefully dabbed my legs clean with a napkin before placing the bandages on for me. He was beyond gentle enough for the job, and I was relieved that he arranged them perfectly, so that none of the sticky parts were attached to actual scrapes.

"It's just, I knew that pulling your mom's glory right out from under you wouldn't be smooth, like yanking a tablecloth and leaving the dishes undisturbed," Dad said, pressing lightly on the last corner of adhesive. "I knew that without some magic to fall back on, you'd have been hurt beyond what's fair for a kid."

"Like surplus suffering?" I said.

"Exactly," he said. "And then I thought about who

you'd want to be like, if not your mom, and I realized it sure wouldn't be your dull, faded dad.

"But I *so* wanted it to be me," he said.

As he tucked the flap on the Band-Aid box shut, I couldn't help but think about Scrabble games and pipe-cleaner scenes and a stupid cell phone and the endless list of ways that Dad had tried to make things good. So many things that M. B. McClean just seemed to be the exclamation point at the end.

"You wanted to be the cheese," I said.

"The what?"

"The cheese, the gooey good stuff that fills in the empty space when a slice is taken away."

"Oh."

I picked at a little crusted honey bun sugar on my palm.

"But it was still wrong to lie to all those people," I said. "And to me."

"I know," he said. "And for that I am truly sorry."

Dad twisted around, lifted the fringy green-and-yellow suit jacket from the back of the driver's seat, and held it up to himself.

"Guess we won't be needing this stuff anymore," he said, feeling for the tarnished chain that was tucked down in the tiny front pocket. Then he hunched over so I couldn't see, gave the chain a good tug, and pried something off the end before tossing the jacket in a lump under the coffee table.

"Hold out your hand," he said.

When I did, he laid a little golden silhouette-head of

a girl in my palm. The head had *Cass* engraved in bad cursive across it. It was so lovely, I gasped out a little squeak.

"This is the one from Mom's bracelet," I said. "I thought she kept it."

"Nope. I've been holding this one close to me," said Dad.

"The whole time?"

"The whole time."

I pinched the charm tight, smushing a perfect thumb-print across its cheek. Then, in the suddenly bearable morning sun, that smudgy silhouette took on a whole new shine. I couldn't believe Dad had been carrying it with him in a secret place all along. Like it was the most important thing in the world to him.

thirty-seven

Nimble Creek . . .
Uh-gane

Dad sat in the driver's seat holding out the map at arm's length like he was fighting off a monster. He'd traced our planned route home across Mississippi and Alabama with beige drippings from a coffee stirrer. For the first hour of the trip I was in charge of drying things off in the back of The Roast, one paper towel square at a time.

"So how's it look back there?" he called.

With all the once-sparkly pieces and parts scattered about, the inside of the RV looked like the sad, littered end of a Fourth of July parade. Even the glitter CASS across my curtain was clumped and unreadable.

"Everything's soggy," I said. "The afghan squishes. My backpack's soaked. Your hat is kinda smushy. And the tambourine won't even jangle."

I didn't mention my wall noodling, which, I was surprised to find, had not been affected in the least. That's the good thing about something being permanent, I suppose. It holds up in a storm.

"Sorry about all your stuff," he said. "But don't worry about M. B. McClean's things. Those fall into the *don't need no more, no how* category anyway, I guess."

And unfortunately, there was a lot of *no more, no how* on the agenda in the The Roast for the next day and a half. No more spying. No calls to make. Nothing to fish for. No soaps to choose from. No reason not to just feel the dampness of the bed under you and enjoy a collection of wet shoes doing their little musty stink dance around your head. In other words, The Roast had become a major snore salad.

"Just a hundred or so more miles," Dad said, and after that, he, Gordon Lightfoot, and I were silent for the rest of the drive, which stretched out into a slow passing of yellow road dashes, mile-marker signs, and cows. I counted all the way up to a hundred and sixty-three cows by the time we finally saw a familiar exit, adding on twenty more that were probably hiding behind bigger cows.

Dad put on his blinker and veered onto the exit ramp.

"Why are we stopping in Nimble Creek?" I said.

"Gas light's on," said Dad. "I just thought we'd fill up somewhere familiar."

It didn't take but a minute for us to be approaching all the old familiar sights of Nimble Creek, Mississippi, this time from the other direction. The decaying minigolf course, the big twirly ice cream cone, the park where . . .

"What in the world?" said Dad, startling me. "Cass, do you see what I see over there? Is that a mirage on that fountain in the park, or is there something weird on top of it?"

I craned my neck to look, but couldn't make out anything beyond the flagpole.

"I don't see anything," I said.

"All right," said Dad, aiming The Roast farther into the park. "It might not be anything, but I want to go check it out."

He found his way to exactly where we'd parked last time and stopped in the lot between the big gazebo and the old minigolf place. The entire park was empty, save for the occasional darting squirrel.

"Looks like the heat's kept everyone inside today," he said.

Sure enough, despite air-conditioning, we must have been in the hottest vehicle in the hottest part of the hottest day in Mississippi ever. Dad and I climbed down from The Roast, and I immediately noticed what a different scene it was from the last time we were here. No banner, no wagon, no tambourine. No moms fanning, and no kids playing. Despite the differences, though, I did notice something strangely familiar at the center of the park. And it was certainly not a mirage.

"No way," said Dad, as he and I approached the fountain gazebo, slow and cautious like a couple of cats. When we got close enough to get a good look, I couldn't even begin to believe my eyes. There, on top of the big fountain, rising up from its middle, was a statue of M. B. McClean, with his happy Cassistant standing right next to him.

Side by side, Dad and I circled the fountain and took in every bit of the monument. Someone had squished a mound of soaps together and carved every last detail—top hat and flip-flops and all. The little Cass even held a tiny tambourine in her hand. It must have taken all the left-over soap in town to do it. Underneath the figures, there was a poster written in green-and-yellow finger paint. It read:

In Honor of Mr. M. B. McClean, for all the fun
—From Michelangelo and the gang

I immediately flashed back to that boy with the Frisbee, the little Spider-Man fan who'd washed with the Michelangelo soap at the tail end of our crazy day in Nimble Creek. How inspired the boy must have been by M. B. McClean that he would be able to sculpt something so grand out of something so ordinary as old soap.

"Wow," Dad said. "I guess sometimes the zingle really does happen later, huh?"

For a few seconds, I saw my dad's smile bust through his sadness. I, too, couldn't help but be somewhat stunned by the exhibit before us. A monument. *Of my dad and me.* It was such a wonder of smoothness and color and detail, it made me feel prouder than anything concrete ever could. In fact, I would have been glad to stand there forever, marveling at the thing.

"Hey," Dad said, with a nudge to my side. "You got a pen I can borrow?" He had to say it twice to distract me from my stare.

"Yeah," I said. "I've got a Sharpie in The Roast."

"Run get it, if you would."

I almost didn't want to leave, for fear of coming back and discovering I'd imagined the whole scene, but I was too curious to know what Dad was going to do with the marker.

When I returned, Dad took the Sharpie and stepped up to the statue, giving it a good look up and down before uncapping the marker and adding a little something to the poster-board inscription. Right next to the *M*, he squeezed in the letters *ake*. After the *B*, he wrote *elieve*. Then he backed himself all the way to the spot next to me, keeping his gaze on the mini-monument the whole time. I just stood there with my mouth hanging open. What he'd just done had most certainly made me forget to breathe.

"But, Dad . . ." I said. "What in the world? You mean you were *Make Believe* all along?"

Dad nodded, slow and smug. "All along."

"Make Believe McClean?"

"Make Believe McClean," he said.

"And those people knew it?"

"Probably."

Dad's peaceful smile lingered for a few seconds more, and then we made our way back to The Roast, thoughtful and silent. Both of us were totally awestruck by what we'd seen, and I was totally dumbstruck by what I'd read. *Make Believe McClean*, I said again and again in my head until it turned almost musical.

"Now, let's get out of here before we have to see ourselves melt," Dad said, as he opened the door of The Roast and gave me a boost. But as bright and joyous as that part of our day had been, as soon as the monument and the park were out of sight, I could feel a gloomy grayness settle back down all around the RV once again. The farther we got from Nimble Creek, the more I wished we'd had the Belfusses' Polaroid camera, so we could have kept a miniversion of the park scene with us the rest of the way home. That statue would have surely made a picture worth displaying on Dad's visor shade.

I ambled back to my room, wondering if Dad was missing Sway half as much as I was. In fact, while Dad navigated us out of Mississippi, I couldn't much think of anything at all except for soap slivers. Worthless as they might have seemed last night, I found myself longing for them in an unmistakably noodle-worthy way.

It doubled the mustiness in my little room when I pulled the curtain shut. Mr. and Mrs. Pizza's freshening powers had been drowned right out of them, but I figured the smell of some Sharpies could overcome all of that. I pulled the black one from my pocket and gathered the rest of his friends. Then I tore the wet corners of the Eiffel Tower poster right off the thumbtacks to expose the whole canvas of blank tree before me. I thought about how Dad would probably want to paint the wall white again if he ever sold the RV, but that thought totally brought some of the grayness down around me too. So instead of doing more thinking, I began to noodle like crazy right there on the wall, hoping that maybe even under future layers of white paint, there would remain a permanent memory of the things that happened on this trip.

At first I drew just a small oval sitting on a branch here

and there. And then one per branch, and then two. And then even more, using every color I had. Before I knew it, I'd drawn at least a hundred soap slivers resting on the branches of that great big tree. And then I felt the need to decorate them. Not with swirlies. Not with paisleys. Not with hearts or sparks. But with letters. Among them were *AJ* for Aunt Jo, *UC* for Uncle Clay, *S* for Syd, *C* for Connie, another *C* for Celeste, *A* for Ambrette, *POW* for Ambrette's husband, and even a *TBN* for Toodi Bleu Nordenhauer.

I labeled a sliver for just about every person I could think of, getting so caught up in my noodling that I hardly noticed when an all-too-familiar buzzing came from below. Opening up the beauty box fast as I could, I found the phone vibrating its way across an otherwise empty compartment. The little screen showed me the same 239 number again, sending a squirt of fear from my head to my toes. Or maybe it was a squirt of courage, because this time I capped my marker and answered. If she was worthy of a sliver, then she was certainly worth talking to.

"Hello?"

"Cass?"

Oh good, it's Mom. Oh no, it's Mom. Oh wow, it's Mom.

"Mom?"

"How are you, baby?"

"Okay, I guess."

"I tried to call you back the other day, but no one answered," she said.

"I know. I was just kind of busy."

"So where in the world are you?" she asked. "What have you been up to?"

There was such a pile of telling to do. I decided to start with the most immediate bits. "Mississippi, and noodling."

"Noodling an in-between?"

"I don't know," I said. "*Is* it an in-between?"

Mom left my question just hanging there in space.

"Hey, I just got your postcard," she said. "That fancy little soap smelled real nice. I've already used it up."

Little did Mom know what an honor she'd had to wash with Make Believe McClean's next-to-last living soap sliver.

"So what did that little *M T* on there stand for?" she said.

"Nothing. It's a secret."

And that's when I swept all my scattering courage into a pile right in the middle of me. I took a deep breath. "Mom, I know all about what happened to you last year. I know about the man you couldn't save. And I know you had to stop being a rescuer."

"Oh, Cass . . ."

I could feel my throat tightening. "The thing is, I just don't know why you had to stop being my mom."

Then Mom wasted half a refill minute trying to put together a sentence. I could tell she was headed in the direction of an apology, but not in the direction of Alabama.

"Please don't say that, baby. You must know, I never, ever meant for things to get this way," she said. "It's just that, sometimes when you mess up one thing and then another—well, you wake up one day and messing up just comes easy to you."

Mom's voice got quieter and quieter, like our time might just poof away into noiselessness.

"But you used to know how to clean up messes," I said. "Right, Mom?"

"*Used to* is right, Cass."

That's when my own supply of words ran so low, I had to use some of Dad's.

"You shouldn't let what you didn't do ruin what you *did*," I said.

"Baby, I'm afraid I've ruined a lot of things," she said. "But no matter what happens, Cass, you need to remember something, okay? You need to know that you're already more of a hero than I'll ever be."

Then Mom must have run out of words too. In her silence, I wondered how in the world somebody could make you so happy and so sad at the same time. And then I thought about what it really meant to be a hero. How maybe it's not just about pulling people from rooftops or flipped-over cars. Or even about having certificates. Maybe even sometimes it's about being the one who snags a ten-year-old's favorite pajamas because you're there to tuck her in every night with your calloused hands.

"Cass." Mom finally spoke. "I guess I better—"

"But wait," I said. "Mom?"

"What, baby?"

"When you used it . . . the soap, I mean . . . did you feel a zingle?"

"A what?"

"Never mind."

"So what's this magic you called me about the other day?" she asked.

295

I picked up one last piece of courage and dusted it off.

"You know, Dad just might have some mercy left over," I said.

"What do you mean by that, hon?" said Mom.

"We're supposed to be home tonight. Maybe you could call and ask him about the magic."

Mom paused so long, I felt nervous the refill minutes would expire right out from under us.

"And if you—*when* you call—be sure and ask him about his statue too," I said.

"Okay, baby. Not tonight, but maybe sometime," she said, in a way that told me it would indeed be *some time* before she realized she'd left *two* heroes behind.

"Bye, Mom. I love you."

"I love you too, Cass."

With that, I dropped the phone to my side and backed myself up, standing as far from my noodling as I could. As I took in every inch of the soapy wonder that had been my week, something suddenly occurred to me: What if the things you always thought were just the in-between junk were actually the good things themselves? Maybe there wasn't such a thing as an in-between at all. No in-between days, no in-between places, no in-between people. Maybe, just maybe, there was some Sway to be found in all of it.

And then I did the best thing I knew to do with the strange concoction of sadness and hope brewing inside me. I prayed. I prayed for the people whose initials were on those slivers. Not just for those people, but for the cave people before them and the robot people after them. For *real* orphans. For all the people who have lost shoes in the road. For kids whose parents play war. For Toodi Bleu Skies and Toodi Bleu Nordenhauer, for M. B. McClean and Douglas Nordenhauer. And all the people who need to find the magic in Make Believe. That, I figured, just about covered the whole world.

Just then, right about the same moment as my *Amen*, I felt Sway slosh over the edge of me, sending a tickle of an idea across my whole self.

thirty-eight
Pink Crumblets

After a quick peek to make sure Dad was focused on the road and the road alone, I snuck the manicure kit from the rolltop desk drawer, grabbed my Toodi Bleu sliver from the pantry cabinet, and set them both on a smoothed-out work spot on my bed. The soap kept sticking to my damp cushion, so I had to find something dry to put under it. Turns out, an airbrushed tank top that's been kept safe and dry inside a plastic beauty box makes a great cushion for the delicate job of restoring a soap sliver.

I slid the nail file from the manicure kit and hovered it in the air for a moment, too scared to lower it, like one false poke would waste the last sliver to be found in all the soap mines in the world. But then I just held my breath and went for it, shaky at first, but then more steady-handed with each stroke. As I worked, I noticed that the minuscule soap scrapings that fell to the side looked like pink crumblets, reminding me of an eraser that's done some forgiving.

Once a lot of scraping and a little carving was complete, I crept out to swipe the encyclopedia volume marked Q R S. I felt sure Dad would hear me bumping around, but he just plodded on, taking his eyes off the road only to glance at the map. Then I opened the book across my bed next to where the soap rested. Its pages were wavy and stuck together. So much so that I had to lick my pointer finger to help me flip through, leaving a flowery soapy taste on my tongue. By the time I'd lip-smacked the taste away, I'd found the listing I was after. I figured the book was ruined anyway, so I tore the whole page right out of there.

I lifted the finished soap carefully with two fingers and placed it right in the middle of the torn-out page. Then I folded the paper around it again and again, concentrating so hard on wrapping the sliver securely without crushing it, I didn't even notice that The Roast had come to a stop. Nor did I notice Dad standing right behind me with my curtain pulled open. I almost jumped out of my skin when he spoke.

"Cass, I thought you'd maybe want a bite to—Wow, what have you been up to?"

"It's a surprise," I said, hiding the bundle behind my back. Then I realized he wasn't even looking at me or the torn book at all. He was staring at my wall.

"Um, it's my noodling," I explained. "I've sort of been working on it the whole trip. See, it's a big, reaching tree. A Castanea dentata tree. And it's all full of soap slivers."

"I see that," Dad said, standing for a minute in silence. I didn't know whether he was just taking it all in, or brewing up a big mad.

"I know it's permanent and all, and I know people

299

aren't supposed to write on walls, but I thought it might be okay."

"I wouldn't call it okay," said Dad, sending a blast of *yeeks* right through me.

"Oh, it's better than okay," he said.

"Really?" I let out a breath I didn't realize I'd been holding.

"Definitely. It's far more beautiful than that old Eiffel Tower, and it's just what this grungy RV has been missing," he said. "Maybe you could expand it and fill the whole wall with it someday. Or who knows? Maybe even the whole Roast."

"You mean we're not going to sell it?"

"No way," he said. "Not in a million years would I part with a *Cassterpiece* like this."

Cassterpiece. Hearing Dad say that word was like the noise a rainbow would make if a rainbow made noise.

"But first," he said, "let's see how much pig meat twelve bucks will buy us."

Moments later, inside the Top Hat BBQ in Blount Springs, Alabama, Dad and I found ourselves sitting in a C-shaped booth that had a deer head looking out over it. I held tight to my little page-wrapped bundle until the food came. Then, while Dad raved on about my noodling between gnawing ribs, I stood crinkle fries on end in my slaw and waited for the right moment. When he ripped open a moist towelette and gave his hands a thorough wipe-down, I saw my opportunity.

"Um, speaking of hand-washing," I said, sliding the bundle to his side of the table.

Dad had all sorts of confusion across his face.

"Be careful when you unwrap it," I said. "Delicate stuff inside there."

He flip-flip-flipped the package until the tiny soap plopped out onto the table.

"The thing is," I said, "I finally decided which sliver I want to use."

Dad took a close look at the soap.

"See there . . . it's an *M B M*," I showed him. "For my partner in Sway-making."

Dad looked as stunned as if the deer head had spoken my words.

"But not just that," I said. "Look at the other side."

He rolled the soap over with one hand.

"Is that a *D N*?" he said.

"For Douglas Nordenhauer," I said. "The *cheese*."

Dad fixed his eyes on that soap like the whole rest of the room blurred out around it.

"But wait, there's something else you need to see, too," I told him, smoothing out the damp-edged encyclopedia page and pinning it down with the salt and pepper. The section highlighted in yellow Sharpie read:

> Soap is formed by mixing common oils with a strong alkaline solution. The most common form of bar soap is made by combining a measure of distilled water, olive oil, and lye.

"What's all this about?" said Dad.

"Well, since I dumped out all the soaps," I explained, "I just figured someday we might want to use those

301

ingredients to make our own. I mean, in case a couple of nuts need a fresh batch of slivers, you know, for fun or something."

Dad smiled so crinkly, he got little twinkles in his eyes.

"And, Dad, there's just one last thing," I said, tucking the sliver gently into my shorts pocket.

"What's that?" he said.

"What I mainly wanted to say—" I stood another fry in my slaw. "What I mainly want to say is that I'm real sorry for making you worry."

"Oh come on, Cass, you know better than that," Dad said. "You don't have a lick of wrength in you."

"But I ran away, just like Mom did."

"True." He nodded. "But you also came back."

"I didn't even realize what I was running away from," I said.

"It takes some people longer than others to figure that out," he said. "All is forgiven, Cass."

Dad rose to his feet and dusted the salt from his legs.

"All?" I said. "Even Mom?"

"One step at a time, okay?" he said, reaching to offer me a hand as I slid out of the booth. Then it was on to the pay area, which was just beyond a long counter full of every kind of candy a person could want. Between the bubble gum and the peppermint sticks sat a no-necked-gallon milk jug that was half full of money, with a note taped to the side. The note simply said: *For the Weston County tornado victims.* Dad plinked our change into the jug and looked out the window at our exhausted RV, which was smoking more than a little from the tailpipe.

"The Roast is done," he said with a grin. "Let's go home."

thirty-nine

Rare and Genuine

"Biiiiiiiiiiiiiig Riiiiiiiiiiiiiiiiight!" Dad shouted, nearly taking out our mailbox as he bumped us into the driveway. I couldn't decide if it felt like we'd been gone for ages, for a few days, or for maybe just long enough. All I knew was that seeing the familiar sites of Olyn, Alabama, through the eyes of a returning hero felt better than I had even hoped it would.

We pulled to a stop in the middle of the driveway, between our house and Syd's. It had been a few hours since lunch, and I suddenly found myself craving a potpie.

"So what do you think?" Dad said. "Should I wear the top hat and glasses for everybody?"

"I don't think so," I said, popping open the glove box and handing him the *It's a dirty job, but somebody's got to do it* ball cap. "How about just this for now?"

I heard Syd's screen door slam shut, so I pinched the little Castanea dentata seed burr out of the cup holder and scrambled to the back to grab my CAN IT! box. Then, seed in hand and can in pocket, I slid down from my side of The Roast at the same time Dad slid down from his.

"Lady and gentlemen of the Nordenhauer persuasion!" Dad called out as he made his way onto the little porch next door. I was about to circle around the rear of the RV to join him, when I was suddenly stopped in my tracks by a figure lunging at me from a hiding place underneath the bumper. *Syd.* Soon as I caught my breath and swallowed my heart back down, I realized how very much I had missed my cousin.

"Syd Nordenhauer! You scared the wits out of me!"

"I couldn't resist," he said. "I heard The Roast as soon as you guys hit the driveway."

I was relieved he didn't say a word about my big zeeyut, probably because he had a humongous red bump on his own forehead that made mine look like a speck.

"So?" he said. "Was it as wackadoo as you thought?"

"More than you could ever imagine," I said. "But it was the *best* kind of wackadoo."

I heard the screen door open as Aunt Jo greeted Dad and called for Uncle Clay to wheel himself out. All the things I wanted to tell Syd swirled around my brain.

"Well then, spill it," said Syd. "I want to hear details."

He leaned in to give me little push on the shoulder. When he did, I caught a glimpse of something behind him across the way, something that made me so mad I couldn't hold back. There was Mom's cloud piñata still dangling, all weather-beaten and frail, expectedly so. But it also had a big ugly gaping hole in the top of it, like somebody's cousin had hit it with a stick.

"Good grief, Syd!" I said. "You just had to go and bust it, didn't you?"

Syd's eyes got wide. "Huh? What'd I do?"

"The piñata. You smacked it open. I know you did, and you did it as soon as I left. Look at that hole!"

Syd looked back over his shoulder. "Shut up dot com! I did not!"

I gave him a nasty look.

"No really," he insisted. "Come here."

Syd pulled me by the arm to the spot right under the cloud and ran to grab a step stool from their porch.

"I didn't bust that hole, I swear it." He placed the stool under the piñata. "Somebody else did."

All scattered around his feet and mine were what looked like tufts of cotton strewn about.

"Now climb up there and have a look," he said.

When I climbed the two steps and took a peek inside the hole, it was lots more of the same. Cotton balls, Q-tips, gauze pads. *Rescue supplies.* So that's what Uncle Clay had filled it with for Mom's party.

But the discovery didn't end there, for in the middle of all that stuff, I saw and heard a rustling around that inspired me to poke my face closer for a better look. When I did, I was delighted to find that in a fluffed-up wad of cotton, there sat three little birds. Three baby birds, just barely feathered, bobbing their heads in near-perfect rhythm with the racing of my heart.

I backed my head away from the hole, to find Syd doing an impatient foot shuffle. Aunt Jo, Uncle Clay, and Dad gave us three hearty waves from the porch.

"There's birds living in here," I said.

"Duhyees," said Syd. "That's what I wanted you to see."

"You mean *they* busted the hole?"

"The mama bird did," he said.

I turned back for another peek. It was amazing how content the little family looked in their custom arrangement of dingy, matted fluff.

"Don't linger all day up there," warned Syd. "The mama bird comes around every once in a while. And you sure don't want to have your head in that cloud when she does. That's how I got this poke on the forehead."

Despite the warning, I stood there watching the tiny birds, marveling at their comfort until my cousin chopped me hard in the back of the left knee.

"Enough already," he said. "I want to see inside The Roast while it's still light out."

"Okay," I said, rolling the concealed seed burr around in my fist. "But there's something I want to do first."

"What?" he said.

"It's kind of a private thing," I said, worried that Syd would make fun of my plan.

"Oh, come on," said Syd.

"All right," I said. "You can watch. That is, if you promise not to laugh."

"Omise-pray," said Syd.

Just a few steps over into our yard, I knelt down where the old dead Castanea dentata tree used to be, noticing that someone had kindly propped the little wire fence back up. Syd squatted close to me as I opened my hand to take a good look at the prickly seed casing inside it. The burr looked like a fuzzy baby alien resting on my palm. Soon as he saw it, Syd started to make his *Twilight Zone* noise, but then stopped short and changed it into a throat-clearing.

"What is it?" he asked.

"Seeds," I said, prying open the prickly burr to reveal the shiny brown chestnuts inside. "They're Castanea dentata seeds. I'm going to grow the tallest and reachingest Castanea dentata tree in the state of Alabama. Maybe in the whole country."

I paused a moment for Syd to slip in some kind of joke, but instead, real quiet, he just said, "Awes."

Then, together, Syd and I scratched out a shallow hole. The ground felt cool and crumbly between my fingers, and as we dug, I noticed a few loose, frail rootlets from the old Castanea dentata tree mixed into the dirt. It made me wonder if the ragged root pieces might somehow actually help the new tree to grow even bigger. While Syd waited, I pinched up the plumpest of the chestnuts and carefully dropped it at the very center of the hole. As I covered the seed with the dug-out dirt, I first made a wish for its safety and strength, and then said a prayer that the wish would come true.

Sappy Castanea Dentata, I thought.

Thankfully, no part of my ritual inspired Syd to do the usual cuckoo-clock doors with his hands. Instead, he just sat there patient and still until my business was done.

"Hey," said Syd, "maybe after this we can wash our hands with some, oh, I don't know, *magic* soap?"

"How do you know about the soaps?" I asked. "Did Uncle Clay tell you?"

"Yeah, he told me," said Syd. "Which is more than I can say for you, holding out on me for like fifteen minutes now." He looked me square in the eyes and said, "All I know is, you need to let me into that RV now. I want to see that stuff."

Syd so had the look of a believer, it made me wonder what exactly Uncle Clay had told him.

"Sorry, we're a little low on inventory right now," I said. "But Dad and I plan to fix that."

"Fair enough," said Syd. "But shoot straight with me, cousin to cousin. Do the soaps really work?"

"Better than you could even imagine," I said.

"Well, you better get me one soon," said Syd, leaning in close to inspect my planting.

"Hold up," he added, scooping some extra dirt from outside the tiny fenced area. "Part of the seed is still showing there."

Syd patted an extra layer of dirt gently onto the mound. "You sure don't want a critter to come dig it all up."

"Thank you," I said, partly for the advice, but mainly for his being such a good permanent.

"Hey, and thanks for the going-away present too," I said. "It came in real handy."

I pulled the CAN IT! box from my pocket to find the one thing I'd left in there—the worn label from our old Castanea dentata tree. I picked out the little paper and pressed it word-side-up into the dirt, right next to the seed mound.

"You plan on that tag staying there forever?" asked Syd.

"Historical marker," I corrected him. "And only until

309

the tree gets huge enough to have a plaque under it. Like someday when my great-grandkids come to see it."

I was imagining mine and Syd's descendants washing with soaps carved with our own initials, when Aunt Jo called us over to the porch for some welcome-home snacks. Maybe a nice big bowl of Funyuns, I hoped, as Syd and I rose to our feet and dusted the loose dirt from our knees.

"So just how high do we expect this thing to grow?" Dad said from behind me and Syd, startling the both of us. He'd walked up so quietly, and now just stood there staring at the clear expanse of the Alabama sky, the pride in his face brightening him like no green-and-yellow suit could ever do.

"That high," I said, pointing sharp and straight into the forever blue above. Soon as I did, I noticed a fat robin flying across the yard in our direction, so low it seemed that if I kept my finger in the air, she might scrape her belly on it.

"That's her!" yelled Syd, covering his face with his hands. "That's the mama! Take cover!"

Dad scooted up close behind and clasped both arms around me tight. Tight like he was telling the world, *This one belongs to me, and don't you even think about messing with her.* Syd bent down to avoid a beak to the noggin, but it didn't even cross my mind to do the same. Instead, I stood firm against my dad as that bird soared right on past, rising and falling on a breeze all the way back to her babies' cloudy, cushy home.

"Come on, Cass," Dad said. "You've got some

seriously muddy planter's hands, there. Let's go wash up for the party."

With the coast clear of birds, Syd took off for his porch, and I turned to follow Dad to our back door. As we climbed the steps, I reached into my pocket to make sure my last little sliver was still there. I squeezed it tight in my palm, and as soon as I locked my fingers around the soap, something happened that caught me by surprise. For the first time ever, I felt it. A *zingle*. And not just any zingle, but the kind that comes from the inside out. The kind that starts at your heart and travels through you with every beat. Like the warm, unmistakable feeling of it being well with your soul.

Acknowledgments

First of all, I thank God for His mercy and for the numerous times He has rescued me from storms. Every name mentioned here represents some sparkly goodness He's seen fit to swirl into my life.

Thank you to Bryan and Lainey, my joy, my inspiration, and my partners in marching forth. To Verv, who taught me there's nothing you can't can. To Foof, for music, and for showing me how to run against the wind. To Julia, Fred, and Jamie for fortitude and Teaduncles. And to Aunt Becky, Tobes, Aunt Jo, and Dee Dee, for your unfailing sweetness to both little Amber and big Amber throughout the years.

Thank you to Abby Ranger, whose editing guidance hasn't a lick of wrength. And to Joanna Stampfel-Volpe, awes agent, for her unwavering belief in this story.

Thank you to Cary Holladay, Summer Dawn Laurie, Liz Schonhorst, Caroline Abbey, and Amy Tipton for opening doors. To Hassen, Gibby, and Edmond, for my first ever review. And, of course, to Mr. Lightfoot for the melancholy.

Day by day, I find myself sloshing over with gratitude for fellow Christians, family, and friends who carried me through my fight with cancer, enabling me to feel the zingle of a lifelong dream come true.

You people are what Sway is all about. You are the glitters that have stuck.